Tell Me You Trust Me

Tell Me You Trust Me

ELLE OWENS

THOMAS & MERCER

Published by Thomas & Mercer, Seattle

www.apub.com

ISBN-13: 9781662525575 (paperback)
ISBN-13: 9781662525582 (digital)

Cover design by Ploy Siripant
Cover image: © Novasphere99, © Atria Borealis, © Ilya_Levchenko / Shutterstock; © Karina Vega / ArcAngel

Printed in the United States of America

To my dad, who not only taught me the power of music, but who handed me my first thriller as an adult and started my obsession with reading (and writing) thrillers

CHAPTER ONE

Monday, 7:00 a.m.

The morning started like any other. The coffee machine whirred as Ethan rushed through getting ready for work. It was always the same routine: shave, shower, kiss the top of Logan's head, and give me a quick hug before shoving a protein bar in his mouth as he left.

"You want me to make you a lunch today?" My sleep-deprived brain hadn't woken up yet, and I frowned at Ethan's appearance. He wore jeans, not slacks. He definitely hadn't shaved. I loved the rougher look on him, but the compliment stuck in my throat as he stared at me with an expression I couldn't decipher. It wasn't longing or anger, but it was intense, and goose bumps broke out on my neck. "What is it?"

He rubbed his lips together before closing the distance between us. He wrapped me in a hug that made it hard to breathe.

I laughed, my stomach twisting in worry over the extra affection. "Ethan, what is this?"

After releasing me, he cupped my face and traced my skin with his fingertips. He lowered his voice, his breath tickling my face. "I need you to trust me. Tell me you understand."

I nodded.

But he shook his head as he backed toward the garage door. "Tell me you trust me, Marissa."

"Of *course* I trust you." I frowned as he gave me one more long look and walked back toward the garage.

I had no idea those words would be the ones I replayed in my head over and over, because that night, everything changed.

My husband never came home.

CHAPTER TWO

Tuesday, 9:00 a.m.—One day missing

At first, my mind came up with a million different scenarios to make sense of what happened. Ethan walked to the store. He mailed a package. He went into work. There was a business trip. A friend had an accident. He was certainly the type to help out a friend in need—hell, even a stranger. He'd once picked up a hitchhiker despite my pleas not to because the guy could've been a killer (he wasn't). Ethan was just that kind of guy.

The longer he didn't answer my calls, the more the absolute terror crept in. Eating became impossible. Breathing, a challenge. Yet our son tried to crawl up my legs with his familiar babble of *mamamama*. He signed the gesture for milk, one of the few signs Ethan and I had taught him. He knew *more* and *please* too. I lifted him to my hip and got him a cup of milk, going through the motions on autopilot.

It felt like a lifetime ago that Ethan and I had taken a sign language course so we could try to teach Logan. It had been just a year.

Gone. Ethan's gone. His phone and wallet weren't at home. His car in the driveway. I'd been the last person to see him when he'd left for work the day before. I swallowed the lump of horror away.

"But he left the keys. That has to be a sign." My dad's voice carried over from the living room. It was our unofficial headquarters since we were approaching the time of reporting a missing person. He and

Mom, along with my brother, Peter, all made camp with their electronic devices. They'd all been on the phone or computer since the previous evening, when Ethan hadn't returned home from work.

They agreed it was unusual. But my mom, the eternal optimist, said there was nothing to worry about quite yet.

It was the word *yet* that made my stomach heave and my hands shake. If that *yet* came to be, I wasn't sure how I could survive. Ethan was my rock, the one to help me when I was stressed. Who did I have without him?

My mom looked up from her spot on the recliner, and her gaze softened. "Marissa, honey, sit down. Have you eaten anything?"

"I can't." My voice sounded like sandpaper going through a blender. Even with the sleeping pills, I couldn't rest with all the possibilities of what could've happened playing in my mind like a horror movie, each one spiraling into something worse.

His car broke down so he hitched a ride. Having an affair. Has a second family. Choked while alone. Dead in a hospital somewhere. Kidnapped for ransom. Random attack. Fled the country.

I took a shaky breath and checked my phone *again*, for the millionth time. No calls were going through to his phone. He didn't have Find My Phone turned on. No texts or emails were answered.

God, I would have to call the police to tell them my husband had never come home. My knees trembled, and I set Logan down before grabbing the chair for support. Should I have asked about the jeans, the beard? Had those been hints?

"Sit. I'll make french toast. It was always your favorite as a kid." My mom rummaged through our pantry. I must've looked pathetic, because my mom never cooked anymore.

"He didn't say anything before he left yesterday? Nothing weird or out of the ordinary?" My dad put his arm around me. I leaned into him, his familiar scent of pine comforting me. He smelled like my childhood, a brief moment of nostalgia intruding on the nightmare. "This isn't like him."

No shit, I wanted to say, but having an attitude wouldn't be helpful. "Nothing weird, no."

That's not true. The same unwelcome goose bumps coated my arms. Ethan had *seemed* different, but saying *he didn't shave* seemed frivolous. The tight hug and the intense look weren't newsworthy . . . unless he'd known something was about to happen. *Tell me you trust me, Marissa.* Had I made that up in my sleep-deprived state, or had he said that? My mind spun.

"What about his computer? Were you able to log in and see if there was a letter or note, anything indicating why he left? I know you're not the best with electronics, but he would've left you instructions or something," my dad said.

His question insinuated this had been planned. The fact my *husband* might've planned to leave me and Logan was not something I could just *get over* or accept. Thinking that way made me feel like my entire chest was filled with cement and my skin was slowly burning. A letter meant he'd chosen to leave.

I gagged, and dashed to the kitchen sink before throwing up. It wasn't much, since I couldn't eat, and the burn made my eyes water. I rinsed the mess and used the faucet to clean my mouth as my brother set his laptop down.

"Marissa, fuck, I'm sorry." Peter got me a glass of orange juice, and I chugged it, knowing I needed something in my system besides sleeping pills. "I can't imagine how tough this is for you and little Lo."

He frowned hard, the lines wrinkling his forehead and making him look older. His jaw tightened as he glanced at our parents, then back to me. His left eye twitched before he masked his face into a smile. He always took care of me, and I knew I was a mess. Damn. I was catastrophizing and needed a breath. Peter was still there for me. This had to be difficult for him too.

"Thanks, Peter." I set the glass down on the counter with shaky hands.

"I'm hoping this will be something wild, and we'll laugh about it later. Like, he wanted to help a family of geese cross the road or something and dropped his phone and is in the wilderness somewhere. Remember how he helped that sick bird when we went camping?" My brother lifted one side of his mouth in a grin, showcasing one dimple, and reached out to squeeze my shoulder.

The problem with his version of the story and the ones my parents had offered was the fact his car was in the driveway. When he'd left the previous morning, I hadn't noticed he didn't have his keys.

It wasn't until that evening, when he wasn't home at six, that I noticed his keys on the counter next to the paper towels and the car in the driveway. Why would he *not* drive to work like he had every other day? Did he get a ride with someone? Car pool? Rideshare?

It would've been simple to tell me *Oh, just getting a ride with Max* or *Taking an Uber since your brother will give me a ride home.*

He'd said none of that, just *Tell me you trust me.*

Ethan knew how hard it had been for me to adjust to having Logan. He knew my lack of confidence about my looks, my ability to be a mom and a wife—the postpartum depression that made me second-guess everything. My once-healthy brown hair had split ends, my "glow" from pregnancy had disappeared, and I always looked tired regardless of how much sleep I had. For him to leave, by choice, right now, would be utter betrayal. *But* that was just one possibility in a sea of them.

Peter rubbed my back for a minute before guiding me to the couch. "I'm calling the police. Screw this *waiting for a certain number of hours* rule. If he's hurt or in danger, we should get people on the case right fucking now. We should be looking for him. He's a dad, for Christ's sake."

"Language," I said on instinct as I searched for Logan's little body to make sure he hadn't heard it. He'd been on a real kick of trying new words that weren't exactly helpful for an eighteen-month-old. *Toaster*, *baboon*, and *damn* were the latest. Parent of the year, here. Logan picked up a box of puzzle pieces and threw them on the ground with a whine.

Peter shrugged and picked up a stuffed elephant to distract Logan. My mom met my dad's gaze across our house. Our kitchen opened to our living room, allowing all of us to interact while my mom cooked. I loved this house because of the open concept. Ethan did, too, when we bought it.

My throat tightened as they shared a dark glance. They'd always protected me from the bad parts of life, so seeing them look grim had my stomach twisting even more. *This is bad.*

"I say we call them." My dad stood and pulled his phone from his pocket. "I said so on the drive over here, didn't I, hon? I have a buddy at the station who can help us out."

He didn't wait before walking into the hallway, and I tried not to listen to his sharp voice. I failed.

Son-in-law.

Missing.

Twenty-four hours.

No contact.

Could be in harm's way.

Logan dropped one of the heavy wooden puzzle pieces of trains on his foot, then screamed in pain, and I bolted up. Holding our son, soothing him, gave me a purpose. "Shh, you're okay, baby. You're okay."

Logan cried into my shoulder as my mom watched us with a tender gaze. She set the spoon next to the stove, the french toast cooking. My mom would help me. She always had. She held my hair the time I had the flu so bad I slept in the bathroom. And during my first heartbreak, she let me cry and gave me pep talks. She'd know what to do.

"We'll get through this, sweetie. I know we can," she said.

My eyes stung again, and the weight on my chest doubled at the morbidity of my next thought: *He has no family to inform.*

I pressed my forehead against Logan, the only living connection I had to Ethan. We were his only family. Logan and I and my parents and brother. He always told me how lucky he was to have found someone who came with a plus-three. For a guy who'd lost both his parents at eighteen and had no extended family, we were the jackpot.

"An officer will be reaching out soon. Since there's been no sign of him anywhere and this is so unlike him, they want to do the initial paperwork just in case there's some foul play." My dad's strong voice commanded the room, and while the words *foul play* made my stomach roll again, the fact there was an investigator coming seemed like the right move. "We should see if we can find anything to help. Has he used a credit card or phone?"

I gulped, shaking my head. "No phone. No credit card."

"You've checked?" The wrinkles on his forehead deepened, and he glanced down the hall. "You want me to look, just to make sure you're not missing anything? Your mind isn't in the right place now, sweetheart. Let me and Peter handle it to be safe. Come on, give Logan to your mother."

My dad was right. Obviously, I knew how to function on a computer, but it was easier to let him take charge.

"Gam Gam!" Logan cheered when my mom picked him up and snuggled him. I followed my dad down the hall into the office and was hit with Ethan's cologne—sandalwood and soap—and the lingering scent of his coffee mug. His office was in the front room of the house, with two large windows facing the neighborhood. Ethan's desk was twice the size of mine. I used to tease him for it, but in reality, he needed extra monitors, whereas I had my nice compact writing table to the left. He encouraged me to have my own setup, but it still felt like his office rather than *ours*. The walls were covered with bookshelves and photos from our relationship. Memories of trips, an old baseball glove, and fake plants lined the shelves, giving it a tasteful yet eccentric look. I loved having our shared space, and I always preferred working in here when he was home. I liked his company and hearing how he spoke on work calls.

"The sooner we can find something to help, the sooner we can find him. If he got caught up with some bad people, maybe they forced him to take funds out? Can you think of anyone upset with Ethan?" My dad stared at the wall, his attention moving from picture to picture.

I sniffed, and my dad handed me a tissue.

"You need to focus, Marissa. I know it's hard, but giving yourself a few things to do will help. Can you do that?" My dad's calm voice provided the support I needed to sit in Ethan's chair. It squeaked when I adjusted it, and I could almost hear Ethan's voice saying, *Oh, I'll get this fixed another time*. A sob threatened to come out, and I bit down on my lip to hold it together.

My dad was right. One task at a time.

My fingers trembled as I booted up Ethan's computer. We shared a couple of passwords with each other for our devices—our anniversary, our favorite movie name, an inside joke about hippos—but none of them worked. They had earlier that morning, when I logged in from my device. "Hmm."

"What's *hmm*?" my dad asked as he stared at the screen. He squinted. "What's the password?"

"I don't know." I frowned. "I thought I did . . . it worked this morning."

"You don't know? Marissa, come on." His impatience made my stomach drop, and I squeezed my eyes shut.

"I—I tried all the ones I could think of." I sniffed and wiped the back of my hand over my face. So many tears. I opened his desk drawer and rifled through the gum wrappers and pens to find a lone sheet of paper with passwords. A hot-pink Post-it stuck to the top, random numbers and a little key drawn on it. Not helpful nor the best way to keep a password. For a techie guy, this was a terrible idea. I brushed it to the side. Maybe I reset the password by accident? Unless . . . no. There was no way Ethan reset it . . . right? I was too tired. "Let me try to—"

My dad took the sheet and sighed. "Good man. Looks like you aren't totally in the dark right now. He left us this. Let me help, sweetie. It's best for everyone."

It was best to let him lead, like he always did. I was in no state to fight with him about who held the paper of passwords or why he always said things that were dismissive to me.

"Now, I don't see *computer* on here, but you should try all the other ones. Netflix, Spotify, gas, water. You should get all this stuff in a file so when the police get here, you can hand it all to them."

"You think they need all this stuff?"

"Yes, sweetheart." He patted my shoulder again. "They *need* to find him. Your husband can't just go missing. He's out there, somewhere."

CHAPTER THREE

Wednesday, 8:00 a.m.—Two days missing

Detective Luna stood in my kitchen the next morning, looking too big for the small room. He was a large man with a soft face. Brown skin, brown eyes, a sturdy nose. With his hands on his hips, he surveyed the house with an air of intelligence.

A part of me watched this play out like a movie, as if this weren't my real life. The other part of me, my soul, hurt. Like something poisonous had seeped its way inside my heart and was slowly eating at me. My dad kept tapping his fingers on the table, and Peter tore a piece of paper into a million little flakes.

"I'm going to ask some questions to get an idea of Ethan, but I'm going to be honest with you all. Since he doesn't have any history of mental illness and there hasn't been any indication that he's in danger, this is just standard paperwork. I'll jot down the details and file it."

"So you won't actually look for him?" Peter said, the disbelief in his voice mirroring my own. "That seems dumb. He could be hurt and need help."

Detective Luna lifted both hands in a *what can you do* gesture. "Statistically, people like your husband either chose to leave or return within a few days. Now, do you want to move to somewhere more comfortable, or are you okay with me asking questions here?"

"Here's fine." My dad squeezed my forearm. That gesture gave me a little confidence boost to get through this.

The detective didn't respond to my father. He narrowed his eyes at me and waited. "Marissa, when was the last time you saw him?"

"Monday morning." My throat grew tight. "I—I didn't realize it at the time, but he left his keys on the counter when he walked out the door. I—I had no idea he didn't drive to work."

"Did he tell you he went to work? Did he say *I'm going to work* before he left?"

"N-no." I clenched my jaw. "He asked me if I trusted him, and I said yes. Then he left. I assumed he'd go to work."

"Was that normal, his asking you if you trusted him?"

All eyes were on me, my dad's the most intense. I shuddered. "Not normal, but not weird."

My dad shifted, clearly wanting to say something. He was a large, toned man with dark, graying hair and broad shoulders. He was infamous for his scowl and sharp gaze, one that did him well in business. He opened his mouth to speak, but my brother beat him to it.

"There's no indication he entered the building on Monday." Peter's voice held the same air of authority my dad's did, only his tone was softer. Kinder. "Ethan works with us, my dad and me. When Marissa called yesterday evening, I checked the security logs, and he never used his key card."

"You didn't notice he wasn't there before?" Detective Luna asked my brother, his eyebrows forming one line on his face. They were dark and strong.

"I was in meetings all day, and there are days, like Monday, where you don't know who's there or not. We didn't have any meetings set up with him, so he went under the radar. That's not uncommon since we work on different floors."

"Do you have a system of how employees call in sick or report being absent? Is there a log you could check?"

Was there? I had no idea. No one talked to me about business because *the men* ran it. My dad played into traditional roles often. My mom played into them, too, telling me to not stress about things that weren't my job. Being a good mom and wife were my priorities. My skin always prickled with annoyance when talking about that, but I'd learned to ignore it. Ethan working full time to support us was beneficial for me. It let me spend time with Logan.

But now? He was gone. What would I do? I couldn't move in with my parents. It was their roof, their rules, and I'd lose my independence.

Desperation gripped me, hysteria close behind it. Fear and worry twisted into a terrible combination. My emotions were out of control.

I took a shaky breath and dug my fingernails into my palms as the detective and my dad continued talking. My brother made a quick call, and before he hung up, he grimaced. "I don't know where he went when he left here, but he never made it to work yesterday. His supervisor confirmed it."

The ringing in my ears grew, and swallowing became impossible. I pushed the back door open and went outside. After a few peaceful minutes in the chilly fall air, I calmed. I had no idea how to move past this. Move on, without Ethan.

But that was if he was truly gone. Which maybe he wasn't?

Fuck.

"Are you okay?" Detective Luna asked, sliding the door shut so it was just him and me on the deck.

"Not really."

I'd always been intimidated by authority figures, but he had a calming presence. "Are there any concerns you have that you might want to share with me *without* your family hearing?"

Great question. Yes. There was. But how could I explain them out loud? "Detective." I found my voice and spoke louder. "Do you trust your gut or intuition often?"

"Yes. I do."

"Why?"

"Because those feelings tend to be some version of correct. Tell me, do you have a gut feeling right now?"

I opened my mouth to say yes when my mom poked her head out the door. "Honey, Logan wants to play outside. Want me to take him?"

"Please." I squeezed my eyes shut. Detective Luna moved closer, not quite touching me but close enough for me to smell his coffee breath. He didn't say anything else, and my fears merged together. The deepest and darkest one. "I'm afraid . . . I'm afraid he did this on purpose. Leaving. And if so, that means we'll never find him."

"Why do you think that?"

I gripped the edge of the railing. How did I explain the late-night calls, the change I'd seen in him, bit by bit? This wasn't a sudden thing, Ethan changing and pulling back. It had been gradual. No specific moment explained why things were different. He led a monotonous life that he enjoyed, so the chance of his getting involved with something horrible clashed with everything I knew. The prickle on my skin when he *worked late* or the second-guessing him when he'd take a *work* call in the other room, though . . . those jumped to the front of my mind. But how much of that was my own insecurities at play? I voiced none of it; I just said, "It's a feeling."

He didn't respond. He adjusted his weight and looked past me through the glass door and into my kitchen. "Are you and your family close?"

"Yes." My grip tightened to the point where my knuckles turned white.

"Was Ethan close with your family too?"

"Yes. He didn't have any family left. He . . . he . . ." I paused, my eyes watering and my voice shaky. "He was so h-happy to join our family. They thought of him as a second son."

"This must be hard on all of you."

"Yes."

"Did Ethan like working for your dad?"

I sighed and curled my toes into my slippers. "He didn't talk about work much, honestly. It was just a job for him."

"How long has he worked for him?"

"Since we've been married. Three years."

"Everything okay out here?" My dad pushed the door open and spoke a little fast. He tended to do that when he got worked up. This situation definitely had us all worked up. "Sweetheart, want me to join you?"

"I guess." I wrapped my arms around my stomach and hugged tight.

"What do you need to know, Officer Luna?"

"Detective," he corrected my father. "I'm going to file the paperwork and jot down some notes."

"You're not going to track his credit card or finances or phone or anything?"

"There's no reason to believe Ethan's in harm's way."

"But he's missing. My daughter needs her husband—their *son* needs his father. I need my son-in-law and employee back. Surely you should be looking for him?"

I glanced at my dad and almost smiled at the intense look on his face. He was fighting for me. He always would.

I put Logan down for a nap, like I always did around noon, and enjoyed his sweet baby smell. He cuddled against me, and his soft brown hair tickled my nose. Everyone said he was a mini me, but all I saw was Ethan: his ears, his brown eyes, his long lashes, and his curved lips. I set him in the crib and went to turn the noise machine on when I noticed the little cubes that tracked his age had been changed to sixty-nine.

I snorted. *Of course* Ethan had done that recently. We always showed little pieces of our immaturity, and it reminded me of the time he'd spelled *BOOBS* on the bathtub wall with the foam letters. We even had a shared playlist we added to on Spotify titled "696969." It was ridiculous.

Something itched at the back of my mind like déjà vu or a memory that was just a whisper. Nerves prickled along my spine, growing more and more apparent as the minutes went by while I stared at the numbers. There was only one way I could relax or settle down or focus.

Music.

Ethan used to tease me for spending hours creating playlists. Writing reviews for an indie magazine was my current part-time job, which I adored, and music was my entire life: piano lessons, concerts, playlists.

I quietly shut the nursery door and entered the hallway. "Mom," I said. She sat with Peter on the couch, watching TV. "I think I need to lie down. Logan's out already, and I need rest. Do you mind . . . if anything happens?"

"Yes, of course, go. Lie down. You need sleep to function, hon." She got up and walked over to me, arms extended. As she hugged me, her familiar floral perfume tickled my nose. "I love you."

Peter nodded at me. "I'll stick around, too, and make sure we order dinner for you and Lo."

"Thanks." I headed back to our bedroom and crawled onto Ethan's side of the bed. I grabbed my phone and went to the "696969" playlist. It had songs from the Killers, the Black Keys, Arctic Monkeys, and Glass Animals. It was our playlist.

All the songs we'd laughed and danced and fallen in love to.

I closed my eyes and hit Shuffle, *needing* to feel him, to know that what we had wasn't in my head. My feet wiggled to the drums, and my heart rate finally calmed down. Music was where my soul lived, and my body was just the physical vessel it borrowed from time to time.

While listening to song after song, I felt like myself again. Like I could breathe.

But the calm vanished when a song I had never heard came on. **"Trust Me" by YOUYA.** I sat up in my bed. Why was this song on our playlist? Was there some meaning to it that I didn't remember?

When had that song been added? My heart pounded in my chest, each beat sending a ripple of adrenaline through me.

I clicked on Date Added. *Monday morning.* Ethan had added the song titled "Trust Me" the morning I last saw him. The last time he added a song to that list had been three months ago.

This was intentional. *Trust me.*

What the *fuck* did that mean?

CHAPTER FOUR

Wednesday, 7:30 p.m.—Two days missing

After searching every single playlist we shared, I found there were no more additions to any of them since the day he'd left. Just the one. *Trust me.*

Trust you after you disappeared on me?

I ground my teeth together in frustration. Sure, the relief at seeing the song helped, but what if it was a fluke? It didn't explain a single thing.

Ethan was intentional in every action—he took his time cleaning, hanging a picture frame, and making outfit choices based on what his day included. For this song to be added the last morning I'd seen him meant something.

I wiped the counter, pushing the remains from dinner into the sink. Peter had ordered Chinese food from our favorite place down the street and helped make sure Logan ate. As I tossed the rag into the washer, my phone went off with an unknown number. My heart leaped in my throat, hope bolting through me.

Ethan!

"Hello? Hi!" I answered, desperation clogging my voice. He'd finally called! "Is this you, Ethan?"

"Is that Ethan?" my dad screamed.

He prowled toward me, his eyes wide and a vein bulging in his forehead. His aggressive stance and roaring voice made me lean away as I strained to hear the other end of the call. "Ethan, is this you?"

Nothing. Silence. A breath. Then they hung up.

What the actual fuck. My gut hollowed out as I scanned every corner of the kitchen and living room. The hairs on the back of my neck stood on end, the feeling of unease sending alarm bells all over my body. *Get out of here,* my gut screamed.

But this was our home! Where was I going to go?

"Who was that?" my dad demanded, yanking my phone out of my hands. "Let me look."

"Was it Ethan? Or someone asking for ransom?" Peter joined us, his face laced with worry.

My dad's expression paled. "Was it, Marissa?"

"I don't know." I cleared my throat and clasped my hands together to stop the trembling. "How do we even know it's Ethan? And why would you think they want ransom?"

"Just a possibility." My dad cussed and tossed my phone on the counter. "Useless." He paced, running a hand through his hair.

My adrenaline needed to escape, and my body shook so much. Peter took a deep breath, his entire body shifting to a more relaxed stance. It unnerved me to see him swing from panicked to calm.

"We have no way of proving that was Ethan or someone asking for ransom, but I'm having a hard time thinking he ran away. He loved Marissa and Logan. God, he talked about Lo all the time," Peter said in a slow radio voice. The same voice he used when our parents fought.

"Peter." My dad lowered his voice, and the two of them shared a look.

Peter fisted his hand at his side before he flexed it.

"What did that mean, Dad?" I asked, marching to the living room to join my mom.

"What, sweetheart?" He met my eyes with a half smile. My dad quickly followed and sat on my couch. "What did you ask?"

"Why did you say Peter's name like that?"

"I'm pissed, honey. I hate how upset you are right now. I don't understand why this is happening, and you know I get mad about shit like that."

I wiped my hands on my thighs.

Trust me.

Did you call me, Ethan?

"I'm hopeful he's okay and healthy. I just . . . cannot see him choosing to leave, you know? He loved you both more than words," my mom said. Her brows drew together, revealing all her wrinkles. "Do you want to talk about it or not? I don't know what to do here to help you, baby."

My eyes prickled with tears again, and I took a shaky breath. My pulse hummed through my body like the thrum of a bass. "I think . . . I think Ethan's okay."

"What?" Peter walked over to the couch and sat, resting his elbows on his knees. "Why? Did he call you?"

"No." I chewed my lip and rubbed my knuckles together. A horrible, guilty feeling ate at my stomach at the thought of telling them. But they were my family. They'd be thrilled he was okay. Heck, they hadn't left my side since this all started. "He added a song to one of our playlists the morning he left."

Silence. My family's wide eyes. My pounding heartbeat.

I wondered if I'd said it out loud or imagined the words, but then Peter tilted his head. "What do you mean?"

"I've been trying to share playlists with all of you for years," I snapped. My part-time job was an ongoing joke in my family. Writing about music was *silly*, something they viewed as a hobby. They revered themselves as tech gods, with all their coding and programming and computer skills.

It didn't matter how I'd begged my father to join the family business. He'd said I was too soft and vulnerable to handle their world. With nothing more than a headshake and a *Tech is a man's field, Marissa*, he'd solidified my weak ambition to amount to nothing more than a part-time writer.

I was proud I had a part-time job and was a mom! I worked fucking hard.

"I've gotten your playlists, Marissa, but what does it mean if Ethan added a song? I'm not tracking," Peter said, the tension in his shoulders visible. The temperature in the room rose. With Ethan being gone and my brother ready to snap . . . maybe I shouldn't have said anything.

"Explain the song addition." My dad's voice came out louder than we'd been speaking, as if he were trying to make sure someone down the hall could eavesdrop. "It must be important if you feel he's communicating with you. Tell us. Maybe it'll help us find him."

The vibration in my gut doubled, and I willed my body to settle down. I didn't know why I held back from sharing the truth, yet the silence grew, and everyone stared at me expectantly. "'Trust Me.' That's the song he added that morning."

"Are you sure? How do you know?" My dad's tone shifted into an *almost too sweet* voice that he used on waiters at restaurants. I always hated it; a normal tone would work fine. I was sure it was effective for him at work, but I wished he wouldn't use it on me.

"My job is music. I know how playlists work and when songs were added," I said louder.

"Were there more songs? Does the playlist give a location? Let's go through your other lists of that indie music and see if there are any other clues," Peter said. "I can help you. Maybe Mom and Dad can leave, and you and I can dive into the playlist?"

"I already did. There's nothing."

"You might've missed something, sweetheart." My dad patted my arm and pushed up from the couch. "You've been known to misplace things, and if this is a clue that can help us find him, I know I'd feel better about it if Peter and I took a glance."

A sticky, gross feeling flared in my stomach, the urge to kick them all out frightening me. I never misplaced things—except for a brief lapse when I'd had pregnancy brain. It was a very real thing, and I hadn't found my keys twice. That was it.

It had to be the stress heightening my emotions. Why else would I be so mad at my dad for trying to help? Sleep. That's what I needed.

"Dad, I think I want to take a bath and go to sleep," I said, sighing.

He frowned and shoved his hands in his pockets. "We can hang out just to be safe."

"No. I think we should leave." Peter met my gaze with a brief nod. He understood. He could always read my moods, and I had to be radiating annoyance. "She needs rest, and we're hovering."

I mouthed *thank you* to him. Peter would always be my protector, my closest friend.

My dad narrowed his eyes at me, his jaw tightening. "Okay, Peter's right. This is horrible, but we can come back first thing in the morning. We've been smothering her for two days now," he said.

"What about work?" I said, hating the thought of them being here all day *again*, stifling me. I hadn't had a moment to myself since this ordeal started. Plus, the nagging feeling that Ethan left more clues for me was something I needed to explore alone.

Not with my parents. Not with Peter.

The sixty-nine in Logan's room had reminded me of the playlist, which led to finding the song he added the morning he left. There had to be more. I *needed* there to be more, and I didn't want an audience.

"Work? Your husband is missing. I can take off until we find him. Peter can too." He let out a chuckle. "I do run the place, so I can do this."

"No, I meant . . . ," I said, unsure how to finish the sentence. "Work. Ethan's work. We should go to the office and see if there's anything there, right? I didn't even think about that. He's been working long hours lately."

Peter stood. "Great idea, Marissa. Yeah, we can head into the office tomorrow and look around."

"You come here to help." My dad gestured to my mom. He didn't ask her. He demanded, per usual. She nodded, always the supportive wife, and leaned down to give me a long hug. Her embrace was the final straw against me holding it together. The scent of her lavender lotion flooded my nose, and I buried my face into her neck and cried.

Ethan was gone, on purpose or not. He'd either be found or not. I'd either be a single parent or not. Those were the possibilities, and even though the addition of the song had provided a brief moment of hope and a step forward, the overwhelming weight of it all crushed me.

My heart physically hurt with each beat, and my mom rubbed her hands up and down my back. "Are you sure you don't want us to stay? We can, baby. Just ask."

"N-no." I sniffed and pulled back. "I need . . . to do this alone tonight."

"I'll be here in the morning, okay? Even if you want to cry all day, I'll help with Logan. Do you want us to take him home tonight, to make sure you get sleep?"

"No." I sniffed again, grateful for the gesture. "He's keeping me sane right now, but thank you. Maybe another night."

She patted my arm before they got their coats and left. Peter pulled me into a hug, whispering that he'd figure out what was going on for me. He would do whatever he could, and I believed him. But I had some solo exploring to do.

There was a pleasant silence with them gone from the house.

It was a long shot. Totally wild. But an idea had struck when my dad seemed to disregard my notion that Ethan tried contacting me. If Ethan had added that song, he might be watching to see if I saw it. That meant he had access to his Spotify account.

He knows how much I'm on there.

I put on "I Miss You" by blink-182 and let myself wallow in the angsty lyrics and familiar timbre of their vocalist. I belted out the words, channeling my turmoil into singing. It soothed me. I bobbed my head to the song and headed to Ethan's office, needing to be around his stuff. I sat in his chair and spun around.

A new book was underneath a picture of us, and I pulled it out. It didn't belong here at all. In fact, dust gathered on the shelf except for this book. My heart about exploded out of my chest like it had when I'd seen the addition of the song. A sign!

He'd bought it for me to read a few months ago, saying it was one of the best books he'd read. *Tell No One* by Harlan Coben. The premise was not one I wanted to escape into now—his wife was presumed dead but showed up years later. A shiver went through me. Years of thinking he's dead, only for him to be alive the whole time?

I couldn't survive that.

I flipped through the pages and stumbled upon a bookmark. Idly, I twisted it between my fingers. On the back, there was something handwritten in Ethan's writing.

CRESCENT BALLROOM.

The name of our favorite concert venue.

There was also a date at the bottom—Monday morning. My pulse spiked like I'd sprinted up the stairs without breathing. If I wasn't mistaken, this was another clue. I just had to decipher it, and I knew *exactly* where to look.

CHAPTER FIVE

Wednesday, 9:30 p.m.—Two days missing

Ethan kept his vinyl records in a box at the back of our closet. It had been months, if not years, since I'd looked at them. Since he'd started working for my father's business, he'd gotten busy. Then, once things leveled out, I got pregnant by accident, and our life revolved around Logan. We didn't have our late-night wine and music parties, where we'd listen to entire albums and compare notes. The last concert we'd gone to before I got pregnant was Jungle. The alt-pop band from the United Kingdom was one of my favorites, and that night was in my top five.

The force of the memory hit me hard, making me breathless as I pulled the box out from under a pile of sweatshirts, which caused Ethan's familiar scent to reach me. He'd always smiled softly at me when I'd worn his clothes. I held his light-gray sweatshirt against my face and inhaled. I'd ordered this one for him three years ago for his birthday, and he'd loved it so much he'd worn a hole in it. After giving myself five seconds of grief, I set it aside and got to work.

The lid of the box clicked open, and I leafed through the records carefully until I found the Jungle album. A bright-green sticky note sat there, and I almost dropped the album. *A clue! Another clue!*

WELLINGTON2007

What the fuck did *Wellington2007* mean? I ripped the note off and flipped it over, desperately needing there to be more than a nonsense word. A key was taped on the back. A small, unhelpful key. It was light; I almost couldn't feel it. Nondescript. I twirled it, hoping to find something that told what it was for. It could've been to a deposit box, a jewelry box, or a safe. Hell, it could be a toy key for Logan.

The utter joy at finding the clue switched to chaos and anger, all within a blink. Why leave me this code word and key? I fisted the piece of paper in my hand, crunching it as I slid onto the floor. I wasn't sure what I'd expected—a hidden cell phone to call him, maybe.

Nada. There was nothing.

Defeated, I dragged myself back to the bedroom. I went to the playlist, scrolling and organizing the songs by add date to reassure myself Ethan had added the song.

The hairs on the back of my neck tingled. I looked again, and my stomach hardened with the same dread I felt watching the news. Or a car crash. A sick feeling in my gut. *It's not here.*

My fingers shook violently as I scanned my friends to the right of my screen. One thing Ethan and I had done when he started working long hours was add each other on Spotify. His last song was "I Love You" by Billie Eilish—listened to two hours ago.

Two hours.

Not two days.

He's alive.

I let out a giggle of relief, and I cupped my hand over my mouth. Even with the disappearance of the "Trust Me" song, he played this song after I played "I Miss You."

I had no idea where the fuck he was or what had happened, but he was somewhere, alive. I played the song **"R U Ok" by Tate McRae** and waited. I chewed the hell out of my thumbnail. He could see I was live, listening to this song.

Seconds ticked by slower than molasses, and the song ended.

He still wasn't actively listening to a song. I could wait him out. It wasn't like I was sleeping well since he'd disappeared.

But then he went active. **"Tell No One about Tonight" by Le Sport.** God, my lips curved into a smile. He was there.

I played **"Our Secret" by the Postal Service**.

Immediately, his song switched to **"Be Careful" by Cardi B**. It played for thirty seconds before he played another one. **"Trust No One" by Space914.**

Goose bumps traveled down my neck, sending a chill through me. For him to choose *that song* . . . he knew I was only close with my family. I had a few online friends, but they were in different states. *Trust no one* . . . my mind went to my mom, dad, brother. They were my rocks. We did a lot of activities with my parents. Did Ethan mean I shouldn't trust the way my dad spoke to me, making me down on myself? Or did he mean not to trust what they said about Ethan? I wasn't sure, but the seed of suspicion took root. Why should I blindly trust Ethan, the man who'd changed in the last few months, the man who'd left me?

Something soft thudded on the other side of the house. *Fuck.* Fear made everything seem more in focus: the sound of the furnace humming, the baby monitor's barely-there frequency, the buzzing of the lights. Our bedroom sat in the back of the house, while the rest of it—the office, living room, kitchen, and nursery—was all on the other side.

That thud happened two more times, and my chest hurt with how fast my heart pounded into my ribs. *Logan.* I'd die for my son, that was no question; if there was an intruder, they'd have to go through me first.

Weapons. I needed weapons.

With my senses in high gear, the thuds seemed like footsteps, and I grabbed the only heavy thing in the room. My lamp. With my pulse racing throughout my body, I tiptoed toward the door and held my breath. The person was *right* there.

I could hear their breathing, the shuffle of their pants. They were headed toward the other wing of the house, where Logan was, and that snapped me into fight mode. I darted out of the room and raised the lamp over my head, ready to crush it on the intruder, when my brother yelped.

"Marissa! God, what are you doing?" He jumped back as he clutched his chest. "Were you going to hit me with that?"

"Yes. I—I thought you were an intruder." My voice broke, and my legs shook as we stood there. Relief flooded me. "What are you doing? You scared the shit out of me."

Peter ran a hand over his face, and he flashed me a smile. "I left my phone here. You know I can't live without that thing."

"Ah, right. The ladies would suffer." I hoped the teasing would make the awkward situation better.

My joke hit the mark. He nodded, and his eyes softened. "I'm sorry to scare you, Mar. I didn't want to come in through the front door and wake Lo up, and I didn't have a way to call you."

Oh, that made sense.

"Was the back door unlocked?"

"I used my key." He held up the red key Ethan and I had made for my parents to have, in case of emergencies. I frowned, pretty confident we hadn't given Peter his yet. "Ethan gave it to me a few weeks ago."

He must've read my face.

Seeing another key nagged something in the back of my mind. I believed in patterns, and it felt like I had seen three keys today . . . but ugh, it didn't make sense.

"Can you grab your phone and call it? Maybe we'll hear it?"

I nodded and went back into my bedroom. I hit Call for my brother's phone, but as I came out into the hallway, he wasn't there. "Peter?"

A thud came from Ethan's office, causing me to head that way. Just before I took a step toward the door, Peter exited the office with his phone in his hands.

"Found her, my sweet, sexy phone."

I snorted. "You're so weird. Where was it?"

"In the office, on the bookshelf. I bet I set it there when we were trying to look at bank accounts or something." He shrugged and pocketed the device. "I'm really sorry about worrying you."

"No, it's fine. I appreciate you not coming in the front door." I wrapped my arms around my stomach. We got along well and never fought. Even though he was four years older than me, we'd always been friends. Always close.

We'd grab dinner all the time before Ethan and I got married, and then the two of them hit it off, and our twosome became a trio. I so badly wanted to tell him about the songs. But **"Tell No One about Tonight"** was a clear message.

"Are you sure you'll be okay? This has to be so hard, Mar. I'm so fucking sorry you're going through this. Mom and Dad aren't helping at all. I wish they'd just . . . shut the hell up sometimes."

I snorted, but my skin prickled. "Trust No One" blared in my head. I forced a smile. "I know. But they help with Logan, and I'm grateful for that."

"I still think you should consider what I said a few weeks ago." His tone got serious, his face hardening. "Dad is toxic, and you don't need to let him do this to you."

"I can't . . . I'm not cutting them off, Peter." My voice shook. I never understood how he could say that shit while continuing to work for our dad and hang out with him. "I know you want to protect me but—"

"I love you, Mar, and they are toxic. You don't need their shit."

It was an ongoing battle we had. Peter had grown more insistent on me cutting off our parents, doing his best to persuade me it was for the better. He meant well, I knew that, but Logan loved his grandparents. They helped me with meals and day care. Any passive-aggressive comment could be shrugged off; there were too many good things about them to let the small stuff prevent a relationship between our parents and Logan. Peter didn't understand the love between a child and his grandparents since we never spent time with our own growing up—it was unmatched—so I ignored his pleas.

His love for me was making me emotional, and I hugged Peter hard. He squeezed me back, the unsaid words comforting me in a way I hadn't expected.

When we ended the embrace, he asked, "Has he added any more songs or done anything to make this all make sense?"

Yes. "No, I think I might've dreamed the other one too. It's gone."

Peter tensed, and frown lines formed around his eyes. "You know you didn't. You wouldn't make that mistake. Now, please get some sleep. I'll be there when Dad searches his office, and we'll find something, I'm sure."

"Okay, yeah."

He left rather quickly, and I was alone again. I did another round of locking every door and window, thinking about my parents, Peter's insistence on my cutting them off, and the "Trust No One" song. They felt . . . related, but I had no idea how or why.

I needed to think. I needed music. I needed Ethan's home office.

I quietly walked in and stilled.

Something felt different. I read once about a prank someone pulled where they moved every piece of furniture in one direction by two inches. Not enough to make it obvious but enough to have someone misjudge where corners and edges were. It felt like that. Like everything had shifted.

I didn't turn on the hallway lights for fear of waking Logan, which meant every little light from Ethan's computer stood out.

And that was the only reason I noticed *the light*. There was a tiny jump drive the size of my nail plugged into the back of his Mac, and the light pulsated like it was working really hard. My stomach lurched.

I could swear that hadn't been there before. Ethan hated jump drives. He was a firm believer in the cloud and online storage, so that begged the question: Did he leave this for me to find, or . . . did someone else put it there? And if it wasn't Ethan . . . then *who*? My brother? Maybe it was a password-decryption thing that would help get us into the computer. Yeah. That made the most sense. We all wanted to get into the device, and he was trying to be helpful.

I'd make sure to ask him about it tomorrow.

CHAPTER SIX

Thursday, 8:00 a.m.—Three days missing

"Home" by Edward Sharpe and the Magnetic Zeros. Our song. That was the final thing Ethan listened to last night, giving me enough peace of mind to sleep, which I desperately needed. Turned out, my brain put together the pieces it had missed the day before.

The hot-pink Post-it note on the password list? My dad had left it on the computer. The random numbers were actually coordinates. I'd woken up with the idea to google the pattern and bam—where did they lead?

To the goddamn post office.

What did the post office contain? PO boxes. And judging by the key drawn on the Post-it, what did this little key probably fit into? Said PO box. All I had to do was figure out which one. That was all. No big deal.

The little thing was in my pocket, and despite it being tiny, it felt like a million pounds of unknowns. My skin prickled as I glanced around the lobby. It felt like someone was watching me, but no one stared at me longer than a second. I glanced out the window and found a big burly man leaning against a pillar with his arms crossed. He had piercing green eyes and wore a black suit, but the second I met his gaze, he turned away.

It was silly. Stupid, probably, but my thoughts weren't rational right now. What if . . . no. There was no way Ethan was involved with the mob . . . right? I brushed it off, ignoring the way the burly guy had seemed to study me.

I had to focus on the PO boxes.

What if there was an answer there that made things worse? What if it was some illegal crime I was now a part of? What if this made me guilty? What if it was nothing? I couldn't be sure. I *hated* not knowing and not *trusting* him.

I wiped my palms on my pants, then secured Lo in his stroller. I had no idea what box to look for, but I hoped like hell I could figure it out.

The bell chimed, and a worker glanced up with a frown. Gulping, I waved and eyed the layout. Older folks lined up waiting to mail packages, the boxes in their hands too large for their bodies. In front of me, there was a packing station.

To the left, there was a hallway. A security camera blinked in the corner. Was it following me, or was I losing it? My palms were sweating against the stroller as I slowly went left, eyeing the walls for anything that jumped out.

Tears of frustration welled in my eyes.

I shouldn't be doing this. I wasn't clever or tough, not like Ethan or my family. This was too much for me. My mouth dried up, my vision blurred as fear took over, but then Logan babbled, "Dad dada."

A man walked in with a hat, and I gasped.

It wasn't Ethan, but the similarity to him was enough to freak me out. The guy had the same broad shoulders and sharp jaw. I stared, my lips parted, and the man frowned at me. *Focus.* My skin prickled. I kept going.

The hallway widened, and on either side, there were boxes built into the wall. There were at least a hundred of them. Did I just . . . try every box? I reached into my pocket for the small key and *shit.* It fell, clanging onto the ground a foot away from me. Logan babbled *dadada* again as I picked it up, my shirt clinging to my back from all the sweat.

I slowed my breathing as I approached the first row of PO boxes. They were in the two thousands.

Wait.

Wellington2007. The word on the Post-it. Was that . . . ? I scanned for 2007 and found it on the top right. *I should try that one first.*

As I reached for the box with sweaty fingers, my phone buzzed.

Dad: Found Ethan's planner. Will show Mar to see if she can help.

Mom: Good. I'll ask her.

Wait. What? Did they not know I was in the group chat?

Marissa: Ask me what?

Mom: Sorry sweetie, I meant about Ethan's plans. See you soon ❤

We'd been texting in our family group message the last few days. Did they . . . have a separate thread without me? Probably. I couldn't worry about that now. I took the key and slid it into 2007 and *holy shit*. It turned, and I was inside the PO box.

My pulse was like punches in my throat, the *thud thud thud* of my heart aching as I pulled out a yellow-brownish envelope. This had to be it. The clues. The explanation. Sounds stopped around me; the only thing I heard was my heartbeat as I stuck my hand inside and found . . . cash. A wad of cash and a scrap of paper that said *KEEP THIS JUST IN CASE.* No other explanation. Just money.

Mafia. He'd stolen this. He was a criminal. This was a theft. My stomach clenched as I fought the urge to fling it across the room. This had to be thousands of dollars for me. But *why*? I glanced outside, and the suited man was gone, but that didn't bring much relief.

"Oh, he is so cute, dear!" An older woman walked up to me, her stale perfume tickling my nose in an unpleasant way. "How old is he?"

"Uh, he's, uh, one and a half." I swallowed and clenched the envelope. Who was this woman? Why was she here, talking to me?

"Adorable." She had gray, curly hair and only stood about five feet tall, but her gaze was sharp and unnerving as she jutted her chin toward the envelope. "Those always remind me of movies, carrying a secret message or money or something from a spy. You know what I mean?"

Does she know? Was she waiting for me? I took a step back, the hairs on the back of my neck standing on end. The security camera moved an inch—pointing directly at us. *Fuck.*

"You're pale. Do you need help?"

"N-no. I'm okay." I needed to get the hell out, now.

I squinted into the box, needing there to be more, but it was empty. Just the envelope and warning. Time to go.

I locked up the box, trying to hold the envelope under my arm. The woman stood too close to me, her wheezy breath making me more nervous by the second. Without a backward glance, I ran us back to the car. Logan was secure in his seat as I stared at the doors of the post office—the woman stood there, watching us. What the absolute fuck.

The second I shut the car door and locked it, my phone rang.

UNKNOWN CALLER.

"Hello?"

The same silence. A breath. A dull ringing. No voice.

Nothing. I hung up, my skin feeling too tight. Two calls, two silences, the old woman. That wasn't good. It was one thing to get a weird call, but *right* after finding cash in a secret PO box? No thank you. Before I could even reverse out of the lot, my phone buzzed.

Mom: Why aren't you home? I'm here early to help!

It was 7:45. She'd planned on coming at nine. What the hell was going on?

Marissa: I had to mail something for my job, be right back.

She was early, intentionally, and sent the text seconds after the call. This was too much. I gripped the wheel, the money pinned against my leg, as I cursed Ethan. He'd set this up. He'd done this, and I had no idea what to do.

"Gam Gam!" Logan cheered as we parked in our driveway, my mom leaning against her car with a frown. She walked over to the car door and pulled it open. After getting Logan out of his car seat, she picked him up and covered him with kisses. I used the time to shove the envelope into my purse.

"Hon, you look tired. I could've dropped something off for you." She clicked her tongue and hoisted Logan on her hip. "I brought lunch, dinner, fruit, and dessert for both of you. You will eat on my watch. You need to lie down. You have circles under your eyes, dear."

I forced a smile. "No, I should get some work done, actually." *And figure out why I have this wad of cash and am getting weird calls.*

My mom stared at me with her lip curled.

"What? I could use the distraction."

"I hate that you feel you *need* to work. Ethan vowed to care for you both for all your lives. Your dad takes care of me; Ethan should take care of you. That is what a husband does."

"Mom." I fought an eye roll. "I enjoy writing. It's not a money thing—it's for me. Ethan supports us financially."

She twisted her face in a scowl before giving her attention back to Logan. This wasn't the first time we'd had this conversation. She had antiquated views of women's roles. She'd always been happy to let my dad lead, steamrolling everyone else, and she'd smile while he did it. Before I'd gotten a degree in creative writing, when I'd wanted to join the business, she'd pulled me aside and said it was hard for her to see me try to join a man's world. I was too sensitive, and I'd just get hurt. She said that she'd known from when I was a baby that I wasn't cut out for it, and she'd protect me from that environment. That I was better off staying out of the family business.

At first, I thought it was a joke. But it definitely hadn't been. My mom didn't want me working there because I wasn't cut out for it. It wasn't my place. Being a mother and a wife was enough of a full-time job for me, and I should be *proud* of being a homemaker. That was still her view.

"Go write, if you must." Her tone was clipped, and while it annoyed me, she was there, helping me with Logan and bringing us food. I walked up to her and gave both her and Lo a hug. The tightness of her shoulders relaxed.

"I love you."

"I love you, too, Marissa. I know you're independent, I just . . . marriage is hard, and I worry if your independent streak caused an unnecessary strain. If you dedicated more time to supporting Ethan, like I do your father . . ." She took a quick breath before breaking our embrace and carrying Logan to the front door. "He wouldn't have stayed late all those nights at work doing god knows what."

Her words hit me in the solar plexus. *Unnecessary strain.*

Was she hinting that I'd caused him to leave? How did she know he stayed late? Did I tell her that? Did my dad mention it to her, expressing concerns about our marriage? *Fuck.*

I chewed my thumbnail and tasted blood as I walked into our office. I shut the door and closed my eyes, trying to settle down. The hints that I caused Ethan to leave were growing, the self-doubt and worry doubling as more mystery clouded his disappearance. I fell into his chair and eyed the damn flash drive. I needed a distraction, so I'd research the shit out of it. *And ask Peter about it.*

Despite searching online, I couldn't figure out if the jump drive was a certain type for a specific purpose.

Like surveillance. It was a real trip to think Ethan put it in there to monitor what I did on his device, but I was never on it. I had my own. *But the password to Ethan's computer had been changed the morning after he disappeared* . . . someone else wanted to monitor Ethan's activity. Who, though? And when? Peter? But why? Had it been my dad?

No. They'd tell me.

But would they? The voice in the back of my mind shouted about all the times they'd downplayed my intelligence and mocked me. Never in an up-front, hurtful way. It was subtle. An eye roll, a scoff.

Trust no one. Ethan's warning gripped me.

The money. The PO box. The song.

I picked up my phone to text Peter about the drive but paused. Maybe, just maybe, he'd thought I wouldn't notice.

I gritted my teeth and pulled the flash drive out. I wanted it out just in case Ethan hadn't put it there. I tensed, waiting for something to happen, but there wasn't a sound or an epiphany. Just the screen saver coming to life on Ethan's computer.

He used to have a picture of the three of us as the background, but now it was a slideshow of photos. One of the two of us from years ago, a couple of Logan, a LEGO tower he'd built with Logan, and then a photo of Minecraft.

What?

Why in the fuck would—wait. Awareness flooded through me, making my skin tingle and my breathing ragged. *Minecraft.* Something we'd done together years ago.

Duke of Wellington was his username when we played. Holy shit.

WELLINGTON2007 was a code for a PO box and now this. *Okay, Ethan.*

My fingers shook like I'd stuck them in an electric socket, and I typed the word found on the vinyl from our best concert together.

It worked. I was in Ethan's computer.

I clicked too fast and opened up ten folders, scanning for a title that jumped out at me. It would've been great if he'd named it *READ THIS, MARISSA*, but that was asking too much.

The guy had left me breadcrumbs, and while they weren't easy to crack, they were only meant for me to understand. Not anyone else. That seemed important. So, what stood out to *me*?

There were finances, photos of Logan and us. Spreadsheets of movies he'd seen from the one summer he promised to watch all IMDb's top 250 movies.

I closed out of the folders and opened one titled *Draft 1*. He wasn't a writer by any means, but *draft* caught my attention.

Dear Marissa.

My breath lodged in my throat. This was meant for me! For me!

It was empty. Just that title. Dear Marissa. Nothing else.

What the fuck are you doing, Ethan? I rubbed my forehead with my fingers and fought the urge to cry, yet again. But I had no more tears left. He knew I hated puzzles.

I rested my head on the table and, in the process, hit the keyboard. I didn't care. There was a knock on the door, and my head snapped up. "Hmm?"

My mom pushed the door open, and her eyes widened when she saw me. "You figured out his password?" There was a lilt to her voice that sounded fake, like she was trying too hard to seem casual.

"No," I lied, still protecting *whatever* journey Ethan had me on. The monitor faced the window, so she wouldn't see the screen. "I signed in as a guest. I think I just . . . wanted to be closer to him. Sit in his chair. Use his stuff."

"Oh, hon." The shine to her eyes remained as she frowned. "Your dad and Peter are heading this way. They said they found something they want to talk to you about. They are geniuses, you know them. They can take another hack at the computer. You shouldn't worry about the tech stuff. I never do. Not with them around."

Her hesitant tone and constant fidgeting with her thumb and pointer had my nerves on edge. Like a loose thread on the hem of a shirt that kept growing and growing the more you pulled.

"Wait, what did they find?" I asked, proud of keeping myself calm. Did I want to throttle my mother to spit out whatever secret she hid? Yes. I knew her tells. "Mom, come on."

I bunched my fists at my sides, remembering all the other times she'd waited until my father got home to share news. Our aunt passing away, our family dog being put down, the rejection letters I got for college, which they'd opened without permission. They preached about transparency yet couldn't function without the other to share bad news. And it defaulted to my dad. The man of the house.

Her gaze moved from me to the window right behind me. *Avoiding eye contact.* Great. "It'll be best if he speaks to you. He can explain it better than me."

"My husband is *missing*. I'm going to be a single parent if we don't find him, so for the love of god, cut the crap, Mom. If you know what he's going to tell me, you need to tell me right now. It's not going to matter for you if it's now or in twenty minutes. Fuck, stop being shady. I hate how you let Dad do this to you all the time. You're an equal, not his submissive."

We both froze. I had never yelled at my mom. I never lost my cool or temper because it wasn't *becoming* of me. Peter could throw a tantrum about anything—someone getting a parking spot he wanted or the outcome of a sporting match. But me? Never.

A second passed, my mom's mouth parting like I'd told her I was a witch who could fly, and I covered my mouth with my hand. Her gaze hardened, and a flash of darkness crossed her face, a look I had never seen before. My veins chilled.

"I didn't mean . . . I'm sorry I yelled."

She righted her face and posture, but the concern and fear in her eyes had me questioning my apology. What was she *afraid* of?

"It's fine. You're stressed. Not yourself. It's understandable." She took a breath, then clasped her hands together and rested them on her gut. It made her look weird, unnatural. It reminded me of the time I'd disappointed her when I was twelve—stole her earrings. She didn't yell; she'd whispered and conveyed her disgust at my behavior.

Mom glanced at the window, then back to me before saying, "Your father found evidence of an affair. Possibly more than one. I think once we go over whatever he found, we should call that detective back."

Affair. Affair. Affair.

My head spun, and the ringing in my ears buzzed like a swarm of bees. My worst fear, come to life. It didn't matter that Ethan left breadcrumbs for me, playing our song and using our inside jokes. The thought that had kept me up at night as he slowly pulled away from me had legs and was growing. I wasn't enough for him. He was always so charismatic, larger than life. I was a wallflower and a pushover, and the thought of never being good enough for him had lived in my head all these years. The words my mom said, that I wasn't a good enough wife, returned, laughing at me. The pain broke me. How could I not think it true when he'd *cheated* on me? *Possibly with more than one woman.*

Time didn't make sense anymore, but Logan appeared next to my mom, and she frowned at me, her eyes narrowed in concern, and her gaze shifted from me to the window again. She blinked, and I swore she looked cheerful for half a second. Like a shadow of a spark.

Why would she be happy? What part of this moment brought her joy? Unless she knew something. But what? Did she *know* Ethan had cheated on me?

She picked up my son, and I found my voice again. "C-could you take him to the park for a bit? Let me gather myself?"

"Of course, hon." She pursed her lips and spun around, her heels clicking on the hardwood floor. She always dressed impeccably, like she was headed to a garden party at any hour of the day. Heels, fun skirts, or beautiful dresses. Her ballroom hair and perfect makeup used to impress me; now, it made me hate myself more when I'd go days without an ounce of makeup. *She must think I'm a sloppy woman.*

But that didn't matter. Ethan mattered. His possible *affairs*.

I gulped down the grapefruit-size ball of emotion and sat back in the chair. It was only then I realized, at some point, all the text had been highlighted, and it was clear now why it looked like a blank document.

The font was in white.

Ethan had left me a message. One that chilled me to my bones.

CHAPTER SEVEN

Thursday, 12:00 p.m.—Three days missing

WE'RE BEING WATCHED.

The white text from the document had sent a shiver through me, starting in my heart and ending at my toes. Was it the mob coming after us? Was that why he'd left me money . . . to run away? I had deleted the document from the device completely. Images of the suited man from the bank intruding in my head and causing a full-body tremble.

"Brought you mac and cheese, sweetheart. It's from your favorite place near the office. Run by the mom-and-pop couple." My dad set the bowl down on the side table next to the couch. My mom's food was still in the kitchen. They all focused on me eating first, since I had barely held it together the last few hours.

"Eat some, dear." My mom handed me a spoon and set the bowl on my lap. "You need it. You need your strength."

She was right. With Logan napping, I could force myself to eat a real meal.

Peter pinched the bridge of his nose and handed me the day planner by sliding it across the coffee table. The smooth leather barely made any sound, and I eyed it, afraid of what I'd find. It felt dirty now. Used. Gross. *Betrayed.*

"You'll want to see this. I don't . . . it's hard to know for sure," Peter said.

"It's pretty clear." My dad glared at my brother.

This happened a lot around me. Peter would speak against my dad, and they'd argue.

"Just tell me the truth. Please. Stop talking in circles." I took a bite, and my body craved more. My taste buds exploded at the first touch of real food today, and I knew I had to take better care of myself to get through this.

My dad had the same reluctant pull of his mouth he'd had when he told me our childhood dog had to be put down. "We found his planner at the office, with some interesting things written down. We tracked his notes to the surveillance footage, and it's . . . not great. He's with another woman, possibly more. Can you take my word for it?"

"No." The macaroni turned to ash in my mouth, each swallow becoming more difficult. I set the bowl on the coffee table. "I need to see it."

My father reached over to pat my forearm. "We asked them to pull footage as far as they could. Max Moore, the head of security, said they keep a loop of about four weeks, but he thinks he can find more in storage. With all the high-end stuff we deal with, it's imperative we save everything."

"Right." I fought the eye roll that almost slipped out. How crass of me. But if I had a bingo card with every mention of how important and techy and top secret their business was, I'd win a million dollars.

My brother took out a laptop from his backpack, and his fingers flew over the keyboard as he signed in. He had dark circles under his eyes, and my attention flashed to my mom. Had she commented about his appearance? Asked him to make his skin better to find a partner?

No.

A bubble of laughter almost snuck out. I, the mild-mannered, quiet daughter was on the verge of calling out my parents. It was the least opportune time, as they were helping me, but the urge was there, lingering just out of reach. To actually tell them what was on my mind.

Maybe another day.

"This first video is from last week. Tuesday night." Peter cleared his throat, his face set in hard lines. My brother never lied to me, so this had to be big.

The momentary hysteria disappeared, and a white-hot sadness erupted, like lava, flowing through my veins as the video snapshot showed my husband with another woman. I hadn't even hit Play yet. It was just a still.

The intent was clear. The pressure in my chest grew exponentially, and I pressed my hand against it to relieve the pain. I'd made shrimp campanelle Tuesday night—his favorite meal—and he missed it because he said he was working. I believed him, and the lie was right in front of me.

I tasted salt before I realized I was crying, but I hit Play. The time stamp said 6:15 p.m., the time he should've been home and eating with me. They were in the elevator, and she stood next to him, her hand on his arm, and his brows drawn.

How dare he look guilty when he knew what he was doing! I took a breath and forced myself to watch as they left the elevator and walked down the narrow hallway toward his office. They went inside, and he shut the door, lowered the shades, but not before their shadows moved closer.

Maybe there was an explanation for it.

"There's three more like that from the past two weeks." Peter's voice came out strained and ragged.

"The s-same woman?"

"No. Different ones." Peter tapped the front of the planner. "I'm not sure if it's a coincidence or not, but there's a certain mark on the dates he's seen with the women. A secret way to meet them so you wouldn't know? They go back a few months, but they picked up the last month. Have you noticed him acting differently?"

Yes.

The songs. The money. The PO box.

Why go through all the steps to send me personal messages if this was happening? I rubbed my palms over my eyes until I saw white spots and felt the heavy stares of my family all around me.

Ethan wouldn't do that . . . but didn't all wives think that? That they were special and that their husband wouldn't step out on them? The reality that I could have no idea was a hard pill to swallow.

The familiar tingling on the back of my neck gave me the motivation needed to get more information. My first reaction to the video was that *this* explained why he'd acted weird. So, I'd known, on some level, something was going on.

"Are there more?" I asked, wanting the proof.

"You're not watching them." My dad grabbed the laptop out of my reach, shutting it. "Trust us on this. It's four women."

"I never would've thought he could do this." My mom placed a hand over her heart, her lips pulled down. "This is so unlike him to hurt you, Marissa. You are such a good wife, right?"

Was I, Mother? You made sure to remind me how bad I was.

I said nothing. I gritted my teeth together, my heart racing as I met Peter's gaze. "Can I see the other videos?"

He shook his head, his shoulders tensing.

"Let me look at the planner then, since you won't show me what I want to see." I opened the leather journal and rubbed my finger over the date for Tuesday. Nothing seemed odd or inexplicable, except for the lone star in the corner of the entry. His schedule was normal. *Conference call. Lunch with L. Financials—3:00.* But the star. I ran the pad of my pointer over it and felt the indentation. He wrote it with aggression, so hard that when I flipped the page, I saw the star had come through it.

This isn't right.

I'd seen Ethan's writing. I'd watched the way he wrote carefully, and I looked at our jar of pens on the counter. This star was made with a ballpoint pen. Our jar held only gel pens that rolled over the paper and often left smudges.

A memory came to light, but it was blurry, like an old film that needed cleaning. I blinked, focused on the gut feeling I was missing something, and traced the star again.

"Do you know what a star means, Marissa?" Peter asked, his voice pulling me back to the moment. "Has he used it before?"

"No." I counted ten other stars from the past two months, all done with a black ballpoint pen. All were indented into the journal. I flipped it more, all the way back to January, and smiled at how he'd written *MARISSA'S BIRTHDAY!* in all caps. He'd bought me a vintage record and had an artist commission an old photo of us at a concert. It was the most thoughtful, loving gift. So for him to have an affair? Stab to the heart.

No stars then, on that day. Nothing written so hard that it bulged through the pages.

"What is it? Why are you smiling?" my dad asked, his accusing tone making me jolt.

"Sorry," I mumbled. I was unsure how to explain my thoughts. "I have no idea what the stars mean, and I've never seen him use them before to indicate anything."

"I think they were a way to document whenever he hooked up with someone." My dad scooted his chair closer to the coffee table. "Innocent enough for you to not catch it."

"I hate to say it, but Dad's right. I think . . . this was his way." Peter swallowed so hard, I heard it across the room, and I met his stare. "We don't have cameras in his office, before you ask. Not that that's helpful."

Right, Peter. It wouldn't be helpful to see my husband sleeping with someone else, but it'd be real great to know what was happening. Did he have a sex addiction and had to get off at work twice a week? Was it the risk factor he wanted? Hell, he'd done it at the office where my dad and brother worked. Risky. A really risky move that clashed with who Ethan was. The guy wore a seat belt, always locked everything twice in the house, and had avoided anything adrenaline inducing our entire time together. He put on sunscreen every day and wouldn't stand outside in a storm because the risk of getting hit by lightning was too high for his comfort. He hated risks. Sleeping with someone other than his wife . . . where his father-in-law could see?

People did stupid things all the time, but this was the height of stupidity. The more I thought about it, the more my confidence grew that I was missing something. This wasn't just a string of random hookups or a couple of affairs. I had no way of asking Ethan about it right now—there weren't enough song titles to adequately ask *Hey, are you sleeping with a bunch of women at the office or no?* But I could try to find the women. Not in a crazy, *I'm going to beat them up* way.

A way to get answers.

"Don't guests have to sign in?" I asked, needing to figure out these women's names. Every time I'd visited the office to see Ethan, Peter, or my dad, they'd made me sign in. They knew who I was, my birthday, and I wouldn't be surprised if they had my social security on file somewhere, but I still had to sign in. *Protocol.*

"What are you getting at?" My dad shifted in the seat and tilted his head at me.

"They would have to sign in. I want the women's names."

"I don't think it'll be healthy to have you cyberstalk the women Ethan was sleeping with, Mar." My dad's voice was tight with anger. "That won't help you."

"I want the women's names," I said again. The growing urge to snap at my family doubled in size. Did they not get it? I *needed* to ask the women questions. They could tell me what was going on since no one else could! "They could have answers about where the hell he is." *About the money! About it all!*

"It won't do you any good, baby, to find out those names. It'll make you obsess over everything, and you need to be strong for Logan." My mom's tone was laced with more aggression than I was accustomed to. I looked from her, to Peter, to my dad. They all wore the same expressions: tight lines around their mouths. Worry lines on their foreheads. Narrowed eyes.

"How can I get the women's names?" I asked for the third time. "Do I need to head down there and talk to the guard myself?"

"You're being difficult right now, but again, you're going through a lot." My dad rubbed his forehead. "The names won't solve anything you're searching for. It'll only cause you pain, and you already have enough of it right now. He cheated on you. It sucks, but going after the other women isn't the right move. We should focus on finding where he is."

"Is there a reason you're ignoring what I'm asking?" I snapped. The silence following my question was strong enough to make anyone cover their ears to avoid the profound nothingness. Just the buzz of the fridge and breathing.

"Mar," Peter said.

I stopped him by raising a hand. "Either get me the names, or I'll find them myself." I got up from the couch and walked over to the back door to go outside. Never in a million years had I thought I'd stand up to my parents when Ethan was missing. I had no one to fall back on, to pat my shoulder and tell me it'd be okay. Yet, with him missing and me being on my own, I'd never felt more capable.

Trust no one.

I might've felt capable, but I had never felt so alone.

I stood on the porch, enjoying the fall weather, with the damp smell of leaves and the slight chill, for a while. No one joined me. I preferred it that way. The sting from Ethan's possible betrayal echoed in my chest, but the sliver of unknown kept me from fully breaking down.

That unknown part was what I needed. Talking to those women would help that.

"Hon." My mom opened the door and poked her head out. "Detective Luna is here."

He walked outside; his height and dark eyes intimidated me into crossing my arms over my stomach. He glanced at my mom, then me before saying, "We found something you need to see."

CHAPTER EIGHT

Thursday, 2:00 p.m.—Three days missing

There was a gravity to his voice that sent a shiver down my spine.

"What did you find?" my dad asked, his words hurried together in one breath as he rushed toward the back door.

"A company car was reported missing yesterday, and we found it." He narrowed his eyes at my father. "It was abandoned on the side of I-10, east of Bloomington, and Ethan's wallet was there with traces of blood."

"*What?*" someone said, either my dad or brother.

The masculine voice was drowned out by the buzzing in my ears. Blood. Not necessarily Ethan's blood . . .

"What time? What time was this found? The blood?" I asked, digging my nails into the palms of my hands. The sharp points dug into my skin, and I waited. The time of this mattered. "Why is this the first we're hearing about it? This happened yesterday, you said?"

My dad raised his voice. "My company car? I didn't know it had been stolen. Who called it in? Why didn't they tell me?"

"I need the time of when you found it." I stared at the detective. My voice sounded off to my own ears, distant and lyrical.

He ignored my father's questions and stared right back, with a slight tilt of his head. "Noon."

My shoulders sagged in relief. Ethan had listened to those songs *after* noon. He'd played various songs last night—so he was okay. But it didn't explain the wallet or blood.

The detective pressed his lips together. But then, with no more than a blink, he shifted his attention to my dad. "A Scott Gerwig called it into the station. The only reason I connected the dots was because the call came through to my buddy who knew I was semi-involved in this."

"Scott. Damn it." My dad huffed. "I'm calling him right now."

"If I can advise you to wait, it would be helpful for the case."

"It's a case now?" I asked.

"We're circulating Ethan's photo, and we have an alert set on his account if he spends anything. His credit cards were missing from the wallet." He turned his back on me. "With the blood and discarding of the wallet, we're forced to be involved at this point. Unless . . ."

Peter slid the back door open and joined the rest of us. "Unless what?" he asked, the three syllables lacking his usual cocky candor. "Any of you have anything to tell me?"

My heart raced, and my palms were sweating so badly, if he saw my hands he'd know I was withholding something. But the silence sent a flutter of nerves to my stomach.

"Are we going to just *not* mention the affairs?" I asked.

"Affairs?" Detective Luna asked, his tone getting higher. "What affairs?"

"Ask him." I pointed to my dad and walked through the doors before plopping down at the kitchen table. My mind spun, and my lungs threatened to collapse. All I wanted to do was get my laptop and search for songs to ask Ethan what the ever-loving hell was going on, but I couldn't. Not with the detective here.

"We found some footage of Ethan and women at the office." My dad followed me, squeezing the back of his neck. Once inside, he tapped his right toe on the floor over and over in a constant beat. *Tap tap tap-tap-tap.* Hearing him explain what we saw, again, wasn't as painful as the first time, and right as he clarified how the footage only lasted a certain amount of time, I found my moment just as everyone else entered the kitchen.

"You could get the list of women from the head of security." I sat up straighter and ignored the narrowing of my father's eyes. He didn't like being interrupted, but la-di-freaking-da. My husband was missing. "Everyone is required to sign in at their building, and, uh, getting their names would be a great start."

Detective Luna studied me with a look that penetrated the glass-like hold I had on my emotions. His dark eyes had seen some shit. That was clear. But there was a soft kindness in his expression that caught me off guard. "Marissa, can I speak to you alone for a moment?"

"She doesn't need to be *alone* right now. Her husband is gone." My mom put her arm around me. "Just talk to her here where we can support her. She needs us; can't you see?"

I stood, but her arm tightened around me. "Mom, it's fine."

Her persistence irritated me, and I dragged my hand through my hair.

"Honey, that's what family does: supports you during the hard times. You're barely hanging on right now." She frowned. "Let us help you. You don't need to be a hero."

"Actually," Detective Luna said. "It's important that it's just her and I right now."

"Sounds like she might need a lawyer present," my dad said, his voice brisk and hard.

"No."

That's all the detective said. The authority in his voice, the way his eyes narrowed at my father and *not* me, sent a chill down my spine.

Peter moved closer to me. "At least let me go with you, Mar."

"I'm sure she appreciates your support, but I need a few moments of her time." The detective focused on me. "Is there somewhere we could chat? Another room?"

We're being watched.

I twisted my hands together before saying, "How about the front porch?"

He gave a curt nod and walked to the front door before opening it and guiding me through. "Your family is protective."

"That's one word for it." I laughed even though it wasn't funny. "Wh-what did you need to ask me?"

He scratched his chin and stared over my shoulder. "The affairs. Did you suspect or know about them?"

"No." I squeezed my eyes shut as the images replayed over and over. "My dad and brother showed me today, the footage from the office."

"I'm going to ask you again—was Ethan acting weird before Monday? Any indication of affairs or some sort of trouble?"

"He's been distant and working later." I rubbed my palms on my thighs. It was right there, the truth of the song titles on the tip of my tongue. But I couldn't do it. Something prevented me from sharing it with him. "Our marriage has been rocky for the past year or so."

"When did it start getting rocky?"

"Our relationship changed when he started working for my dad, but it's worsened over the past year. It's a stressful job. I got pregnant two years ago and had a rough time, and I kept thinking everything would go back to what it had been after I recovered and Logan wasn't a newborn baby, but it hasn't. Though there is one thing that I keep thinking about."

"What's that?" he asked, his tone high again.

I wrung my hands and looked him in the eye. "He told me to trust him before he walked out the door. I think that means something."

He sighed and crouched, looking over his shoulder toward the side window, where my parents lurked in the hallway. "I think so too. I have to show you a photo of what we found in the car."

He held his phone out, and I squinted at the image. The familiar navy company car sat on the side of the road; Ethan's wallet sat open right on the driver's seat. I scanned the car, expecting to see a knife or something. "Is there something I'm supposed to be looking at?"

He swiped to the next picture. It was a close-up of the wallet. There was a note. A white index card.

CASIO.

I felt the detective's gaze, and my skin flushed—not out of guilt or embarrassment but out of utter confusion. Casio. A type of tape. A keyboard. A watch. "Am I—am I supposed to know what this means?"

"That was my question for you." He put his phone back in his pocket. There was a tightness to his eyes now. "Think about it, and get back to me when you figure it out."

"What makes you sure I can?"

"Just a gut feeling." He echoed my words from the day before. He stared at me as a strum of music carried over from the house next door. The melodies were like an air horn, screaming the truth at me.

I knew what Ethan's note meant.

CHAPTER NINE

Thursday, 9:00 p.m.—Three days missing

The second I locked the door behind my parents and brother, I grabbed the laptop and beelined it toward Ethan's album collection. They had stayed for hours after the detective left, hovering over me to the point I was annoyed. It had taken a lot of convincing, but after I snapped at my mom and dad, they must've sensed I needed time to cope. I played into the emotional-woman trope, and they wanted nothing to do with it. Peter had even suggested he'd be a phone call away and it'd be good for me to have some "me" time tonight.

Now I could deal with a huge clue: the note.

"Casio" was our favorite song from the band Jungle. Maybe he'd left another note for me, explaining all the madness.

With my laptop on a box next to me, I played **"What Is Going On?" by Sophisticated Dingo**. His last song was still from hours ago, but I had bigger things to worry about than a song.

Like the wallet and blood and cash and affairs.

I combed through every record, and not a single note, Post-it, or clue was there. I stared at the albums everywhere on the closet floor. Nothing was there for me. *CASIO* was not in reference to this album from that band.

Ethan wasn't mysterious or adventurous, so this new phase of clues and lies hurt on a visceral level. Who was this man?

I put the records back in place, content on digging back into his computer. With one pathetic sigh, I pushed up from the floor, but a shoebox caught my eye. It sat just to the right of the records and had a layer of dust with a fresh handprint on top that seemed out of place.

I bent down to take off the lid, and a little of the tension in my shoulders left at the box of photos. That's all it was. A part of me thought there'd be a chance this was a gun or something insane that matched the current narrative of my life. A hidden passport. Drugs, maybe.

My heart swelled as photos of young Ethan looked up at me. He had the same wide smile and sparkling eyes. His arm was around a woman who had to be his mom. She had the same eyes, nose, and face shape. *God, is this right before she died?*

There were photos of him and his parents. When we'd met at nineteen, he said his family died in a horrible car accident that made him an orphan. His face got all red, and his eyes watered, and that was that. I never questioned him about it much over the years. He'd share a memory about his mom or dad, but he never went into detail. He'd always change the subject.

I checked Spotify and sucked in a breath at the song he was listening to *right* now: **the Del McCoury Band's "I Need More Time."**

I responded with **Annie Lennox's "Why."**

The fact we were communicating by song titles was almost enough to make me laugh-cry. While it was clever, it just made everything clouded in more mystery. Yes, I should've been thankful he was alive, but the question about those women kept returning into my head. Why go to this effort? Did he *want* me to find out about the women?

My husband was missing, but he was cheating on me. My priorities were fucked. This not-eating, not-sleeping stress was messing with my mind. I rubbed my temples and watched his song title *not* change. A few minutes went by without a new song, and my throat closed. *Did something happen?*

Or was choosing the song title hard?

I sighed, keeping the screen in view as I leafed through a few more photos. They all were older, *before we got together* old, and the familiar stuffy, dusty smell filled the small closet. I sneezed and was about to put the box back when a vibrant blue background caught my eye. It was just the corner of a photo peeking out under the stack, but there was no way that blue had lasted ten years in a box.

Setting a large stack of photos to the side, I eyed the photo that had to be new. Two young boys wore identical huge smiles. They looked familiar but not in a way that I'd met them before. Almost like . . . no. I stopped the thought. That was . . . I kept looking. Were they *his* children? God. My stomach rolled like I was on a downward descent on a roller coaster and the seat belt didn't hold. My pulse pounded in my temples, and I focused on taking three deep breaths to settle the pending freak-out. Underneath it, there were stacks of photos of the boys.

Someone had given Ethan photos, and he'd shoved them down in this shoebox covered in dust. Why? I added it to my ongoing list of questions that would probably never get answered.

So not only was this weird exchange still happening, it'd been going on for years. Was this an affair from before, one he couldn't let go of?

I shoved the photos back in the box and set it back in its spot, hidden in plain view like before. Still no song from Ethan's end as I made my way toward his office. That little flash drive sat on the desk, not plugged in, and I eyed it like this entire scenario was *its* fault.

"How to Fix Everything" by Fantasy Camp played on Ethan's username, and I stared at it. He needed time to *fix* everything. Did that mean letting go of the women? The photos with the two boys I'd never met? I rubbed my forehead, debating my next move.

I could try to ask the question eating me up, making me feel gross and used and unwanted. **"Are You Cheating on Me?" by All City Affairs.** There. I'd put it in the universe.

Every hair on my body stood on end as I waited for him to put on a song.

There had to be a song titled "No, Never! I Love You, Marissa!" That would be great, actually.

"Only You" by Yaz.

"Where Are You" by Silverstein. I typed the song title and hit Play, turning down the music because the heavy metal vibes did *not* fit the mood. A melancholic, sad tune fit the vibe in the room.

Instead of waiting on Ethan to respond, I logged in to the computer with the weird Minecraft picture and did a quick scan of the room. Nothing jumped out at me like a camera or a blinking light to signify that I was being watched, yet my skin seemed too tight for my body. A whirring sound had me sitting up straighter, but it had to be the computer starting up. God, my frayed nerves were on edge.

Oh, how he was so organized. Each folder labeled and color coded based on the use. Red for finances, yellow for photos, green for hobbies, and so on. I squeezed my eyes shut, hoping a memory would strike me as to where to start first, but the only thing I could think of was *follow the money.*

Always follow the money.

I clicked the red folder and scanned the spreadsheets and receipts. I'd be lying if I said it all made sense to me, because I had no idea what we paid every month for each utility.

How un-twenty-first-century woman of me. My frowned deepened as I saw how much we paid for water, power, waste management, and internet. It seemed silly that we paid that much for everything, but we needed all of it. There was a line for *401(k)* and *BBB.*

The 401(k) made sense. I'd heard of that and caught my dad and brother blabbing on about how great theirs was and blah, blah. But *BBB*? That wasn't an acronym I knew. I typed it in and came up with Better Business Bureau, which meant nothing to me. Why would Ethan pay two thousand a month to them? That sounded like a shit ton of money to just give to a business. God, would I have to learn all this on top of being a single parent? *Fuck.*

Because my husband was so detailed, I pulled up a sheet from seven years ago, before we'd gotten married, when we'd just barely started living together. The same line, *BBB*, was there but for less money. He had dates going back all the way to when we'd first met, and the same three letters were there. If this had been going on since before me, could it be child support? A secret mortgage?

My body tightened, and my stomach heaved. Years of this. *BBB.* Why?

I swallowed the bile and flicked my attention to my laptop; the newest song on Ethan's end was **"Close to You" by Collie Buddz**.

Was he really *close* to me? With all these lies and secrets? I shook my head even though he couldn't see me and put on **"Agnes" by Glass Animals**. Ethan knew what that song meant to me. It was my cry song, my desperate song. The song I listened to when I felt low and hopeless. The sad song hit me in the soul, and I wanted him to know I was bleeding.

Not five seconds later, he changed the song to **"Stay Strong" by Dj Rufio**, but I blinked back tears. How could I stay strong when my world was blowing up? Affairs, disappearances, cash, pictures of kids I had never seen, and *BBB*.

I was missing something huge. I knew it in my bones, like I'd known we were going to have a boy. Just a feeling I couldn't explain but would bet my life on it. *Something* would make all this make sense; I just had to figure out what that thing was.

Follow the money.

It was a horrible combination of horror and embarrassment that made my cheeks flush and my throat tighten; I hadn't even known we were missing a huge chunk of money each month. All those months of budgeting and not eating out to save a bit were a joke if Ethan put two grand somewhere. How fucking insulting. I'd almost canceled my Spotify subscription to save money.

Where was it coming from? Did he have a side hustle I didn't know about? Did it involve the other women? Drugs? Something worse?

I pulled out our white sheet of paper with all the passwords, though I knew I wouldn't find any recent trace of bank use since the police said they were watching Ethan's accounts. He had been very deliberate every step of the way, so he wouldn't start messing up now. I logged in to our joint account.

His direct deposit every month was more than I'd thought. Quite a bit. But there wasn't an explanation as to where the money went. I scrolled and searched the details to find a clue of sorts. A hint of an account or *BBB*. I came up blank. But I paused. There was a username EHawkins2 at the top of the page, which struck me as odd.

I rarely did banking. We agreed that finances would be Ethan, and I'd do housework. We had an account we shared—the one I was in. Why would Ethan create a separate one with another username? One I didn't know about?

The buzz came back, and I logged out and hit Forgot My Username with the new username. With a few clicks and a password reset, I was in *his secret* bank account.

But it didn't look the same as our joint one. There was checking and savings and *BBB*. Thousands and thousands of our dollars sat in a *BBB* account, and with shaky hands, I clicked it for more details.

Every month, money was wired from this secret account to a PayPal account.

What the actual fuck?

CHAPTER TEN

Friday, 9:00 a.m.—Four days missing

To think I was angry at Ethan a few weeks ago for not changing the toilet paper roll. It was *laughable.* The list of all the crazy shit I'd found in four days was enough to make the most sensible person lose her mind.

Affairs. Hidden photos. PO box with cash. Secret bank account with *thousands* of dollars. Oh, and the simple fact he'd up and disappeared. My stomach would have ulcers for the rest of my life at this point.

"Mama!" Logan said, grabbing one of his favorite books and running over to me after finishing breakfast. He was clearly Ethan's son, with his soft brown hair and large eyes. My throat tightened just thinking about having to explain why his daddy wasn't coming home. "Book book!" Logan said, jumping into my lap.

Ethan played outside with our son, but cuddling with a fun book was Logan and Mama's time, so I shoved all thoughts out of my brain and focused on Logan. My baby. We read ten kid books before his attention moved to blocks, and I sat on the couch with my laptop. My mom promised to come over in the morning to help, but I couldn't wait until then to dive deeper into this *BBB* account. What was the PayPal account used for? How did it work?

I'd found no other clues in his computer or around his desk to indicate if he owned the PayPal account or if someone else did. The account name in the transaction log was just a string of numbers—which added to the level of shady that I wasn't comfortable accepting. The more I thought about it, the more this whole thing seemed like it could point to a secret affair or child support.

But . . . I couldn't recall any work trips that had lasted more than a day. If Ethan really had this *secret* family, when would he have seen them? I bit my bottom lip too hard and tasted a hint of metal as blood seeped into my mouth. "Damn it." I got up to get a tissue and noticed the damn planner sat unopened on the counter since my dad had dropped it off.

I grabbed that on my way back to the couch and settled in. There had to be a trail for me to follow. I didn't know what it was, but I hoped I'd find it when I saw it. Each entry for the past month was normal except for those stars that aligned with the *affairs*. On a whim, I called Hawkins Associates and asked for the head of security.

"Who's calling?"

"This is Ethan's wife, Marissa. I'm hoping to get a few questions answered."

"Ah, I'm so sorry to hear about his disappearance, ma'am. We're all hoping he'll be back safe soon," the operator said. "I'll connect you to Max."

"Thank you."

The phone rang, and I paced the living room as Logan moved from blocks to cars. He zoomed them all over the carpet and up the side of the couch, a goofy smile on his squishy face. I ran a hand through his hair. I'd do whatever I had to, for him. So he could have a good life and know love, with or without his dad.

Because despite the song titles, my gut kept telling me this went deeper than affairs and thieving, and the more stones I overturned, the worse it'd be.

"This is Max."

"Hi, Max. This is Ethan Creighton's wife, Marissa. I was hoping to get some information from you, if you don't mind."

"Marissa." Sympathy laced his tone. "What can I do for you?"

"Ethan had some visitors on certain dates. I—I'm hoping you could give me their names."

"I'm sorry. I can't do that." He sighed, and I genuinely felt his sorrow. "It's confidential, and I'm not allowed."

"My husband is missing, and I found out about his *affairs*, okay? I'd like to know about specific visitors so I can try to figure out where he is!" My voice shook at the end, unintentionally, and he sucked in a breath.

"Affairs? Marissa, I have a hard time believing that. He loved you and your boy. Talked about you both all the time."

My eyes stung, and I slammed them shut. "I've seen a video, okay? This is . . . painful. Please, the woman's name from last Tuesday. Who is she?"

Papers shuffled in the background, and his resigned sigh sent a flicker of hope through me. *He's giving it to me.* "Becky Smith. Now I gotta go."

He hung up, and victory rang through my blood. I had a name. A place to start. Sure, it was generic, and there were probably a million Becky Smiths, but that put a name to a face. I wrote the name down in the planner next to that goddamn star and clicked my tongue. Why would Ethan put a *star* on the days he'd potentially cheated? That seemed dumb. Way too dumb. He'd been so careful with the secret bank accounts and hiding those photos, so putting a symbol in the planner he used all the time seemed . . . careless.

Ethan wasn't careless at all.

Logan walked up to me with a magnetic board that said *E* + *M* = *<3*, and it was like a punch to the gut. Ethan had played with that toy Sunday before everything went to shit, and the conflicting thoughts in my mind were enough to make me sick. My stomach cramped just as my mom walked in.

"Oh, honey." She set her purse and phone on the coffee table. "You look like hell. I'm so sorry. I am just as appalled by Ethan as you are."

"It's unbelievable," I whispered.

"It feels that way, but once the truth comes out, you see things in a different light. All those late nights you told me about? You told me how he forgot a few date nights?" She arched her brows. "It's hard but not unbelievable. You're strong. You'll be okay. I know it."

I washed my mouth out with water as Logan stared at me with furrowed brows, and then I took a shaky breath. "I'm not sure I will."

"Nonsense. You have Logan and us."

I slid her a look, a sarcastic reply *right* there on my tongue, but she was right. Logan would keep me focused, yet that didn't take away the absolute gut-wrenching hurt. "Thanks for coming over to help with Lo again."

"Of course. He's my favorite grandson ever. Aren't you?" She bent down in her black dress and heels, and my son ran up to her. The image of a messy Logan throwing himself at my always-put-together mom had me smiling. The two of them were adorable together. Lo was more comfortable around her than anyone else.

I could do this. I *would* survive this. "Is Dad or Peter coming over today? Just curious if they got a list of names for me."

She narrowed her eyes, and her jaw tightened just a bit. "It's not wise for you to get those names, baby. You'll just hurt yourself. And it's not worth you seeing who the other women are. What is that going to do besides cause pain? But I think that detective is visiting the office today."

Irritation had my eyes twitching.

Logan let out a loud grunt, and seconds later, a horrible smell surrounded us. "Oh, kid. Damn." I laughed at the timing of his poop, and my mom shooed me away as I reached for him.

"Nonsense. I'll do it. Make yourself a cup of tea. Have some crackers. The bags under your eyes are getting worse. You need rest." My mom cupped my face for a second before walking toward the nursery with Logan.

I got up and leaned against the counter, rubbing my puffy eyes. I'd gotten decent sleep last night, but that damn account kept flashing through my mind. It was easier to focus on than Ethan's betrayal. I had a PayPal account so I could get paid for writing articles, but I had it connected to our bank account, not a secret one I hid from my spouse.

Wait . . . I pushed up from the counter and paced the hardwood floor. It was a bit of a pain to send money *from* the bank *into* the PayPal account. That meant . . .

There had to be a secret email account somewhere too. That account would be able to log in to PayPal and set up the connection to the *BBB* account. Unless he'd *given* someone else the bank information, but that went against everything I knew about Ethan.

So do the affairs.

Affairs my mom had believed in instantly.

I groaned and pressed the heels of my hands into my eyes until I saw white spots. I was so close to *almost* figuring it out when my mom's phone buzzed. I walked over to make sure it wasn't a call and saw my dad's text pop up.

It's done.

I frowned. What was done? I had her phone in my hands when the insane idea to read her messages to him hit me. Was I just being a superspy now? Convinced secrets lay everywhere? I felt creepy, guilty that she'd catch me. Did my microwave have a hidden camera or the sink have a secret mic? I set my mom's phone down, convinced she was right. Maybe I did need to take care of myself more. My thoughts were spiraling and not productive.

She returned with Logan, setting him on the ground. He sprinted toward his toys, and she laughed. "He really is go, go, go."

"That's Logan. Thanks for changing him."

"No thanks needed." She scanned the counter. "Why aren't you eating or drinking?"

"Sorry. I . . . I can't seem to get over all the lies." I almost told her everything, but the "Tell No One about Tonight" song still felt important. Plus, it was mortifying to learn he might not have had affairs but a secret life I knew nothing about. What kind of wife would I be once the truth got out?

I could easily imagine the insults people would have, twisting this entire thing to make it my fault. *You aren't good enough, so Ethan stepped out. You weren't attractive enough or smart enough to know two grand went to a secret account. That was men's business, not yours, but a good wife would've known.*

My mom pursed her lips, and tight lines formed around her eyes. "Baby, we will get through this as a family. I loved Ethan, but when everything comes to light, just know we'll always have your back."

My lips quirked up in a half smile. "Thanks. Hey, Dad texted you."

"Oh." She moved so quickly, I blinked in surprise. She was more a *glider* when she walked, with swaying hips, but she dove for the phone and held it close to her face.

"What's so important?" I asked.

"It's not." She moved her fingers fast over the screen and pocketed her phone. She looked at me with a closed-mouth smile. "He gets worried when I don't respond right away. It's silly. There was a time I'd forget my phone for hours, and it'd worry him. You know how protective he is of me—of all of us, really. He'd do anything for us, Marissa. I hope you know that." The soft lines on her face returned. "Now, come on, baby. Make some ginger tea."

I nodded and started the kettle, analyzing her words. My dad *did* go nuclear when we didn't respond to a text or call within a time frame he deemed soon enough. I'd seen my mom vacuum and not respond, and he'd berate her. Her job was to be available to him. My shoulders relaxed—that text had to mean nothing. Just my dad's controlling nature being consistent. Food would help. Eating would help rationalize my insane thoughts.

I got a granola bar just as the doorbell rang three times. Maybe it was intuition or the fact no one had rung the doorbell in months, but goose bumps broke out over my skin.

My mom frowned, and we shared a look that said *What now?* I set the mug down on the hall table and opened the door. A teenager, maybe six feet tall and all skin and bones, stood there. My first thought was that he should be in school. "How can I help you?"

"Are you Marissa?" he asked, not meeting my gaze.

"Yes, why?"

"I was paid to hand you this if you were home alone." He handed me a yellow envelope and took a step back. "Have a great day."

"Wait . . . Who told you to give this to me? What is it?" I asked, my voice on the edge of hysteria. Was this another Ethan clue? A trick? A message?

"No idea. Just earning some cash." He waved and hopped onto a bike. My heart ricocheted in my chest, and I clutched the envelope tightly. *I was paid to hand this to you if you were home alone.*

Home alone.

Not home *with* someone else.

"Who was that?" My mom appeared, and her eyes widened as she stared at the envelope. "Honey, what is that?"

"N-nothing."

She reached for it. "Let me see."

"No, no." I backed up a step and ran to the bathroom. Her voice carried through the door, but I blocked it out. It could be a message from Ethan, one I didn't want my mom seeing.

My heart raced as I tore open the yellow envelope. *What is it, Ethan?* My fingers shook as I realized what it was. My blood chilled, and I gasped.

CHAPTER ELEVEN

Friday, 12:00 p.m.—Four days missing

Tell him to stop, or we'll make him stop.

This was a threat to Logan. My baby.

That's what was written on the note on top of a family photo. The writing was black and choppy, and I checked the baby monitor every three seconds to make sure Lo was safe in his crib. The sound of the coffee maker filled the silence with its dripping and bubbling. It was better than listening to my parents' haggard breaths or my own heart trying to run me to an early grave. My dad had arrived an hour ago after my mom demanded he come help.

I checked the monitor *again* as I walked over to ensure the front door was bolted. When I returned to the main room, Detective Luna stood near a bookcase with his hands in his pockets. He'd just finished processing the photo as evidence. Because that's what it was now. Evidence.

He stared at a photo of Ethan and I, taken years ago, and he sighed before meeting my gaze. "You shouldn't have opened the envelope. We'll test for prints, but we'll need to take yours to eliminate them as the suspect's."

"That's fine. Up until now, I wasn't given any indication we, my *son* and I, were in danger. Forgive me for thinking it was a note from Ethan."

"Are you expecting a note from him?" he asked, those dark brows remaining furrowed. It was a great question.

"Yes, hon, are you thinking Ethan will contact you? Has he? That would mean he's okay if so." My mom brought her hand over her chest and closed her eyes, the entire gesture making me snort. She always acted on the dramatic side.

The detective saw my reaction.

I shrugged at his intense stare. Did he suspect me? Great. Bring it.

That's where I was at mentally, so not great. The photo meant Ethan might not be okay. That he hadn't planned this as a way to help his secret family.

Unless one of his mistresses has an angry husband?

Or he's in money trouble?

What if the affairs and money are two separate issues?

Fuck. This was too much. I rubbed my temples and focused on the picture Detective Luna had stared at. I loved that photo. Ethan held Logan, smiling down at me, and you could tell I love them with my whole body. The way I leaned into Ethan, tilted my face closer to my boys. This was my favorite photo I'd ever taken. I'd printed it and kept a copy on my desk too.

Wait.

Hold on.

A ripple of energy flowed through me from head to toe, and I rushed into the office. That photo with the terrifying words written on it wasn't just *out there*. That wasn't a common, easy-to-find picture. My Facebook profile was private and set to friends and family.

Only friends and family.

Eighty people, which honestly was about seventy-five too many. I logged in to my account settings and confirmed what was visible to the world. My gut churned. Either Ethan had given a copy of that photo to someone, which didn't seem likely to me, or . . . whoever had sent this note was my friend.

A soft knock on the door caught my attention. Detective Luna stood there. "May I come in?"

I nodded.

"I asked your parents to give us another minute."

His large frame intimidated me from the sheer size but not in a way I felt I was in danger. He wasn't someone I'd ever want to piss off. I chewed the side of my lip and turned my laptop toward him.

"This picture is only accessible to my friends online. That's it. This isn't anywhere else."

"Ah, but everything on the internet is forever." He squinted at the photo in question, and I wanted to scream at him.

He needed to get the list of all my friends and search their homes for Ethan! He needed to get rid of the psycho who'd threatened Logan! "Sir, trust me, no one would have this."

"I'll look into your list of friends, sure." He spoke without hurry, and I thought about taking his shoulders and shaking him to make him understand the urgency. "But before we do that, I need you to be honest with me."

That shut me up. The anger moved to the background, and worry took over, making me adjust my position in the office chair and hope I looked casual. I crossed one leg over the other. There. I looked chill. "Okay."

"What can you tell me about Ethan's work?"

"Oh, that." I laughed. "Well, he works at my father's business and does technology for them. Honestly, it's all computers and tech and boring stuff I don't pay attention to. My dad or brother would be able to help you more there. They handle that stuff, not me." My stomach dropped at the fact I should know more. Maybe that would explain the affairs, bank accounts, money. My face heated at the thought he would know I kept something from him, so I asked, "Could we focus on why this person is targeting my son?"

"Honestly, I don't think you and Logan are targets here. But for your safety, I am going to keep a patrol outside overnight just until we get more details of the case."

"I disagree. They came to my door. They could've attacked me or taken Logan right then. How do you think we're *not* in danger?" I fired back, my face flushing with anger.

"I didn't say that. I'm saying, with the patrol outside, I'm not worried." He scratched his jaw as he eyed the book on Ethan's desk. "Have you read that story?"

"No—sir, Detective." I blinked a few times, still not satisfied with his answer.

"Either is fine. Don't need to use both." He flashed a grin and picked up the Harlan Coben book. He flipped through it and sucked in a breath before setting it down. There was a spark to his eyes that wasn't there before, and the hairs on the back of my neck stood on end.

What in the hell had made him get excited in two seconds?

My mouth felt like it had a million cotton balls in it, and with a quick glance at my laptop, I noticed Ethan's song changed to **"What's Going On" by Teddy Swims**. I glanced out the window, like he was out there, watching this unfold.

"Marissa." The detective's tone was more aggressive. "Do you know where Ethan is?"

"No." My voice cracked. I had no idea. "What makes you think I would know?"

"Because." He held up the book and opened his mouth just as the door swung open.

My dad stood there with wide eyes and a flushed face.

"Dad, what is it?"

"You shouldn't talk to him without a lawyer present." He stumbled into the room, and without thinking about it, I shut my laptop. My dad put a hand on my shoulder and squeezed. "If you can't talk to all of us about what's going on, then we'll find representation, and you'll need to go through them for *any* discussion."

For one brief moment, I swore a dark shadow crossed the detective's face. But he relaxed and smiled. "We can move into the other room, then."

"Great." My dad released his grip on me, and I winced at the damp feeling. It made sense, though. My parents were always weird when it came to authority figures. Made them nervous. They'd coached me at a young age to never answer questions without them or a lawyer present. They'd made me practice as far back as I could remember. It was weird that they weren't following the same behavior now—maybe Ethan's disappearance shook them up too much.

I waited until my dad and the detective left the room. Then I flipped the laptop open and typed as fast as I could into the search bar on Spotify.

How could I tell him Logan was being threatened? I searched all variations of threats, threatened, help, and *nothing* communicated it. My heart worked twice as hard to find a title when my dad poked his head in. "What are you doing?"

"Shutting this down real quick. S-sorry."

He frowned and came toward me when I finally found the song I needed: **"We're All in Danger" by Dangerkids**. I played it, hit Mute, and shut it down. If Ethan didn't understand that, then I didn't know what to do.

I checked the front door locks on the way to meet the rest of the group. My mom and dad sat next to each other on the couch, while the detective stood by the window overlooking the backyard. My first thought was *Oh, everyone's used to talking to the police,* because we did this now—had tense conversations with the detective about my missing husband. My new normal.

My legs shook, and I had too much adrenaline to sit down.

"It's been four days since Ethan disappeared, and my daughter and grandson were threatened. Where are you in this investigation? You must've found something." My dad's tone held a hint of irritation, and

I waited for the detective's response. He hadn't really provided updates to us.

"The company car contained Ethan's fingerprints. Still no trace of his credit cards or phone signal. Until today, I had no true reason to believe he was in danger."

"The threat changed that, right? It'll make you try harder to find him?" my dad asked, his left hand making a fist on his knee. "Because you need to locate Ethan and bring him back. We need to ask him questions."

"What sort of questions?"

"What the hell was he doing? Leaving like this?" My dad's voice shook. "He didn't finish projects at work and left us in a shitty situation. And Marissa and Logan need him back too."

"What can you tell me about Ethan's work, Mr. Hawkins?" The detective switched gears, and the temperature in the room cooled.

"His job?" my dad asked, his brows coming together. "What do you mean?"

"What does Ethan do for you at Hawkins Associates? Marissa didn't seem to know, and I'd like more details about it."

"You . . . you think his work has something to do with all this? The disappearing? The note?" My dad flexed and relaxed his left fist every few seconds.

"I'm not ruling out a single option. Now, are you able to explain it to me, or shall I head to the offices and ask around?"

"Christ, no." My dad ran his right hand over his forehead. "He was head of design and communication for our midwestern clients. Took lead on projects from clients, made sure to communicate all changes. Led a team of five programmers."

"Okay." The detective nodded. "Any problematic clients?"

"No, none. Again, do you think this is about work?"

"Could be but maybe not. You also just said he dropped the ball on projects, so I'm looking into every angle right now." The detective had that look in his eyes, the one he'd had after he held up the Harlan Coben book. "What do any of you know about Ethan's past?"

My mom frowned. "Could you clarify what you mean?"

"How did he grow up? What is his family like?"

"He doesn't have a family, right, Marissa? They died in a car accident or something when he was eighteen. You met him soon after." My dad spoke for me. He always did that.

It was *my* husband who was missing. I should answer the questions. "Yes, that's correct."

"Here's the thing." The detective narrowed his eyes at us. "I did a background check on him to see if anything stood out, and there is no trace of Ethan Creighton until you met him."

"Hmm?" I said, blinking a few times to clear my senses. "What does that mean?"

"It means . . . Ethan Creighton didn't exist ten years ago."

CHAPTER TWELVE

Friday, 9:00 p.m.—Four days missing

"What Do You Mean?" by Justin Bieber.

"You Lied to Me" by Chuck Colbert was my reply. I didn't wait more than thirty seconds before playing the next song: **"Who Are You" by the Who**. Rage coursed through me like someone had turned the faucet on high blast.

Anger at the lies, secrets, *song titles* that were my only way of communication. Was his name even Ethan? **"What's Your Name" by Lynyrd Skynyrd** seemed fitting. I played it and chewed on my cuticle, welcoming the sting of pulling a piece of skin.

"You Know Me" by Robbie Williams.

I gritted my teeth and glanced at the ceiling, my eyes stinging with unshed tears. I wanted to punch the laptop into pieces, scream into the void, and cry. All at the same time.

I sucked in a breath when Peter tapped on the doorframe of the office. I looked up, wiped under my eyes, and gave him a pathetic smile. "Hey."

"Came to make sure you're okay. You've been in here awhile." He frowned and put his hands in his pockets. He eyed the computer. "This can't be easy for you, and Mom and Dad aren't making things easier."

"It's not." I tapped my finger on the side of the desk and relaxed when he sat in my chair. While I'd told him and my parents no one needed to stay here to *watch over* us, I did feel settled having Peter there. His strength and protectiveness had always helped me in the past, and without Ethan around, I'd been more nervous than normal. "Thanks again for staying over."

"Come on. Of course, I'll be here for you. And Logan." He shook his head and locked both his hands behind it. "I keep thinking about the name change. That has to be it, right? Like, what else does that mean? There's no fucking way he had no footprint before turning nineteen. Social media was exploding then. We all had dumb accounts and emails."

It felt like a large hand was wrapped around my neck, and each second that went by, it squeezed just a little tighter. Not a full choke, but a slow death. Death by a thousand small grips. "I don't . . . it sickens me that I don't even know my husband."

"Psh, you know him, Mar. You know how to make him laugh. You know how much he cares for you and Logan. Don't let all these unfinished truths have you doubt him."

"But the affairs. The videos."

"Videos can be misleading," he said, his tone hard. He wouldn't look at me. "Do you remember that time Dad showed us a video of our neighbor kicking their dog?"

I sucked in a breath, disgusted at the memory. Peter and I had stolen the dog because we felt so bad, and we'd found another home for it. "What about . . . ? Why bring that up?"

"The video was faked. Dad was annoyed at the dog barking all the time and wanted it gone. He knew how to manipulate us to do the work for him." His jaw tensed as his dark eyes pierced mine. They were wide, almost like a warning.

"The video of the affairs was *faked*?"

"I tried diving into it to see but couldn't tell. There is a log of a woman coming to visit him, but all I'm saying is, until we find him, don't believe everything. Understand me?"

I nodded. Another piece of the puzzle that I didn't want to solve. My dad faked videos to manipulate us. Because of a video, I'd helped steal someone's dog, and holy shit, I wanted to throw up. The owner had never known what happened.

"Mar," Peter said, drawing my attention back to him. "There has to be a reason for the name change, you know? Maybe there was too much attention from his parents' car crash. Or . . ."

"Or he witnessed a crime? Has another family somewhere? Leads a life I have no fucking clue about? Yeah, I don't know." My fingers shook, and my gaze landed on the Harlan Coben book. I'd been so distracted from Ethan's missing identity, I forgot to flip through the book that had gotten the detective all weird. I held it in my hands and opened the front flap.

"You going to try and read? Get lost in another world for a bit? We can chill in the living room if you want."

"Not sure. I like being in here, though. Makes me feel . . . closer, somehow." I fanned through some of the pages, hoping something would jump out like *HERE IS THE MAGIC EXPLANATION THAT MAKES ALL THIS OKAY.* Or maybe a code to a safe that had a cell phone I could call for some answers.

"Can I ask you a question?"

"Peter, don't waste my brain space. Of course you can." I snorted but tensed when his expression twisted into disgust. "Wait. What is it?"

"Did he . . . talk about work or anything he saw? In the weeks leading up to his disappearance?"

"No." I sighed, annoyed that his question wasn't helpful. I wasn't sure what I'd expected, but it hadn't been that. Work talk. *Again.* "This is like the third time work has been brought up. Did someone get murdered there or what? Are you into dark web shit I should know about?"

Peter laughed. "No. No, nothing like that." His tone rose an octave. He scanned the outer corner of the room, and I followed his gaze. A blank corner met us, and it wasn't all that interesting.

"You have a theory." I sat forward. *That* was why his mannerisms seemed too forced, like he was trying to be chill. The awkward smile and tense eyes. "Tell me."

"It's not so much a theory. More like a guess." He met my gaze and spoke with the same intensity he used when talking about sports. "I have a feeling he saw something or found information that he felt put him in danger. And by chance, possibly you and Lo."

Breathe in, breathe out. "So you think he ran?"

"Possibly." He put both elbows on my desk and rested his chin on his hands. The innocent position clashed with our dark topic of conversation, and the hairs on the back of my neck stood up.

Found something. I chewed the side of my lip and moved all the clues that swirled in my mind. The affairs, the pictures, the bank account, the fact the Ethan Creighton I knew had no recorded past before nineteen. The potentially doctored video my dad might've created. My skin tingled at a key question I needed answered. Peter's theory could work two ways, and I wasn't sure which one he was referring to. "Peter, are you talking about now or when he was nineteen?"

My brother blinked before shrugging. "I guess either one."

"If he saw something at nineteen, changed his name, then that means whatever that event was might be back." I sucked in air. If *this* was the situation, the threat to Logan and me could be more severe.

"Right."

"What bothers me, though, about all this is that . . . this wasn't just a random moment." It felt good getting this off my chest, even without sharing all the details I'd found. I hadn't really talked about it with anyone. I'd bottled it up, searching for clues and for any bit that meant I could save my marriage if we found Ethan. "It was almost like he knew something would happen and planned it."

"I need you to really think about the last few weeks, Mar. You're more perceptive than you think, and you know it. Fuck what Mom and Dad say. You're smart as hell and study people all the time. You pick up on things us numbers and analytic guys don't." My brother's face tightened as a grave seriousness entered his tone. "You know something. Even if it doesn't feel like a big moment, you might have some clues about where he went."

For a slight second, I had the feeling my brother was accusing me. But it vanished when I nodded. He was right. "I've been replaying every conversation and moment, trying to find this *thing* that would explain it all. Trust me. No one feels more guilty than me. How could this all go on and his *wife* had no idea?"

"Men are capable of doing anything given the right motivation." He cracked his knuckles.

What a horrible thought. "People, you mean." I arched a brow. "Not just men. Women need to be looped into that dark statement as well."

"True. I wouldn't want to cross you. I still remember that time you lit my baseball cards on fire."

"Hey." I laughed at the memory. "You *beheaded* my dolls. You deserved it."

He chuckled. "Probably."

My muscles relaxed at our change of tone, and I sat farther back into Ethan's chair. The book still rested in my hands, and I glanced down at its cover during the break in conversation. Nothing looked awry, but there was a slight bolding of a letter. Like it printed poorly. I frowned and ran my finger over the letter and felt the indentation.

Someone wrote in here. Ethan did. I gasped.

"What's up?"

Shit. "Uh, nothing." I shut the book and set it down, hoping he couldn't see the flurry of adrenaline coursing through me. There was a message in that book, one the detective had partially seen and one I needed to figure out right now without my brother asking too many questions. "It's all just so much. I remembered another time Ethan canceled on me when I got a babysitter for date night. Makes me feel gross." I swallowed, hoping the lie took root. "I might try reading to relax."

"Good idea. Want me to stay in here with you?"

No. But that answer would draw suspicion. "If you don't mind." I offered a shy smile. Peter returned it and pulled out his phone.

I was desperate to get back to the book and mentally scolded myself for not looking harder the day I'd found the bookmark. When I took a quick glance at the laptop, Ethan's latest message distracted me.

"(Everything I Do) I Do It for You" by Bryan Adams.

The same ire from earlier came back. If I ever saw my husband again, I would smack him. How could he say *this* with the layers of bullshit I was shoveling through? For me? Yeah, okay.

"Fuck You" by CeeLo Green. There, take that, Ethan. Wonder why I'm pissed and unable to do anything. My entire body shook like I'd had way too much caffeine, and without looking at my brother, I could feel him watching me. I had no explanation for why I was sweating and shaking, as I was on my computer, so if he asked, I had to be quick on my feet.

But he didn't. A minute of silence went by, no song from Ethan, and I went back to the book. It was three hundred pages, and I began on the first one. I had a process: start at the top and run my fingers over the text as my eyes searched for anything that stood out. I stumbled upon bolded letters, then wrote them down on a Post-it.

It was a terrible way to leave a message, and I'd gotten halfway through the book with only ten letters when I opened to a page that had *I LOVE YOU* written in pen. *This* might've been what the detective flipped to at first glance—a love note from Ethan. I ignored it. I wasn't feeling very *loved* right now.

C H R I S T O P H E R M A L I N O W S K I

A name.

Ethan could've left a Post-it or an email or spelled this out with pretzels, but he'd bolded a million letters to spell out a long name. Irritation had me clenching my jaw because, for some dumb reason, I'd thought this book would give me answers, not more questions. I gritted my teeth and did a quick scan through the final pages, and even though the clues were small, there were numbers bolded.

Weird.

2017.

Okay. A name, a proclamation of love, and a date.

I could just add it to the tab of *what the fuck is going on* and hope I'd find the answer someday. I leaned back in the chair, the squeaks the only sound in the office, and I stared at my friends' playlists on Spotify. I had over three hundred friends I'd connected with through my freelance writing. They all listened to various indie-pop or alt artists or were trying to discover the next new thing, but I didn't even care to look at their current songs.

Just user anu8390ub. Ethan.

Nothing new.

Since I was already on my laptop, I opened Google and typed in the name from the book, along with the date, and hit Enter.

Come on, Christopher Malinowski 2017. Give me something.

Articles popped up about investigations, about his disappearance, about how they'd found his body. My heart thudded so loudly, I was shocked Peter couldn't hear it across the room.

Focus.

This name was important enough to hide in a three-hundred-page book, so it deserved proper research. I clicked the first article.

LOCAL MAN GOES MISSING ON FISHING TRIP—LOST ON THE LAKE?

On Thursday afternoon, Callie Malinowski said goodbye to her husband before he went on a fishing trip with some friends. Three days later, she helped the search team identify his body. What happened in those three days?

"Marissa."

I jumped, my eyes flashing at Peter. "Hmm?"

"What are you doing? You're mumbling to yourself over there."

Was I? I frowned. I swore I hadn't made a noise. "Just messing around online."

"You're not looking up news articles about Ethan, right? That won't help you. It'll just make you worry more." His jaw tightened, and his brows were set in a hard line.

His question had to be a coincidence. He couldn't *see* my online search.

"Of course not." I rolled my eyes.

He narrowed his, and I went back to the screen, scanning the article for more information. Christopher had been a great guy, a family man; he was survived by his wife and sons and his parents. The official cause of death was drowning, but none of his friends had seen him go into the water. They went to bed one night, and the next morning, he wasn't in his tent. No signs, no warning.

When he never returned that morning, they called the police and eventually found him in the water. He'd been an experienced hiker, hunter, camper, and swimmer. No one could think of any reason he'd go in the lake at night, by himself. Very unusual of him.

But as I neared the bottom of the web page, a quote stood out to me like a brightly colored misuse of WordArt.

> "He was an exceptional employee. Hawkins Associates will feel Christopher's loss hard, and we'll be helping out his family any way we can," said Franklin Hawkins, the CEO of Hawkins Associates.

Wait.

Three years ago, an employee from my dad's company had drowned while camping, essentially without any explanation. Ethan had left me the name in code. Ethan was missing. I was going to be sick.

I shut down the device and bolted into the guest bathroom before throwing up in the toilet. It was like my mind refused to finish the thought that had started forming. My body rebelled against the abhorrent thought that Ethan and Christopher were linked because there was only one thing connecting them besides *disappearing* without a warning.

Hawkins Associates. My dad's company.

The place where my brother also worked. The hairs on the back of my neck stood on end.

"You okay?" Peter asked.

"No." I wiped my hand over my mouth and flushed. Then I washed my hands and leveled my stare at him in the mirror. He frowned, like my behavior annoyed him. Could I trust him anymore, with how closely he was involved in my dad's company? My heart sped up at the shadow on his face. I was potentially losing my ability to focus. "I need to sleep."

"Good idea. I'll keep an eye on things out here."

I nodded and headed for the office to grab my laptop and phone. Then I went into the main suite of the house. I felt gross, dirty even. I hopped into the shower and refused to make the connection. I *couldn't.*

The steaming hot water helped relax my shoulders temporarily as I went through the motions. Once I was done, I put on an old shirt of Ethan's. It still smelled like him, and despite all the lies, I still *loved* him. That hadn't gone away. My mind was in a haze, and I needed sleep before trying to make sense of my new information. I went through my aggressive skincare routine, then wanted a glass of water before going to bed.

I padded through the doorway and stopped at the sound of Peter speaking to someone in the living room. His tone sent up the hairs on the back of my neck. I put my hand over my mouth to cover my breathing, and I listened.

"She didn't say. Yes, I know. I'll try tonight soon. I think she's communicating with him."

Silence.

Soft footsteps padded down the hall, nearing me, and I jumped back into my room with my heart racing to the point of pain. Had he seen me?

Does he know about Christopher?

Wait. Was I afraid of *my brother*? It was Peter. The guy who'd held me when the first guy broke my heart at sixteen, the guy who'd cried when he held Logan for the first time. The guy who told my parents to fuck off when they treated me poorly. I tried to control my breathing, but it came out in pants. Every sense was on high alert, and without overanalyzing it, I sprinted toward the baby monitor. Logan slept, undisturbed, but I couldn't say I'd be able to sleep a wink.

Who was my brother talking to, and what the *fuck* was he going to try tonight?

CHAPTER THIRTEEN

Friday, 11:45 p.m.—Four days missing

It was strange slinking around my own house, where I'd always thought I was safe. It had been a long time since I'd needed sneaking skills. My soft socks prevented my feet from making any noise as I tiptoed out of the bedroom once it seemed like Peter was asleep on the couch. There were no more shuffling sounds or him walking around the kitchen. If I was going to sneak over to Ethan's computer, I had to do it immediately.

My conscience poked at me like a dull warning in my gut saying *Now*. I'd always thought of it as a mother's intuition, but I wondered if our bodies had a way of knowing danger lurked around the corner. With my heart pounding violently against my rib cage, I took one step into the hallway. Then another.

No sounds coming from the living room. No indication Peter heard me.

I kept going, with my phone in my hand and the monitor—turned down—in the other.

My backup plan if this all went to shit was to blame Logan. Poor guy didn't know he was my scapegoat, but it'd work. Peter couldn't possibly know if Logan had woken up or not. I had to trust that explanation would work if he caught me in the office at midnight.

Lying in the bedroom, alone, confused, and freaking out . . . I hadn't managed to sleep a wink. The longer I tried to figure out what the hell was going on, the more I freaked out, and sitting idly by wasn't a choice anymore.

Secrets were *everywhere*, just out of reach. I could almost taste the bitter flavor of deceit. I needed to write everything down, explore every single piece of information on Ethan's computer, and make a plan. There was a reason he'd left me clues. I had to find out what it was.

I got to Ethan's office and held my breath as I ducked inside, shut the door, and turned the lock. There was a small desktop lamp I switched on, and my adrenaline spiked like the time right before the gun went off for a 5K. The rush of endorphins, the excitement. It was go time.

I got a sheet of yellow paper from one of Ethan's legal pads and wrote everything down.

Affair—Becky Smith

Potentially faked video—my dad

Stars in the planner

The Harlan Coben book with former employee's name

The photos of the kids

Secret bank account

Ethan's last name not being around before he was nineteen

Peter trying something tonight while at my house

The staged wallet with the word CASIO

The song titles

The weird jump drive plugged into Ethan's Mac

The We're being watched *document*

The threatening envelope

They all had to be connected *somehow*.

I fired up Ethan's computer and logged in and leaned back in the chair. A squeak echoed in the room, and I tensed, half expecting Peter to pound on the door and demand to know what was going on. Which still didn't sit well. *Why* would he suspect I was talking to Ethan? He was my brother. I loved him. He protected me.

Being afraid of him, even if it was temporary, was a new and jarring feeling. It had to be the news story of Christopher Malinowski and the fact he'd worked at Hawkins.

"Come on, Ethan," I said to the empty room, pushing away the melancholic mood suffocating me. All the memories of us in here flashed behind my eyes. The happiness, the music, the moments we'd made together. The time we cried from laughing so hard over a silly joke. Or the time we slow danced as he hummed melodies in my ear. Those memories felt like a lifetime ago.

The more and more I found out, the less and less likely things would ever be the same between us. My heart was slowly breaking, and soon enough, there wasn't going to be anything left for Ethan to put back together.

If he ever returns.

With so many directions to choose from, the one that kept hitting at my soul was the photos of the kids. I was a fool to *not* think of the secret bank account, but even if Ethan did have an affair or previous children, it wouldn't be like him to not be a part of their lives. There had been no long business trips where he could've stopped by. Ethan and I had done everything together. Before spiraling into a sobbing mess, I had to keep searching for clues. For anything to explain this all away.

He had a secret bank account and photos in a shoebox, so why wouldn't he have a secret email too?

I got the password sheet out and logged in to his personal Gmail account, EthanCreighton1293. The one he used to pay bills and plan get-togethers with my extended family. Nothing fancy. I combed through the Inbox, Spam, and Sent folders, hoping something stood out.

There was nothing. He sorted his emails with tags into every category imaginable. I snorted. He wasn't this organized in real life. The garage had boxes of unlabeled things that he'd *get to later*, and the number of times I had to pick up his dang dirty socks? A million.

But at least my digital life is squeaky clean. That's what he'd always say, and now, I wondered if that was intentional. Had he been planning this moment for years and leaving me breadcrumbs by means of ridiculous comments? It would make him a level-ten psychopath, but my kind, thoughtful, charming husband was turning out to not be who I'd thought.

I swallowed the ball of emotion and powered on. With my personal and work emails, I chose them to each be the recovery email for the other. I'd thought he must've done the same for his, but I went into the settings and found an email I hadn't seen before.

JSGCasio

CASIO!

This had to be it. With the same rush of nervousness I'd gotten when I found out I was pregnant, I opened a window and signed into a new account. But the weirdest thing happened when I clicked on the *Enter Your Email Here* box.

A list of *three emails* I had never seen before autofilled. That meant . . .

I slammed my eyes shut and took a breath.

A year ago, I'd combined all my email addresses onto my Chrome extensions bar. When I needed to log out of one, I removed it, but even though I deleted that email from a previous job, the username still popped up when I tried to autofill. Ethan had given me so much grief about not *clearing my cache*, and I'd rolled my eyes.

So either Ethan had *intentionally* left these emails available, or he'd forgotten to follow his own advice.

I wrote them all down on my sheet: *SmithEAnon. AlexES987. BobSmithson.*

I had four emails to dive into. This was insane. Not just because of my uncovering more fucking secrets, but how did one person juggle a work email, a personal one, and *four fucking more*?

I rubbed my temples and tried logging in to the first one.

It couldn't find your email address.

Okay, he'd deleted the account. Awesome. With a quick search, I found that once you deleted an account, you only had twenty days to recover it before it was gone forever. That meant this account was dead. Moving on to the next one, I did the same thing.

It couldn't find your email address.

My husband had *burner* email addresses, and despite all the warnings and clues, this scared me. The song titles had reassured me that *maybe* there was something that tied this all together, but fake emails that were *deleted*? The envelope of money *just in case*? This had *shady* written all over it.

BobSmithson was next.

It couldn't find your email address.

Fuck.

I ground my teeth, on the verge of screaming. What was the point of finding these if I couldn't get *into* them?

JSGCasio was my final hope, and I went to log on, and *holy shit.* It worked. The password was autosaved, and if I ever saw Ethan again, I'd give him hell for this.

Total hell.

I just broke in to my techy husband's secret email. I felt like a character on a soap opera, hearing loud music in my ears as the crowd gasped. The momentary relief didn't last long. I had shit to do, and that started by going into his inbox . . . which was empty.

No already-read emails in an endless list, like me. I was in the thousands. Ethan had no unread messages because he sorted them all like a neat freak.

His organization could've had its own show on Netflix; the folders were each labeled with two initials: *DM*, *WS*, *BS*, *PP*, *CM*. All different initials that I thought were states at first. I clicked through *DM*, but there were only promotional emails, which, okay . . . I guess if you had a secret email, signing up for camping ads made sense. *Not.*

BS wasn't filled with bullshit. This folder had hundreds of emails, all starting with the subject line *UPDATE.* And what was weird was that they were always sent to Ethan on Friday afternoons. Friday, Friday, Friday. I scrolled down the web page, and my vision blurred. Without thinking, I clicked on the one from last Friday.

Three days before Ethan never took his car to work.

The email came from a random combination of letters and numbers—not helpful.

From: ma8p7yh

Be careful. We love you. You're doing the right thing, again.

Jesus fucking Christ.

So many layers to unpack. My mind whirled like someone had pulled ten fire alarms inside my skull, all at the same time.

Be careful. Did that mean *ma8p7yh* knew his plans? Had he confided in this person that he was about to leave his family?

We love you. We? WHO IS THE WE? WHY DO THEY LOVE MY HUSBAND? I felt ill reading these messages. Betrayed. A fool. This happened, and I'd had no idea.

You're doing the right thing, again.

Okay, cool, so Ethan has abandoned his family before without warning and left clues for the poor wife to wade through?

I was going to lose my mind. Truly. I took a picture of the email with my phone, unsure what I'd do with it later. It could go onto my *fucking deal with this when I have a goddamn second* list. I went to another email from *ma8p7yh* from two weeks ago.

From: ma8p7yh

We always knew it could happen this way.

Ethan replied to her with a simple almost done.

WHAT HAD BEEN ALMOST DONE?

I had to settle down. I wasn't an angry person and never had the aggressive urges Peter did, where he shared how he fantasized about punching people in the face. Nothing had ever gotten me worked up enough, but this did. I paced the office floor, careful to not hit anything or make noise, and counted to thirty.

Thirty seconds of repeating *what the fuck is my life* in a whisper did little to calm me down, but I went back to the computer and wanted more. I went into *focus* mode, not letting my emotions chime in. One by one, I clicked each labeled folder, selected all, and forwarded them as an attachment to my email. It was tedious, but that way, I wouldn't be rooted to his device.

Not that I couldn't come in and use it.

Peter's weird comment and the unsettling vibes from my family had me pausing. I wasn't sure *why* I mistrusted them or was frightened by my brother, but I wouldn't ignore the feeling. I'd continue to trust my gut even though I was more than confused.

Each folder told another part of Ethan's hidden life.

WS contained hundreds of confirmation emails that the payment had been sent to the mysterious user, dating years back. Since we'd started dating.

PP was all the emails from PayPal.

Forwarded to mine to overanalyze.

I clicked on *CM* and sucked in a breath. Only two emails sat in that folder, but the sender's name stuck out to me.

CHRISTOPHER MALINOWSKI.

The guy who'd showed up dead while camping, who'd worked for my dad, had emailed Ethan on this mysterious account. Twice. Three years ago.

Wait.

Shit. The date!

I opened up the article again and saw the exact dates.

The emails had been sent the day *before* he went missing. The afternoon before the article said he'd gone camping with his buddies and never returned.

Holy shit.

Thud. Thud. Thud.

Peter!

I desperately needed to read those messages, so I forwarded them to my email and clicked the browser closed *just* as the footsteps stopped right outside the office door. Why the fuck had I turned the light on? How could I explain this?

Think.

"Mar?" he said, his voice even and *not* sleepy. I scanned the desk for *anything* to talk my way out of this. I couldn't explain the locked door or the computer. I reached around the monitor and powered it off—the device made a loud chiming sound.

DAMN IT!

"Hold on." I was terrified out of my fucking mind. He'd caught me in the office, at midnight, with a locked door. It wasn't like I'd made any noise.

The door handle shook, and I sucked in a breath, almost yelping. Then the *perfect* idea came. Brilliant. Ethan's old green plaid shirt hung on the back of the computer chair. I slipped it on over my shirt as I unlocked the door and stared up at my brother. I didn't need to fake the moisture in my eyes because I had some fear-induced tears going on. "Come in. Don't wake Logan." I ushered him into the office and shut the door.

He wore sleep pants and a grim expression, one I wasn't used to seeing directed at me. "Why are you up?"

"Logan stirred," I lied. My original plan came to the rescue. "I settled him down, and honestly . . ." I made my voice soft as I looked around the office. "Ethan spent more time in here than anywhere else."

I hugged his shirt against me and stopped preventing myself from crying. I let the tears fall, and my brother's expression softened.

"You came in here to be close to him." He nodded, the muscles around his shoulders relaxing just a bit. His gaze moved to the computer.

"I listened to his playlists. We were both so weird about music and always creating lists for each other. I just . . . wanted to feel near him, okay? I wanted to just deal with this on my own." I prayed Peter bought it.

I didn't want to chance setting him off, so I couldn't follow the intensity of his stare as he studied something on the desk. *Did I leave something out?* The paper with my notes sat folded in my pocket, so it couldn't be that.

He moved closer to me, and I fought a shudder as he put a hand on my shoulder. "You're so strong, Mar. You really are."

"Don't always feel that way." I meant it, and a shadow crossed his eyes. "Anyway, why are you up?"

"Couch isn't comfortable—no offense."

"None taken."

The following silence was awkward. Too long, too filled with tension. Peter took a step closer to the back of Ethan's desk, and he leaned against it as he stared at a photo of Ethan and me on the bookshelf. "You guys were so happy."

I followed his gaze to our wedding photo. It was in a glass frame, and as I admired Ethan's smile in it, there was movement. The frame acted as a mirror with how the light hit it, and I stood there, frozen, as Peter moved his right hand subtly a few inches to the right to grab the small jump drive that I'd left on the desk.

He then put it into the back of the computer, the entire process taking two seconds. I could've stopped him, asked him about it, confronted him, but the best option seemed to be to *let* it happen. Peter did say on the phone he'd try something tonight.

Maybe I'd just witnessed what that thing was.

"Let's try to get some sleep, hmm? Go back to bed, Mar." He yawned and stretched his arms over his head.

"Great idea." I waited for him to leave the office first, and I followed, shutting the door and holding the baby monitor close to my chest. Peter's footsteps carried him toward the couch as I went into my bedroom, my heart racing and mind in overdrive.

The most abhorrent thought kept bouncing around, even though I didn't know the *why* yet: *Christopher Malinowski emailed Ethan the day before he went missing. Then he showed up dead.*

Ethan left me a document that said we're being watched, and four days after his disappearance, my brother has secret conversations with someone on the phone and puts a mysterious flash drive into my husband's computer. Hawkins Associates seemed to be the common denominator of everything—the place of affairs, the reason Ethan had been so stressed out, and . . . my dad's business. It was time to accept the truth: my family was involved. Somehow, someway, they knew something, and I was going to find out what.

CHAPTER FOURTEEN

Saturday, 8:00 a.m.—Five days missing

"We Need to Talk" by Waterparks. That was the song I played on repeat, with the sound off, all morning. My head pounded like I'd downed a bottle of whiskey, but I knew it was from stress and little sleep.

Once his music went live, I switched to **"SOS" by Rihanna**. There couldn't be a clearer message. Ethan could *clearly* keep secrets from me for years, so he could find a way to talk to me. I was sure of it. I was getting sick of the damn song titles.

"You" by Chris Young was his reply. Then, after twenty seconds, he played **"Safe and Sound" by Capital Cities**. Huh. "You" and "Safe and Sound."

He'd asked me a question.

Are you safe and sound?

Ha, no. No, Ethan.

"Working already?" Peter asked, making me jump a bit in my chair. His gaze moved over me and my laptop as he tensed his jaw. He was in front of me, not able to see my screen, but that didn't stop my anxiety one bit. He'd gone to shower ten minutes ago, and I'd hoped to dive into the forwarded emails before he got out. I needed to focus while not giving anything away. I'd overslept out of pure exhaustion, and that had cost me some investigating time.

I looked up from my screen and forced a tight smile. "I'm all up in my feelings, might as well write about them for an article."

It'd be easy to put on some melancholic playlists, losing myself in the voices of Rob Thomas and Hozier.

He nodded. His eyes were darker than normal, and my entire body shivered at the change. I ran my hand over my jaw, willing the shakes to settle. I had no reason to suspect Peter of anything, minus the weird phone call I'd overheard. He'd never hurt me or Logan.

Trust no one.

But can I trust you, "Ethan"?

"Hey, so Dad called and wants me to head into the office to catch up on stuff since we took so much time off this week. Mom said she'll be here in an hour, but I told her you're good without them. Unless you want me to have them come?"

Me? Alone? Please! Get the fuck out!

"No, I don't want them here." My pulse doubled at the thought of finally being by myself. My brother smiled, and unease flowed down my spine like a continual drip from the faucet. He'd *wanted* me to say that. He *wanted* me to be alone at the house.

Why?

Because he knew how my parents made me feel, or was this about the call?

Would it be better to have one of them here? Was this about the flash drive he'd put into Ethan's computer? My body hummed, almost sure that was the answer. I kept my face neutral and checked the baby monitor. Logan stirred. "I'm getting Lo up, but feel free to take some coffee if you want."

"Sure. Hey." He waited until I looked at him before speaking. "I'm doing everything I can at the office to find him. Dad is being . . . Dad, but I'll find the truth for you. I owe it to you and Ethan. You believe me, yeah?"

I closed my eyes and nodded.

"If any of the affair stuff is true, I'm punching him right in the face."

Right behind you.

"Mar, trust your gut. If you get a feeling, follow it. Even if it goes against Mom and Dad." His eyes darkened, and his tone went deep like a dire warning.

Accusations about the flash drive and the phone call were on the tip of my tongue, but I couldn't say the words. My gut churned. Peter had moved into my do-not-trust category, even after years of depending on him. The conflict caused an unwanted pang.

He seemed to understand my hesitancy and patted my shoulder. "Give the little guy a hug."

"Will do." I needed him to get *out* of my house. It was a foreign feeling to want my brother to leave. I loved him. Ethan and I had hung out with him all the time. Twice, sometimes three times a week. We'd taken trips together, gone to concerts. It gutted me to think Ethan's disappearance would cause a rift between Peter and me too.

Peter left through the garage; I locked the door and took a deep breath.

Yes, there was a flash drive in Ethan's computer, but that was it. I was free to do whatever I wanted without worrying someone was going to walk in. I cracked my knuckles and got Logan's breakfast ready, since the kid went zero to sixty when it came to hunger. He got that from me, for sure. I chopped up a banana and made toast. Then I set the meal on his high chair as my mind tried to piece together all the clues: Peter putting the flash drive into Ethan's device, the secret phone call, my uneasy feeling around him . . .

Fuck. This had to do with Ethan's work. I was certain of it. It was the only thing that made sense as to why my own family was so involved.

I headed for the nursery to get Logan and put him in a new outfit for the day. I smiled at his large eyes and curly hair. He was the spitting image of Ethan, and I hoped there'd be a day our family of three would be together again. I wasn't sure it was possible. With the affairs, lies, and identity of a man I wasn't even sure I knew, the chances were slim we'd ever go back to what I considered normal.

"Mi mi mi mi," Logan chanted. The hungry little chunk wanted his milk.

"Hold on, baby." I kissed his head and brought him to the kitchen. As I buckled him into his high chair, I checked every corner and crevice of the kitchen. I didn't even know what I was looking for, just anything suspect, and as I bent to look under the cabinets, a door creaked.

What is that?

I stood, tensed, and slowly spun around. The creak came from the side of the house. Our garage had a side door that opened to the back-yard. I hated that alleyway; it was always covered in dirt. Why did that door creak? I never opened it. The wind was calm today.

"Mama! Mama!" Logan screamed at the top of his lungs, making me jump out of my skin. I glanced over my shoulder, making sure he was okay. With my heart pounding and my senses elevated, I stared at the window that led to the alley, waiting for someone to appear. Who? I had no idea. But someone had to have opened the door.

"Mama!" Logan wailed, the sound so loud that it pierced my soul. Without taking my attention away from the window, searching for any movement, I walked backward toward Logan.

"It's okay, baby. Deep breaths," I said, attempting to keep my voice soft and even. "Mama is right here."

"No! No! No!" He threw his bowl of food onto the floor. Mess exploded everywhere, and the urge to scream clawed up my throat.

"Logan, be quiet, please." I swallowed as a shadow danced against the brick wall. *What the fuck is that?* My ears rang as I grabbed a knife from the holder on the counter. My car keys were in the bedroom, and I wouldn't leave Logan here to grab them. If we had to run for it, the front door would be the safest choice if someone was in the garage or in the backyard.

He cried louder, and my stress was reaching max capacity. I couldn't breathe as I leaned against the wall, out of view from the window. I had to check. With one final gulp of air, I peered through the window to find a large bird attacking an old take-out wrapper. The bird's wings hit the door, causing it to creak as he tried to eat whatever crumbs were left.

I slid onto the floor, the knife still in my hands, as the reality of the situation hit me. *Logan is safe. I'm safe. We're okay.*

Fuck. I scrubbed a hand over my face, wiping the beaded sweat off my forehead. Would I always be like this now, trembling and scared of harmless sounds? I put the knife away and cleaned up the mess, letting myself settle down. One memory tickled the back of my mind, probing me to think deeper on it.

What else had Peter done before I suspected *him*? He'd had free rein in the house after all this started, so he could've planted anything. A microphone, a camera.

Jesus. Was my brother spying on me?

I think she's communicating with him.

Okay, okay. That *had* to be the reason my own family would violate my house. They wanted to know for sure if I was talking to Ethan. If they'd go to those lengths, then that meant they could've hacked my computer too. Lord knew my brother and dad were tech geniuses, so there could be a way for them to do it.

That meant . . . fuck. I quickly went to my room and grabbed my laptop. I glared at it like everything was its fault. I *shouldn't* use that to check my emails. The music could be fine because my family had made it *abundantly* clear that my job was frivolous and silly. In the battle of STEAM versus STEM, they were very much advocates for only focusing on science, technology, engineering, and math and getting rid of the arts.

I'd only use this device to talk to Ethan through music. I'd have to find another way to research. I found a segment from comedian Isaac Witty titled **"Suspicious Behavior"** and let it play for a few minutes before switching to **"My Family" by Pa Salieu and BackRoad Gee**.

I *needed* to comb through those emails. I changed the song to **"Research" by Big Sean and Ariana Grande**.

"Do Nothing Till You Hear from Me" by Ella Fitzgerald.

If only my husband could see me roll my eyes. **"I Have No Choice" by Rupert Gregson-Williams and Lorne Balfe.** We'd never watched *The Crown*, but the soundtrack was lovely. While Logan settled down and finished his breakfast, I made a plan of attack.

We'd go to the library. They had free internet where I could comb through the emails. I frowned at Logan and chewed my lip. I'd have to bring him with because calling my mom to babysit didn't feel like the right move.

"Bah!" Logan shouted, taking a piece of banana and throwing it over his head. It landed on the living room carpet, and despite the mess, I laughed. The adrenaline from earlier had to escape somehow.

My laughter caused him to do it again.

"Food is for eating, Lolo. Where's your mouth? Show me your mouth." I motioned to put it toward his lips.

He mocked me and put the food in his chubby cheeks. He was too cute and stubborn for his own good. While he ate the fruit, I picked up the rogue banana slices. Once, I'd forgotten to clean one up under the couch, and it had rotted in a horrible science-experiment type of way. *Never again. Learned my lesson on that one.*

I bent down onto the carpet to search under the TV stand. Logan could find a way to throw things just about anywhere. My scan came up empty for food, but there was *something* under the wooden stand. It was dark, small, and had a tiny red light in the corner.

I first thought it was a cable product Ethan had set up.

But the placement of this small black item seemed deliberate. Hidden. Out of sight.

Like a secret camera.

If that was true, the more pressing question was how long it had been in our house. Who had put it there? My husband who didn't exist before age nineteen? My brother who inserted fishy jump drives?

I needed to get out of this damn house and to think. Think without worrying who was watching. Even if I was acting weird and out of character, I couldn't trust my own home. I pushed up on my elbows and said with a shaky voice, "I found your banana, silly."

If Peter had put this there . . . then it could've been this week. If it had been before, though . . . shit. I should've studied it more. It'd be too obvious if I went down again to look for dust.

Unless . . . "Lo, where are your bananas, baby?"

I pretended to throw the banana, and he copied my movement, like I'd known he would.

The piece didn't go far enough toward the TV. Damn. I didn't have patience. I tossed the banana on my own to land near the device again, and boom. I repeated my actions, and this time, when I dropped down, I swept my hand under there, putting on a real show if someone was listening or watching. "Lo, again? You need to stop throwing these!"

My face sweat, and my stomach cramped with nerves, but as I pretended to grab the fruit, I hit the device. "Damn, Ethan. Putting shit where you shouldn't." I retracted my hand and stared at the amount of dust that came from the device.

Too much dust to collect from this week.

It made my skin crawl. How long *had* it been here?

I couldn't focus. I needed to know what it was. Was it a listening device? A camera? A motion detector? A *bomb*? I needed to call Detective Luna but without being seen or heard. The fear gripped me again, this time tickling down my spine like a thousand spiders. I repositioned Logan's high chair to face the backyard, turned the TV on for background noise, and discreetly slid the detective's card off the counter into my pocket.

"Mommy needs some fresh air, okay, baby? I'm standing outside for two minutes." I left the door open and stood at the end of the deck. The cool air hit my face, making me shiver, but this had to be done. I dialed.

He answered on the second ring with a brisk tone. "This is Luna."

"Hi, Detective, this is Marissa Creighton. Uh, I found something weird under our TV stand, and honestly, I'm terrified to find out what it is." I spoke as quietly as I could.

"I'll be right over. Are you alone?"

"Yes, just Logan is here with me."

"Good. Keep it that way, you understand?" His tone held no room for disagreement, and if he had said that yesterday, I would've asked why.

Not anymore.

"Yes, sir." I hung up and came back inside the house. I paced the kitchen, feeling my soul shatter piece by piece. With Ethan gone and my family as my only support system, who did I have left? Why was my world falling apart?

I forced myself to eat some plain toast as I counted the minutes until the detective arrived. *Right over* could mean in an hour or when he had time. Until then, I had to act normal. Ha. Normal. What the fuck did that even mean anymore?

The familiar sounds of the Who chimed from my phone—it was my dad. The timing of his call startled me. Why now? Why minutes after I'd called the detective?

My body tensed, preparing for a fight that I didn't even know if I wanted to win. "Hey, Dad." My voice hid my inner turmoil.

"*Don't* talk to the detective without us or a lawyer there. I mean it." His words came out in a rush like he was mid-run. The same feeling I'd gotten when I'd overheard Peter returned. Panic. Disgust. Betrayal. Fear. Then, a prickle of annoyance.

"Why are you calling to tell me this right fucking now?" I said in a very un-Marissa-like response. I didn't regret it despite the two-second delay of silence.

"Excuse me, Marissa, but that isn't how you talk to your father, who has spent all week worrying and taking care of you and Logan. That is not how you show respect. I don't need a reason to tell you to be careful. Isn't my job to protect you? Are you suggesting I don't want what's best for you and Logan?"

"What? Th-that's not what I was saying," I stuttered, my eyes watering.

"Hon." A more urgent tone entered his voice. "I'm not the one with a missing spouse. I have my head on right, and I would just hate for you to say something you shouldn't in front of him. We should be there to protect you. I'll call the family lawyer in two seconds. He could be there to meet you and Luna."

He knew Luna was coming over.

It was like I was dancing on a frozen lake and each movement caused another crack in the surface, but instead of making my way toward the shore, I kept going farther from safety. "How did . . . Why do you know he's coming over here?"

Silence.

"Dad," I urged again. I *knew* the answer, but he was going to have to talk his way out of this. I needed him to have an explanation, something tangible to make sense of this. My dad and brother had a way to *spy* on me, and even if their intentions were to just find Ethan, it was fucked up. "There is no reason—"

"Luna called me, told me he was coming over to talk to you about a new development. Said it'd be better if one of us was there."

Detective Luna had told me it'd be better if it was *just* us. My dad said he had friends at the station, so there was a way he knew, from one of them. I gripped the back of my neck and squeezed, unsure how to handle his lie. He'd said it so easily, so well, if I hadn't *just* gotten off the phone with the detective myself, I would've believed him. So that begged the question—how many more smooth lies had my dad told me?

And how many had I fell for so easily?

"Marissa." He cleared his throat and spoke louder. "I'm sending over the family lawyer. They have no right to question you without one."

"I'm not guilty of anything, Dad, so I don't need one." Especially not the family lawyer, who could be aware or involved in all this tomfoolery. I didn't know what was true and what wasn't, but I couldn't trust anyone besides myself. *What a terrifying thought.*

Logan whined in a high-pitched babble, and I used the excuse. "I gotta go, but it'll be fine. I'll let you know when he leaves, because I need to run an errand."

"Let Peter go with you. It's not safe until we find out who sent that threat."

Knock knock.

The detective was here. "Talk to you later, Dad. Love you." I let the words slip out of habit and in some blind attempt to reassure him. With one quick glance at Logan in the high chair, I grabbed a sheet of paper and wrote the question I needed to ask the detective with a desperation that frightened me.

I'd ignored the signs, excused them, and refused to believe it. But now, it was clear.

DID YOU TELL MY DAD YOU WERE COMING HERE? I wrote on a paper, then grabbed another one. I prayed that maybe the detective had called my dad and I'd gotten it wrong. I wanted that to avoid the reality crashing over me.

I had my two pieces of paper and opened the door, holding my hand out to stop him from coming inside all the way. I held up the first one.

He frowned, then stared at me and over my shoulder before shaking his head.

Fuck. Dread filled me, rooting me to the ground. Then, with a deep breath, I held up the second note.

I THINK MY FAMILY IS WATCHING INSIDE THE HOUSE.

"Want to go for a walk with me?" he asked, taking the papers from my hand and putting them in his pocket.

CHAPTER FIFTEEN

Saturday, 11:00 a.m.—Five days missing

With Logan in the stroller and my phone back home where it couldn't spy on me, I liked being outside; getting away from it all felt good. The fresh air and sun made it a little easier to breathe, and I closed my eyes, stared up at the sky, and inhaled.

"We got some information on who sent you that photo," the detective said in a kind voice. "After we took your statement on what the kid looked like, we found him. He's a local high school kid who had a chance to earn a hundred bucks."

Just a teenager. I breathed a little easier.

"And what did you find?" I asked. With the way he dragged his words, they felt heavy. Important.

"I followed a hunch and showed him about ten pictures. Most of them were guys from Hawkins Associates, security—the entry-level position, so to speak—just to see if they were doing dirty work. But I added photos of your dad and brother."

I swallowed, hard. My throat made a clicking sound, and my grip on the stroller slipped. I *knew* the answer before he said it. Just like the weird tingling fear I had around my family lately—a suspicion. "It was one of them."

"Your brother." Disappointment seeped out of his voice. "He paid him to *deliver the photo but do zero harm*. That was the kid's statement.

He's terrified he's getting charged, but we let him off with a warning. If he comes near you again, which I don't think he will, call me."

The betrayal felt like multiple punches to the gut. I nodded, digesting the information. My brother had paid someone to scare me into thinking Logan and I were in danger. My son. His nephew and godson. Peter was the person who'd get Logan if anything happened to me or Ethan. *God.* I needed to rectify our will, but who else would I leave my son with? Why would Peter do this? It just didn't make any sense.

"What I'm about to ask is important, Marissa."

Shit. His tone made me uncomfortable.

I stared up at the sun, letting it warm my bones and give me strength to hear what he would say. The armor continued to crack around me, threatening to make me succumb to the ice-cold truth, but I stayed above water. For now.

"Okay, what is it?"

"Until I know more, I don't think you should give any indication that you know your brother is involved. Or your father."

"Yeah." I reached out to run my fingers through Logan's curly hair. Whenever I felt like I'd lost too much or couldn't survive this, his presence grounded me. I might not have a family or a marriage to come back to, but I had Logan. I stood straighter, meeting the detective's gaze, and nodded. "I understand."

"It's been hard to get you alone since your family has been around. Have you noticed?"

"Now that you mention it, yes. I should also be up front with you about them." I was *still* not ready to tell him about Ethan's codes. "My brother insisted on spending the night to *protect* me last night, but now that we know he sent the photo, that meant he needed to be inside the house."

The detective sighed and ran a hand over his face. "Your call originally said you found something."

"Yes." I explained how Peter had put in the flash drive and I'd found the device under the TV stand. "This might sound crazy, but at this point, my life is a shit show, and I think . . ." I paused, remembering that document Ethan had left me.

WE'RE BEING WATCHED.

"My family is spying on me, us, Ethan, any combination, and I have no idea why."

"I think so, too, and until I figure out why, you need to be careful. Do you feel threatened at all?" he asked, his calm voice a sliver of reassurance amid the chaos. "Is there somewhere you could go for a bit?"

"No, not threatened." I thought about the absolute terror paralyzing me at overhearing my brother on the phone and even seeing the shadow from a bird. "Not yet, at least. Plus, they'd know something was going on."

"True. But the second you feel unsafe, you call me."

I nodded, and we continued our walk down the street, nearing the park where Ethan and I would take Logan. He'd run around with our son, chasing him in the grass and making him giggle so loudly it echoed around us. That had been before. Before I knew about the secrets, secrets that he'd had since we met. The pang in my chest doubled in size as those images of the two kids popped into my mind. The idea that Logan could have family he'd never meet hurt me, deeply. Maybe it was because motherhood had changed who I was. My core and soul shifted to love Logan.

"Have you found out anything more on Ethan's past? What his . . . other name was or why there's no trace of him?" The words felt like glass cutting my throat.

"No. It's not in any database, but we're working on it." He shoved his hands in his pockets, and we came to a stop right at the edge of the playground. "Marissa, is Ethan contacting you in *any* way?"

Tell no one.

But the lies . . . the affairs, the bank account, the photos, the money, Christopher Malinowski . . . I sucked in a breath. "He left me clues. They don't make sense to me yet, but I'm figuring them out."

"Clues, *how*?"

"You saw the Harlan Coben book. I watched your reaction." I slid my gaze to the detective. My gut said to trust him, but it was hard when everyone around me had layers of secrets. And my dad was too connected to everyone. It might've been foolish to *not* mention the songs, but I wasn't ready. I had a list of shit I needed to uncover *first*, and then I'd share more. Plus, I didn't want to share about the money in case it had been illegally obtained. "Ethan left me a document that said we were being watched. I had no idea at the time it meant my own family, but it checks out."

The detective nodded. "Anything else?"

"The *CASIO* note . . . our favorite song by an indie-pop band has that name, and we saw them in concert. It was one of the best nights we had, so was that his way of reassuring me he's fine, or is there a letter explaining what the hell is going on in a Casio keyboard? I don't know. It's maddening." I felt better I could give the detective more than nothing.

He was silent for a good minute, and my poor cracked lip would bleed soon from how much I gnawed on it. He wore his intelligence like an accessory, always studying and watching, and it made me feel small and unprotected. Not that he scared me, but I would *never* have that sort of strength.

"Here's my theory if you want it." He narrowed his eyes at me just a bit. The movement made him look older, more intense. "I think Ethan planned this, wanted you to figure out *why* on your own, and whatever is going on . . . your family is involved. My gut thinks it's something work related, but I have nothing to prove it. Now, are there any details you're not telling me? It might help put all the pieces together."

The detective knew I had something, and my stomach twisted with guilt when I said, "No, just the clues I mentioned."

That was most of the truth, anyway.

He scanned the park. He didn't seem mad or annoyed. Just curious. "You strike me as an intelligent person, Marissa. Now, have there been any coincidences that struck you as odd?"

Coincidences, my ass. A hidden box of photos of children, money in a lockbox, deleted email accounts, at least one possible affair with Becky Smith, payments, yeah . . . none of those were *coincidences*. I ran a hand over my hair when one major detail jumped out at me.

The *CM* folder. The emails sent from Christopher Malinowski *to* Ethan the day before he went missing.

This one seemed like too much of a coincidence, but disclosing how I knew meant I'd have to open up more to the detective, which I wasn't ready to do. Ethan trusted me enough to leave me breadcrumbs and, call me foolish, I'd follow them.

"What can you tell me about the Christopher Malinowski case from a few years ago, an experienced hiker and camper who showed up dead in a lake?" I asked.

"Oh yeah, what about him?" He spun all the way to look at me, his dark eyes wider than I'd seen before.

Shit. I'd caught his attention.

I looked at the sidewalk and pretended to look at an anthill. Anything to divert my gaze away from his penetrating stare. "I remembered hearing about it a couple of years ago. The guy worked for Hawkins Associates."

I snuck a glance to see his reaction.

The detective's stance went rigid, like someone pressed a freeze button. It didn't last long, though. Just two seconds. "What made you bring up that name, Mrs. Creighton?" The use of my married name made my eye twitch.

"Uh—"

"I ask you about coincidences, and the next question you ask is about Christopher Malinowski. Tell me why."

I shrunk back at his raised tone, and his face softened.

"I'm sorry. I'm not yelling at you. This is just . . . I can't help you if you don't tell me everything." He frowned and stared at Logan. "I get that you're trying to protect yourself. I really do. But I can't protect you and Logan if I don't know what's going on."

"The name was bolded in the Harlan Coben book, each letter bolded, and a date." I sucked in a breath like I'd been underwater for two minutes, and my face flushed. It was dumb to feel like I'd betrayed Ethan by telling him that, but I didn't regret it.

The detective sighed, his face breaking out into a grin. "This helps. This helps *a lot*, Marissa. Come on, let's head back home. Looks like it might storm."

He was right. The dark clouds weren't far off in the west, and I snorted at the irony. Logan babbled and pointed his little hand at every tree we passed, and a comfortable silence grew between us.

It was a good thing, too, since my father's car sat in my driveway. My stomach cramped, and my feet cemented onto the sidewalk once I realized he was in the house, but the detective put a reassuring hand on my back. "You'll be fine. You're not the one in danger."

Meaning . . . Ethan is? And what about Logan?

I kept that to myself and forced my feet to move. There was no way I could pull this off. My dad would see right through me, and then what? Would he destroy my laptop so I couldn't communicate with Ethan? No, that didn't make sense. He needed me to find Ethan.

Just like that, a weird confidence cloaked over me. Dad *needed* me to help whatever weird shit he and Peter were up to. Not the other way around. That meant I was in control. The soft artistic girl without the brain for *numbers* was the one in charge—god, that had to piss him off.

Plus, how much did my mom know about this? They bulldozed over her, so I couldn't trust her, but I wished I could ask her.

"Marissa, Christ." My dad panted as he ran out the front door of my house. His eyes drilled the detective. "I told you *no* talking to her without a lawyer."

"But, Dad, you said it yourself, he had a new development in the case. I wanted to hear it and get out of the house. It's so hard being in there without knowing if Ethan's alive." I made my voice shake.

The moisture in my eyes was real.

"New development," my dad repeated. His eyes glossed over.

Busted.

"Yes, sir. We were looking into Ethan's whereabouts the past few months. Looking for trends. Did he attend the same happy hour place or have a favorite bar? That sort of thing. All of it is pertinent information because we've found people typically return to their comfort places."

"So you're thinking he's for sure alive," my dad said as a bead of sweat pooled on his forehead despite the chilly air.

"Yes, we have no other reason to believe otherwise."

"So why'd you talk to Marissa? You could've looked at his work email or his planner. He always had that fucking thing."

Whoa. The tightwire around my spine stiffened, making me stand up straighter with worry. My dad was *not* acting cool. But something he'd said sparked a roaring fire inside me. Ever since I'd seen emails from Christopher Malinowski, I'd had a question I couldn't quite form.

I knew how to find out, though. Both men just needed to be gone.

The detective nodded and stared at me for a beat. "You're right, Franklin. We should get copies of all those too. Digital and hard copy. Now, since it's the weekend, you up for a drive to your business?"

"Why?"

"Well, I want to get a feel for his office, see what I can find. I figured it'd be better for the business to go when there are fewer employees. I think this will help us figure out where Ethan went."

My dad nodded and didn't even look at me as he got his car keys from his pocket. "Fine, as long as you think it'll help."

"It will, Dad, please. Go with him, and let me know what you can find, okay?" I made my voice extra sweet. It was insane how, within twenty-four hours, the trust between my family and me had shifted. I'd be mad later, but right now, I wanted to understand what was going on so I could decide what to do with the information.

I waited for them to both leave. Then I scrambled inside and handed Logan a snack in his high chair. I needed him *busy*. Attuned to something that wasn't me. My heart thudded in my chest as I went into my closet and found exactly what I was looking for—our old planners. I loved keeping them to go back and look at memories, and I made Ethan do it too.

But my dad had a great point. Why *didn't* we look for trends? But not in the past six months. Years. I needed to look at years. But the word *coincidence* was in bubble letters over my head, flashing over and over ever since the detective had asked about them.

There was a huge one.

I found the planner from three years ago. I flipped to May and ran my finger over the dates when Christopher Malinowski had gone camping and died. *Fuck.*

Fuck.

Ethan's choppy handwriting was right there, in blue ink.

GOLF (Hawkins Associates Outing)—Lakewood

On the Saturday Christopher had gone *missing*, Ethan had been *golfing* in the same town with Hawkins Associates. That meant Christopher Malinowski died near a work event, one that Ethan attended. That wasn't just a singular coincidence—that was a lead.

CHAPTER SIXTEEN

Saturday, 3:00 p.m.—Five days missing

"At the Library" by Green Day. I played that on my laptop before getting Logan into his car seat and heading toward the local library a few blocks away. I *needed* to read those emails away from the house and potential eyes of my family.

God, the unanswered texts from my dad, brother, and mom weighed on me. The most disturbing thing about this was I always hated how my parents spoke to me or gaslighted me in minor conversations. Like when I'd explain how I was upset, but they'd turn it around and say I was ungrateful and selfish for hurting my mom's feelings.

They were always overbearing, but it was the path of least resistance. Until Peter kept planting the seed to cut them off, I truly hadn't realized how bad it was. *Peter.*

The fact he was a part of this hurt. I'd never considered him in the same part of my heart as my parents. He was different, yet he was just as much a part of this as them. *Do I even know anyone anymore?* Perhaps all the stress had messed with my mind.

What about Ethan disappearing had my parents and brother so interested in finding him? I snorted as I drove down the road and stopped at a red light. Like any daughter, I'd assumed they wanted to find him because they loved him and wanted the father of their grandchild or nephew back safely. That wasn't the case here; I was certain. Not with the lying, spying, and threatening note.

My phone rang, again, and my mom's name flashed across the dashboard. I wanted them to leave me alone for one goddamn hour, but right before I dragged my thumb over the Decline button, fear gripped me.

What if they'd put a GPS in my car? Or Ethan's? If they'd put a camera or listening device in the house, was a GPS that far off?

I chewed on my lip for a second before making the rash decision to answer. I needed to ease their minds without giving them any indication to suspect me. The delicate balance of deceit was enough to make my nerves fray. "Hello?"

"Where are you? We've been texting you. You had us worried, honey. You can't forget your phone and be a space cadet today. Not now." She spoke way too fast and loud.

"I'm driving, Mom, so I can't look at my phone."

"Where are you going? You need to be careful. Dad says me or Peter should join you if you go anywhere. Can't say I disagree. You got that threat . . ."

Which Peter sent.

I didn't want to say I was going to the library without a good reason, and I did a quick scan of the front seat. I spotted an old Steak 'n Shake wrapper on the ground. "I wanted a burger, okay? A greasy burger. And then Logan kept saying *book*, so we're doing a quick trip to the library."

My mom sighed and mumbled to someone in the distance. "You'll come back home when you're done?"

"Yes, Mom." I rolled my eyes as I pulled into a parking spot at the library. It was busy, cars and people lining up all over the expansive new parking garage. "Are you at the house?"

"We all are. When you didn't text back, we worried. Your dad had an interesting chat with the detective. We'll fill you in when you get back."

The ball of nerves in my gut doubled in size as my mom hung up without letting me reply. I blew out a frustrated breath. An interesting chat with the detective? What the hell did she mean? Had he told my dad about Christopher Malinowski? Or the clues? Or the suspicions I had about my own parents?

No, he wouldn't do that . . . because he'd told me to be careful. My dad had said he had a *buddy* at the station . . . was Luna that buddy? *What if he's in on it, somehow?* I frowned and rubbed my thumb over the worry wrinkles between my brows. I needed to focus on one thing at a time. I was alone, without eyes watching me, and I had shit to do.

There was a red car that followed me to the library, the windows tinted so I couldn't see who drove. I wasn't sure when they started trailing me, but as I parked, they kept going. *Thank god.* I was paranoid. Totally paranoid.

Logan and I entered the library, and his excitement was contagious. It'd be tricky to keep him entertained *while* I logged in to the computer, but it could happen in ten-minute bursts. That's all I needed. Ten minutes to login, take a picture of the emails, and out. But before I could do that, we went to the kids' section. The same prickly feeling of being watched hit me, and I scanned the library for someone staring at me. Nothing stood out, but there was a large dude who had his back to me in the DVD section.

Was that the mob guy? I clutched my throat, absolutely sure it was him. He looked up, the same piercing green eyes, and I gasped. *It's him.* The man from the post office. Was he . . . stalking me? What the fuck was Ethan into?

Before I could scream or freak out, the man disappeared into an aisle without looking at me, and I sighed. *Calm down.* Just a coincidence. It had to be. The other possibilities were too terrifying.

"Whatcha think, baby?" I said, kissing his sweet head and pulling out some of the kid books.

Logan blabbed and pointed to the moons on the covers. He signed *more* by tapping his cute chubby hands together, and I picked up every book I could find with a moon—his latest obsession—and brought him, and the books, over to the computer center right in the middle of the library. With him occupied for a few minutes, I pulled out my library card for my ID and logged in.

Step one, done.

Step two, open my email.

I typed my username and password as my muscles tensed, waiting to see if those Christopher Malinowski emails helped at all. Bright-red letters greeted me.

> You have entered the incorrect password. Please try again.

I must've typed too fast. I did it again, certain I didn't have any errors.

> You have entered the incorrect password. Please try again.

What the actual fuck?

Logan stood up right as I wanted to punch the computer screen, and I chased him. He saw some puzzles and wanted to touch them, so I grabbed the wooden farm-animal one and brought him back toward the computer. This password nonsense wasted time and pissed me off. Unease melted through my soul, causing my pulse to rise.

I never changed my password. Ethan had made fun of me for using the same one for everything, and I hadn't edited it in years. Which meant . . . *someone* else had. My mouth fell open as a paralyzing dread rooted me to the metal chair. Had my dad or brother or Ethan hacked into my account to read these? Could they?

Yes. They all had tools and gadgets that could mirror every possible thing I did on my device.

That damn password list sat in the top drawer of Ethan's desk, so all my information was there. The yellow sheet of paper with the clues and my suspicions written down remained in my pocket, though. That would never be off my person.

This new password meant I had to reset this immediately using the verification on my phone. I clicked and typed all the necessary items to create a new password, and after two minutes, I was in.

Sweat covered my arms and chest, forming an awkward dark stain on my orange shirt, but I didn't care. I was *finally* back into my email. Logan sat, entertained by a wooden giraffe, and I scanned my inbox for the Christopher Malinowski emails. They weren't right at the top.

My breathing picked up as I scanned each line, *not* seeing what I needed. Was there a chance the original emails had never come through? Or they'd gone to spam? Or they'd been deleted?

No, I'd sent them. That meant . . . I pinched the bridge of my nose and checked the spam folder. Not there.

Next was my trash folder.

It was empty. *Not* the hundreds of promotional emails I deleted on the daily. I had never gone to my trash folder and permanently deleted anything, ever, but someone had, erasing the emails from Christopher Malinowski with them. Shit. Had I potentially put Ethan in danger by exposing all those emails? What did this mean? It was clear someone didn't want me reading them, but who?

Who could've done that besides someone in my family? Fuck. Disappointment hit me *hard*. The whole point of coming to the goddamn library was to *read* those emails.

That was step one of my plan, meaning all my other plans were waiting on this one. The pressure building in my body was going to burst, taking me with it, if this was my life now. Secrets, lies, betrayal, and disappointment. I hung my head, sinking into the hopelessness. Those emails felt crucial, and the only way to read them again was to log into Ethan's computer, which might be bugged by my family.

While they weren't gone forever, it might be too risky. I needed fucking answers, and I needed them *now*.

The Christopher emails were important, but the other nagging feeling I had was about the entire folder from the *ma8p7yh* email address that I took a picture of—the one with emails saying *we love you*. While I didn't necessarily think this person was connected to Christopher Malinowski, it was also an area I wanted to explore away from my family.

My gut churned at the notion I was emailing Ethan's mistress or the mother of his previous children. This was risky, but what choice did I have? Really? It was my only lead. I created a new email, totally fake and untraceable back to me so no one could hack it. Then I emailed the mystery person.

> To: ma8p7yh
>
> This is Ethan's wife. Can we talk please?

I typed it and stared, ruffling Logan's hair for a minute before I scolded myself. This was a horrible email. What if they didn't know he was missing?

We love you. Be careful. You're doing the right thing. That was their email. They *knew* what he was going to do, which pissed me off. I couldn't be trusted enough, but his sidepiece could? Something prickled at the back of my mind, nagging me to make excuses for Ethan. My family *was somehow* involved, so maybe that's why he didn't trust me?

I was seriously losing my mind to be making excuses for why my husband kept secrets from me. If I really was talking to the *other* woman, then maybe I didn't need to be so nice? Fuck, this was hard.

> To: ma8p7yh
>
> This is Ethan's wife. We need to talk asap. It's important.

There, that sent a better tone of urgency. Should I leave a number to call me? Or would she just email back? I chewed my thumbnail and said fuck it. I put my number on there. They would call or not. I hit Send before I overanalyzed it, and sat back in the chair. It let out a horrible squeak, and I winced.

"Da da da," Logan said. The sound of those syllables caused my chest to cave in with pain. He'd just started speaking more words right before Ethan disappeared, and hearing him call for his dad was a cruel form of punishment.

"What are you saying, Lo?" I squeezed my eyes shut to stop the moisture. I couldn't break down every time Logan did something that reminded me of Ethan. I'd never be able to function—the kid was a carbon copy of him. And the worst part about all this? I still loved my husband. I loved him so much. And even though every time I breathed, it hurt because of the lies and betrayal, the love didn't just disappear.

"You liking the puzzle? Can you show me the hippo? Where's the hippo?" I asked, my voice watery. I cleared my throat to try to get ahold of the tears.

Logan looked at me with a toothy smile and pointed toward the bookshelves to his right. I followed his little finger and forced a smile. "You want to go look in the shelves?"

"Da da da," he babbled again.

"Let me sign off, baby, then we can go walk around." I sighed, pushed my hair out of my face, and then gasped at the email in my inbox. *They responded!*

From: ma8p7yh

How did you find my email?

Wow, underwhelming. My jaw clenched from the lack of anything useful from this besides her getting defensive. I pictured some cartoon-villain woman, and I sneered at her as I wrote back.

To: ma8p7yh

I don't want trouble, I want answers. My son could be in danger and I'm sure you understand that.

The tone of my email impressed me. I normally wasn't aggressive or dramatic. I was always calm and found the solutions in times of drama. The peacekeeper. My dad always said Peter was a rain cloud and I was a warm summer day. Did he mean it or merely want me to get it in my head that I could never make trouble? I shook the thought away. I'd need therapy after all this, regardless of the outcome.

"Da da da da," Logan said *again*. It caused my left eye to twitch. He had to stop saying that. It wasn't good for my mental health or his.

"Dada is on a trip, baby. He'll be back soon." I reached over to soothe him with my right hand. If this ma8p7yh (whom I now referred to in my mind as *May*) was not going to be friendly, I needed to up my game.

"Baba mmm dada ma," Logan continued. His little voice was so damn cute that I glanced at him, taking a second to admire how wonderful Logan really was. But something caught my eye.

In the bookshelves.

An envelope jutting out with a large *M* on it.

Wild guess, but I assumed the *M* meant *Marissa.* My mind raced through every person who knew I was here. It unnerved me. The list was short. My mom, which meant my dad and Peter did, and Ethan. If he saw my song choice. I'd even chosen the Green Day version of "At the Library" because he had a lot of feelings about that band.

That meant one of those four people had left me that envelope. *WE'RE BEING WATCHED* seemed to play like a dark theme song in my gut. My spine tingled, and the hairs on the back of my neck stood on end as I hoped, prayed, and wished on every star I could that it was Ethan. Logan's continual saying of *da da da* and pointing . . . I struggled to breathe because of the hope pulsing through me. I quickly set up the new email address on my phone so that I would receive notices if a new email came in. I logged off the computer, picked Logan up, and walked as fast as I could to the envelope.

MARGARITA was written on the back of it. *EVAN WILLIAMS* was on the bottom.

Our nicknames.

One night out, Ethan and I'd had too much to drink after a concert and thought, in our drunken minds, that having alter egos would be fun. All night, he'd called me Margarita, and I'd called him Evan Williams. So dumb, yet so funny. But more importantly—so *us*.

If he'd left this clue, that meant he was here. So close to me. I shoved the envelope in my pocket and ran farther into the aisle. There were people all around, which made my frantic search difficult. *Come on, Ethan. Please, please be here.*

I jogged through each aisle, with Logan bouncing in my arms. This *had* to mean Ethan was here. I was sure of it. I hadn't seen the note before, but I'd only been there a short time. Had he snuck it in? Had someone else dropped it off? My pulse pounded against my throat to the point of pain, the sheer desperation in my body driving me forward to find him. Why wouldn't he say something? Why?

I continued to the nonfiction section in the farthest corner of the library when someone stepped out of the shadows. I almost screamed but turned it into a whisper to avoid attention. *"Ethan!"*

He *crushed me* in a hug, putting his large arms around me and Logan, resting his forehead against mine. His entire body trembled against me, and I took in his familiar scent, his warmth, the way he kissed the top of my head four times. "Marissa," he breathed. His voice broke.

My tears fell freely now.

"My boy." He sniffed as he kissed Logan's face, forehead, and head. "I don't have long." His deep voice filled with emotion that matched mine. His eyes watered.

He seemed older. Rougher. He hadn't shaved, and there were dark circles under his eyes. It seemed like the past five days had been absolute hell. His dark hat, black T-shirt, and faded jeans blended in with what everyone else wore at the library, but it was the look in his eyes that gutted me. He looked miserable, worried. Ethan cupped my face and dragged his thumb over my bottom lip, his face softening as he stared at me. "Are you and Logan okay? You said you weren't safe in the songs?"

"We got a threatening note, which actually came from Peter. I think this guy might be following us too. Are you in the mob? What . . . Ethan, what the fuck is going on?" I wanted to snuggle into my husband. He had been my comfort for so long, the physical need to be near him overwhelmed me.

He shook his head. "Not enough time. I promise it'll all make sense soon. I need you to do something for me, for all this to end. I wrote it in the letter, but once you read it, burn it."

I nodded as he continued to touch every part of me. My hips, sides, arms, shoulders, neck. He couldn't stop touching me, and my battered soul had to ask questions. "Why do you have secret emails? And payments spanning almost a decade? And pictures of kids in our closet?"

My husband paled and opened his mouth, but no sound came out. That wasn't reassuring.

I took a step back, hurt and relieved, happy and devastated. It was a real shit show of an emotional roller coaster, seeing my husband alive, yet not getting any answers. "Ethan," I said again, stronger this time. "I need you to answer me."

He blinked and wiped a hand over his face before he met my eyes again; this time, he looked miserable. Guilty. Regretful. His lips pressed together, and the lines around his eyes increased, but then he stood taller. "Fuck." He straightened his hat and moved back into the shadows. "Mar, I *love* you. You and Lo are my life. No matter *what* you find out, please, believe me on this. I'm doing whatever I can to protect you and my son. Read the note."

"Where are you . . . ? No, Ethan, don't leave us again. Please." I reached for him.

He yanked my arm closer to him and pressed his lips against mine. It was a quick, hard kiss, and then he let go.

His voice came out gruff and direct. "Take Logan toward the kid section. Pretend he walked over here."

"Wait, what—"

"Your mom's here, Mar. They're *always* fucking watching." His piercing tone sent a flurry of anxiety through me; he had hatred for my parents. "Please, I promise this will all make sense. But I need you to continue trusting me, even if it's hard." And with that, he darted to the side and was out of view.

It was a lot to process, but the biggest one of all was *why* my mom was at the library. They were trailing me, for what? To catch Ethan?

I'd told her I needed space, to get out. I hadn't asked for help.

I took a second to calm myself down, and as I made sure the note was out of view, I settled my growing nerves. My family *kept* showing up, watching me, and involving themselves. The people I was supposed to trust the most in my life were all becoming strangers.

CHAPTER SEVENTEEN

Saturday, 3:30 p.m.—"Found"

"Honey, honey, oh, there you are." My mom put a hand over her chest and sighed really loud. She wore a pastel pink dress, one I'd always referred to as the Easter outfit, and she stood out at the library with her curled hair and large sunglasses on the top of her head. She looked like she'd walked here from a yacht party or the derby, and people stared as she let out a half sob. "I tried calling you *six* times."

"What?" I'd *literally* had my phone out less than five minutes ago when I sat at the computer emailing May—Ethan's secret email pen pal. I would've seen, heard, or felt the vibration. Logan reached for my mom, and she picked him up, snuggling her nose into his neck and going on about how much she loved him.

I'd always *loved* how she'd taken to being a grandma. She might look chic, but she was never afraid to get dirty with Logan, play in the mud or with rocks, but all that trust had broken. Gone. I stayed *right* next to them as she held my son, the gross feeling in my gut doubling in size. How could I act normal right now, when Ethan had just been here, alive?

I reached into my pocket for my phone and sucked in a breath.

Missed calls (Mom)

Six of them.

But I'd never heard it, felt it. Not once. I frowned at my phone. "I never heard it go off."

"That's all right. I'm just glad you're both okay. Ever since that picture showed up at the door—ugh—your father and I have been so worried. Peter too. Your big brother is beside himself, hating anyone coming after you and Lo." Peter had sent the photo. He wasn't worried about shit.

She kissed Logan's head and ran her manicured fingers over his hair. Her mouth pinched with concern, and I found myself doubting my gut. She looked genuinely worried—like maybe she wasn't in on the entire thing. She made a goofy face at Logan, making him giggle, and I pressed my palms against my eyes until I saw white spots. My dad and brother were acting shady, but was she?

I didn't know. I didn't know anything anymore.

Ethan was *here*. At the library.

He'd risked giving me the letter that seemed to grow in my back pocket. It felt like it was the size of a helmet and that if I turned around, my mom would know what it was. I had a choice. Did I trust her enough to watch Logan for a minute while I went to the restroom, or did I wait to get to the car and hope my dad or brother weren't watching from somewhere else?

Once you read it, burn it.

Flushing it might be just as effective. I sighed and swallowed, hoping my voice didn't give away my erratic emotions. "Mom, could you watch him for just a minute? I need to use the restroom."

She reached over and squeezed my forearm. "Of course, go. We'll go look at the puppets. I can relive my high-school-acting glory days."

I forced a smile and even managed to produce something that sounded like a laugh. Then I was off. I tried to be natural, to keep up my front. That meant being creative. *Don't reach around to touch the letter. Just be cool.*

I scanned the library, searching to see if Ethan blended in or if my dad was creeping around a corner. The dark hat and shirt Ethan wore weren't in sight, nor was any man resembling my family members. I had to hope that Ethan had a reason for doing this *and* that he'd gotten out okay.

I had this letter and song titles. Hopefully, it would clear stuff up. Maybe not the guilt in his eyes, consuming him and not reassuring me in any way. But the other stuff? God, I needed answers.

I pushed into the ladies' room and found an empty stall. Locking it and taking a deep breath, I pulled the letter from my pocket. My damp hands opened the note, and the messy scrawl of Ethan's handwriting soothed me in a nostalgic way, like when he'd left me notes when we'd first started dating.

> Mar,
>
> I need you to know that I love you and Logan more than ANYTHING in the world. That has never changed nor will it ever. Despite all the secrets and chaos, PLEASE know that you are my favorite person. I promise there is an explanation for all this, but I need more time. I'm so close—then we can pick up the pieces and go back to being a family again.
>
> I need two things from you. The first—I need you to get onto my computer and open my work emails. Click through all the ones that say HAWKINS in the subject. They aren't important for you to read, but if I'm right, which I think I am, it'll set things in motion.
>
> The second—it might be tricky, but you're smart. That's the one thing your family never thought to value about you. You are shrewd and quick on your feet. God, I still remember the time you talked us out

of getting a speeding ticket. I miss you more than you know.

And not just the past week, the past year or so. I know things have been different. This is my fault, and I own that.

PLEASE be careful, but I need you to find out if Dennis Paulson met with Lexington LLC three months ago. Dennis is an adviser for the company.

Again, I can't get into why, but when you find the answer, play a song with a YEAH or a NO.

I'm sorry we're going through this. I assure you, it was never supposed to happen this way. I love you and Logan, and I hope you'll forgive me when this is all done. Don't trust your folks. This'll be over soon, I promise.

E

I read it again. There was so much to unpack. Layers upon layers. He said not to trust my folks. Not . . . my brother and dad. My folks. The unease about my mom took root again.

But the truth was I had a decision to make. Was I going to help him, turn him in to the detective, or do nothing?

I ripped up the note, piece by piece, and let them fall into the toilet as I ground my teeth together. He could've written a full book to explain what was going on, and yet he'd written this? Half answers?

He knew my family would follow me. I sighed as the muscles in my gut eased. He'd clearly written the note in a rush, but his words were specific, intentional. He seemed to be running out of time, so I focused on the facts.

He needed two things from me, and I'd do both. Getting onto his computer was easy enough . . . and I had a theory on *why* it would set things in motion. There was information there, and if he knew my family was *always fucking watching*, then that info was important.

The second . . . hmm, I wouldn't find the information at home, so that meant I had to get into the office without raising suspicion. My chest puffed with confidence at Ethan's words—I was smart, but I didn't like math and technology like my family. I liked music and arts, so they naturally assumed I was *airy*. Ditzy. That was their mistake.

I watched the last piece flush away, and I was about to pocket my phone when the nagging thing in my mind returned. It was the time. I planned everything around Logan's downtime and snacks, so I knew I had to be quick to get him back home by four.

I checked my call log and saw when my mom had first rung—3:06 p.m. I'd told her I was going to the library and had gotten food.

I opened my email and saw when I'd gotten the recovery message, asking me to confirm my authentication code. That was at 3:15 p.m.—there had been ZERO missed calls then. I went to my sent box and saw the emails I'd sent to the mystery May person, and that read 3:19 p.m.

The missed calls came at 3:20 p.m. when I was sitting at the computer with my phone on the desk. I shook my head, doing mental math. It would've taken more than a minute for me to have six missed calls, then for my mom to get into her car *and* drive to the library. There was no way she would've done all that within ten minutes.

Which meant . . . she or all of them started driving here the second I told them I was coming. She could've seen Ethan . . . been waiting for him . . . or my dad could've been. I left the stall and washed my hands before going back out to find my mom and Logan. They were sitting on a couch as my mom read him a book about clouds, and a rush of fury hit me.

For a brief moment, I'd thought she might not be involved. It was fleeting but filled me with hope that maybe my entire family wasn't betraying me. But for her to have called and shown up here . . . it had to have been planned. "Thanks." I walked up to her, my pulse radiating anger through my body.

"Sure you're all right, sweetie? You're pale." She frowned and turned the page for Logan. "Do you need a snack?"

"No. Let's go home."

"Okay, yeah." She studied me for a moment. "Are you sure you're all right?"

"Fine, given the circumstances of having a missing husband," I said through clenched teeth. I needed to GET IT TOGETHER, or she'd know I was on to them. I never played poker because my face had too many tells, and this was slightly harder than just a card game. They always told me I was a shit liar. Even as a kid, I could never keep a secret, and my family often made fun of me for it. "It's just . . . a lot. Sorry I snapped."

"Baby, don't be sorry. I can't imagine what you're going through. Just know you can lean on me for anything, okay? I'll always be there for you. Even when your dad and brother get a little overbearing." She stood up and hugged me, her once-comforting floral perfume now irritating me.

I patted her back and tried to relax my tense muscles. Thankfully, Logan babbled in between us, so he gave me the perfect excuse. "How's my little man?"

"Da da!" he said, pointing over my shoulder, and everything froze.

My breath, my heart, my stance.

Ethan, run! I thought, feeling the blood leave my face as my mom followed his finger with her gaze. A line appeared between her brows, but she picked him up and bounced him on her hip.

"You miss your daddy, Lo?" She kissed his cheek.

Logan kept his chubby finger pointed toward the stairs, where a man with a ball cap stood with his back to us. *What the fuck, Ethan?* He stood there, unmoving, right where my mom could see.

She sucked in a breath and grabbed my wrist, digging her nails into my forearm as the man spun around.

Not Ethan.

Jesus. I ran a shaky hand over my forehead as my mom watched. Her eyes twinkled like she *knew* why I was sweating, and I went into recovery mode. "He kept saying it earlier, and I know it's stupid, but for a second, I thought Ethan would be there, and when he wasn't . . ." My voice broke. "It was dumb. I know he wouldn't be here."

"Oh, honey." My mom's sympathetic voice *seemed* genuine. It hit the right notes. Logan loved his grandma, but with Ethan's explicit note to not trust my parents . . . I couldn't leave my son with her anymore. It was like looking at a stranger now. "I'll make some strong margaritas when we get home. That'll help."

A chill drafted down my spine at her use of the word *margarita.* Never in my life had the two of us made margaritas, so was it a coincidence that *my secret* fake name with Ethan was the drink suggestion she made?

I wasn't sure.

"A margarita sounds great, Mom."

With that, we left the library and went home.

My father paced the living room with his hands in his pockets. The tips of his ears were red, and the continual thud of his gait seemed to echo in the silence. The TV wasn't on, Logan wasn't babbling, and no one said a word. My mind kept repeating the note Ethan had left me, the things he'd asked me to do. The computer would be easy, but there just wasn't a way to do it. Not with my family *here.*

Don't trust your folks.

Tell no one.

We're being watched.

I scanned the recently played music. **"Stay Alert" by D. Savage.**

"Who Can I Trust" by Blacc Zacc.

"Your Guts (I Hate 'Em)" by Reel Big Fish.

Ethan told me to trust my gut. Problem was, she was a hot-ass mess without direction.

"I don't understand why he needs the records." My dad spat out the words. It was clear who the *he* was in the situation. Detective Luna. Apparently, my dad didn't like the fact a detective had gone into Hawkins Associates. It got people talking. Got them asking questions. I knew for a fact he didn't like being questioned for any reason.

The excuse that he *was nervous* around authority figures didn't cut it anymore.

"If it will help find Ethan, then it's important," Peter reassured him. "Didn't he say he thinks Ethan's life is in danger?"

"Wait, *what*?" I snapped, clutching my throat. Logan stopped playing with his stuffed animals and stared at me. "It's okay, bub, go play with your guys." I picked one up off the ground and made some silly sounds.

That did the trick, and he went back to playing at my feet. Call me paranoid, but Logan wasn't going to be out of my sight again . . . even if it was past his nap time. Not until I figured this out.

I widened my eyes at my dad. Even though I'd just *seen* Ethan, the threat was new. The detective had *not* told me that. "What do you mean?"

My mom cleared her throat and shifted her weight as my dad stared at her, and just like that, my father relaxed his stance and glanced at me. The same weathered face and intelligent eyes looked familiar, but there was a wildness to him now that either I'd ignored or hadn't been there before: a slight bulging vein on his forehead, a flush over his skin. It was clear he hadn't been sleeping.

A surge of fury went through me that he was hiding something from me, forcing my hands to form fists on my lap.

His gaze dropped to them, and I unfurled them. *Act weak. Act scared.* I made my lip tremble (which the adrenaline of getting caught made easy) and blinked a lot. "Dad, please, what did he mean?"

He ran a hand over his face and sighed. "He asked to see Ethan's calendar for the past six months. Digital calendar, I guess. Said people add more details to their digital files than paper. Also wanted our work production schedule, which is *fucking* confidential."

"Franklin," my mom snapped. It was sharp, aggressive, like my dad was a disobedient child. "Logan is here—please, no cussing. We're all stressed and missing Ethan. We have to be there for each other."

"Let me speak how I want. Logan can't understand." He glared at her, and she righted her posture, staring at her hands.

He was an ass.

"Why is the production schedule a big deal?" I kept my tone from sounding too desperate. Ethan had shown me the spreadsheet and tried to explain the Scrum process to me once—which was an agile project management framework tactic that seemed complicated—but I tuned out. It had been too many details all at once, and now I felt stupid. "Was he working on something dangerous?"

My dad scoffed. "Production schedule is just that, Marissa. The schedule of the projects he was managing or working on." He pinched the bridge of his nose. "I need a drink."

If the detective had the production schedule or Ethan's calendar . . . I could find something. I was sure. I chewed on the inside of my cheek and watched Logan play with the stuffed animals. He loved the elephant and hugged him tight.

I felt trapped. Trapped with my family, stuck about how to help Ethan—and what about all the unanswered questions? There were too many unknowns and too many paths this could take. My phone buzzed against my thigh, and I pulled it out, half expecting it to be my boss.

I'd never once thought to let her know what was happening.

But it wasn't Claudia asking me where my articles were for the month. It was the secret email. May had responded.

> To: Marissa
>
> Are you threatening me? Not a good move when I have all the answers. Accept defeat, MARISSA HAWKINS. You deserve it. You deserve ALL the things coming your way. Don't email me again. I'm deleting this account. You're interfering in something that goes FAR beyond your sad little life.

What the *fuck*?

The all caps. The use of my maiden name. The attack on me. My eyes prickled with tears at why this person had this anger. Did they view me as the other woman? Did Ethan lie to them, and they blamed me?

My breath lodged in my throat, and the pressure in my chest grew. I'd thought I could get answers from the person my husband had been emailing for years. But this . . . this was angry. The thing that bothered me most was the fact this secret affair might not have anything to do with what was going on with my family.

There could be two scandals rocking my world that didn't connect. Ethan had paled when I asked about the photos and emails, and never responded, almost like . . . *that* didn't matter at the moment. The shit with my family did first.

Then we could wade through the decades' worth of lies. I bolted up from the couch, making all of them look at me. *Shit.* Peter perked up from his spot on the couch, sitting straighter and staring at me with excitement.

Like . . . they all thought I'd figured something out.

Oh, how wrong they were.

"We should head out. Give her some space." Peter stared at our parents. "We could come back in a bit, let Marissa rest."

"We're not leaving now, Peter. Stop suggesting dumb shit. I need you on your game. The last thing we need to do is leave," my dad fired back.

"He's worried about Marissa, like a good older brother." My mom patted my dad's arm. "She needs us to support her right now. With the affairs and disappearance, who else can help her? She can't take care of herself."

"Yes, I can," I said.

"No, hon, you can't. You're a mess." My dad's mouth flattened. "The front door was unlocked when I arrived, and the faucet was left on. You don't make enough on your own to afford payments, and with Ethan gone, he's not getting paid. You can't be on your own. It's not fair to Logan."

Were they insinuating I couldn't take care of my own son? I was gonna kill them. Peter met my gaze, his eyes darkening as he looked at our dad.

"I just . . . need a minute." I picked up my son and breathed him in as I walked down the hall and into Ethan's office, then leaned against the wall. My parents sucked. How dare they suggest I wasn't good for Logan? I would always be there for him. I'd *kill* for my son.

I had a choice to make, one that really mattered, and that needed a clear head. I either focused on the secret emails and payments or helped Ethan with whatever shit he'd set in motion.

One could destroy our marriage, but the other . . . could be more dangerous. I had to let the emails, the payments, and the photos go. No searching for the visitor Becky Smith. No worrying about the secret family.

Get on my computer and search for the emails with HAWKINS in the subject. That, I could do. "Want to play office, Lo?"

Because I could survive this on my own, keeping my son safe. He'd never be out of my sight now.

I'd bought a fake keyboard and mouse for him to play with when I had to work and couldn't distract him, so he thought he was *working* as I logged in to Ethan's computer. I went to his work email account and signed in with the autosaved password.

Just like the secret emails, there were organized folders, labeled. HAWKINS was there, blue, and I clicked it. Showtime.

I opened each one, scrolled down, and repeated the process. The text itself blurred since it was just confirming proofs for projects. Test runs. Design reviews. Meetings with clients to ensure they liked the product. None of the names stood out to me, nor the dates. But this was what Ethan wanted.

Logan typed away on the fake keyboard, his chubby little fingers smashing the keys way too hard. For one second, I smiled at him. He was so damn cute. *I have to solve this mystery for Logan's safety. To give him a chance at a normal life.* I went through the emails at a furious pace, making sure to hit each one, and sighed when I finished. There weren't more than fifty in there.

I relaxed back into the computer chair, listened for any approaching footsteps, and almost laughed. Of *course* they didn't barge in on me now. They wanted me on his computer. They had some spyware on it, I was sure, and were probably watching me as I clicked on Ethan's photo booth.

Photos of the three of us filled the screen, and my heart clenched. *Focus.* I opened Ethan's drawer to see if he still kept our first photo together in there. I'd asked him once, postpartum, if he ever regretted doing life with me. It had been a low moment, but he'd reassured me by showing the photo. Us, young and happy, with the youthful fullness to our cheeks.

It was still there. I pulled it out and smiled. It gave me the strength I needed. Which was well timed because it was then I noticed something was missing.

Something major.

The white sheet of paper with ALL our passwords wasn't in the drawer where I left it. That meant *someone* in my family was getting sloppy and desperately didn't want me accessing Ethan's accounts. I couldn't trust my phone anymore. Hell, I couldn't trust any of my electronics. That meant no digital trail. Nothing to hack. I needed to document everything I had on my phone, right fucking now. Because I knew, without a doubt, someone was watching my every move.

CHAPTER EIGHTEEN

Saturday, 10:00 p.m.—One day "found"

It took forever to convince my parents and brother to get the hell out of my house. After years of not caring that my dad was manipulating me, something finally broke in my soul. I was *fine* being home alone with Logan, and for any of them to suggest I couldn't handle it was almost enough for me to cut them out of my life.

Which I couldn't do *now*. Not when I had to act like I didn't suspect them. And a part of me still dreamed and wished this was all reparable. A flicker of hope remained that Ethan and I would work it out, that there was a legit reason for all this. Or that maybe my family was stressed about something at work, and it caused them to spiral out of control.

But I wasn't naive—everything had changed.

How could I not suspect them? The password sheet that had been missing a few hours ago? Yeah. It had returned to the drawer before they left. Did they think I wouldn't check? Or that I'd think the lone sheet of paper had grown legs and just gone for a walk?

They probably thought I was too emotional to realize they'd snuck it right by me. The thought that I'd caught them made my lips curve in a half smile for just a second. It disappeared at the reality crashing around me. I wished I knew *why* this was even happening.

"I Miss You, I'm Sorry" by Gracie Abrams. Ethan had last listened to that song one hour ago. I rubbed my temples and returned with **"Falling Apart" by Papa Roach**.

"Stay Strong" by Newsboys.

"I'm Trying" by Yeek and Dominic Fike.

Ethan put on **"Heavy, California" by Jungle**, my favorite song from that album. The thrill of seeing him in person faded as my life continued down the maze. Why the games? Why not confide in me? He had to know I'd have helped him. Annoyance crept in, and I wanted to demand answers. I used to listen to that song on repeat for hours, and it had always made me smile. The music videos were incredible with all the dancing. A better time, for sure.

I checked the baby monitor and watched Logan's chest move up and down. He was on his back, something he only did when he was exhausted, and it comforted me. He could still sleep without nightmares of what-ifs.

Being stuck in my house with watchful eyes in every direction put my every sense on high alert. The wind would hit a window and shake the screen, making me jump. Everything was amplified, and I jumped when my email pinged.

My personal email. Not the burner account.

With a new message from May.

Franklin Hawkins, St. Louis, 2008

Delete this now.

I read it again and again and still couldn't make sense of why Ethan's potential affair had emailed *my personal* email with my dad's name, a city, and a year. None of it made sense, and a chill gripped its way down my body, making me shiver. I deleted it, unsure why I was following her instructions when she'd gotten a real attitude before, but I added this information to the master list I kept in my pocket.

The clues kept on coming.

I was insistent on not letting the two paths collide, Ethan's secret life and the current issues with my family, but this . . . this changed that, right? Why would his secret friend/partner/person he emailed every Friday say my dad's name?

I typed in the name, city, and year, and nothing came up. No news stories, no scandalous headlines that would explain why these details were important. I scanned the first page of results, hoping for something to connect the dots between the two situations, but nothing stood out. Not even a word.

God, what had I even been doing in 2008? I was in high school, about to graduate. Doing senior spirit weeks and drinking on the weekends, hoping my parents didn't notice. An ad on the side of the screen caught my attention . . . *HOW TO TELL IF YOUR COMPUTER IS BEING MONITORED RIGHT NOW.*

Well, shit. The back of my neck tingled as I remembered Ethan's words from years ago about bait. Phishing scams. What if this was a trap? I exited out of the window and started a new search. *HOW TO KNOW IF YOUR DEVICE IS BEING MONITORED.*

First one—internet connection.

Check the open ports.

Install a trial spyware program.

View active connections on the internet.

Review installed programs on the device.

Jesus, this was so much.

The room got a million degrees hotter when Ethan's song changed.

"Driveway" by Lil Peep.

Did that mean he was here?

I jumped from the chair and glanced out the small front window, but there wasn't a car or any sign of a person. The hairs on the back of my neck stood on end at the silence of the night. We lived on a road removed from busy streets and surrounded by a lot of retired people who traveled all the time. That meant we were often the only people home on the whole block.

A shadow danced across the driveway from the streetlight, and I jumped. Who the fuck was out there? A coyote? A squirrel? A person . . . But *why*?

A slight thud had me whipping my gaze to the other side of the front yard. It could've been someone jumping onto the ground or someone dropping something. Like a bag?

Thunk.

The metal screen door hit the doorframe. I bit my lip so hard, I tasted blood. The trees weren't blowing in the wind, so *why* would it thunk like that?

What could anyone possibly want from the house? *Unless* it was Ethan? Sneaking in?

My heart rate tripled, and breathing hurt from my absolute indecision.

"Be Careful" by Jason Derulo.

"Call the Police" by John Wayne.

Wait, Ethan was telling me to call the police? *He's watching the house. He's nearby.*

"Come Inside" by Crazy Town. I played it, my adrenaline spiking off the charts. Each limb shook as I changed the song.

"Call the Police" by LCD Soundsystem. "NOW" by Olivia O'Brien. "Im Serious" by Nino Man. "You're Not Alone" by Saosin.

Fuck. An ice-cold chill ran up and down my spine as I stood up. I picked up my phone and called the detective. It rang three times.

"This is Luna."

"Detective, this is Marissa." The words scraped against my throat.

Logan. Must protect Logan.

"What is it?"

"I . . . I think someone might be breaking in to the house." My fingers shook the phone, and I stared through the window. I gripped a pair of scissors with my other hand and turned the computer monitor on so it wouldn't fade after thirty seconds.

"Did you call 911?"

"No, I called you."

"Marissa, hang up and call 911. I'll head over right now." Something shuffled in the background, and I prayed he was close.

I heard a soft thud from the other end of the house, and it felt like ants raced from my skull to my toes. A current went through me. White hot. "Someone's inside."

"Do you have a weapon?"

"N-no." The scissors slipped from my grip. I stood at the edge of Ethan's office now, Logan's nursery to my immediate right. Whoever it was wouldn't get to him without going through me first. "Should I take Logan and run?"

"I'm three minutes out." His voice was clipped. Radio chatter carried through the speaker. "Marissa, get Logan into a room and lock the door."

"Okay." I tiptoed the six feet to Logan's room and went inside before locking it. I scooted his dresser in front of it, hoping to barricade us in. "I'm inside." The sound machine roared, stopping all sounds from outside the door. That meant Logan wouldn't wake up, but . . . "I can't hear anything, though."

"Two minutes away."

I couldn't hear anything, but I felt vibrations. Footsteps. Movement. My teeth chattered together, and I had to protect my baby. No matter what. If the person was here for Ethan's computer, they could have it. I didn't care. I just needed to survive this and protect Logan.

This couldn't have been my family. They would never hurt us . . . right?

The fact I even questioned it had me almost throwing up. What had happened to my world?

"Marissa?" the detective said, his tone urgent. "What's going on?"

I couldn't risk answering. Not with the footsteps so close to the door. The hallway had a night-light for those *middle of the night* wake-ups from Logan, and shadows danced under the doorway.

Oh my god.

Lots of shadows.

There's more than one person.

"Marissa, answer me. I'm a minute out," he yelled.

I couldn't answer him. I hit a button, hoping it made a tone.

"Fuck. Hit one for no, two for yes. Are they close?"

Beep beep.

"Can you get out with Logan?"

Beep beep.

"Do it. Sixty seconds, I'm there. Get out of the house."

I had to get Logan up without alerting the intruders. My feet curled in the soft carpet. I'd have to make a run for it barefoot. I tiptoed toward the window and unlocked it without making a sound. *Check.*

I pushed it up and took a deep breath of the cool night air. Next, I removed the screen with one hand and set it against Logan's closet. Okay. Fuck. This was happening. I was escaping the house with my baby into the middle of the cool night with no shoes. I looked out toward the neighborhood, the empty streets and houses without lights.

Here goes nothing. I swallowed the absolute terror gripping my lungs and picked Logan up from the crib. He stirred but rested his head against my chest. I grabbed a blanket and wrapped him with it before figuring out how I could move both of us out the window.

It'd be hard but doable.

Something loud hit the wall—like the intruders knocked something over—and muffled voices carried through the thin plaster. *Fuck.*

"I'm pulling onto your street. Lights are off. Backup is on the way," the detective said.

"Okay." I took a huge breath to find courage. Then two things happened at once—the sound machine *stopped*. For three seconds.

During that three-second glitch, there was absolute silence, and someone muttered, "Shit, we need to go."

The thuds moved from the office toward the center of the house, and I spoke into the phone just as the machine reset. "They're going to escape! They're leaving!"

"Shit. *Stay* in the room."

The sirens came on, and Logan stirred in my arms, his sleepy eyes searching for whatever had woken him up. I soothed him against my chest as my body trembled with adrenaline. Fear, relief, worry. It was like my blood itched and I had no way to scratch it. It was unsettling in the same way an anxiety attack was. There wasn't a button or trick to get rid of it; I just had to endure it and hope I survived.

I hummed a lullaby to Logan over and over until he fell asleep in my arms. Time seemed to still, and I wasn't sure how many times I hummed "Snuggle Puppy." It could've been three or thirty-three. All I knew was that eventually someone knocked on the door, and a familiar strong voice said my name.

"It's Luna. You can come out now."

Tears spilled out as I set Logan down in his crib, secured the window, and moved the dresser to leave the nursery. I had never been so thankful to see someone else; I threw my arms around him without thinking.

He patted my back a few times. "They got away, whoever it was. We're collecting fingerprints, shoe prints, any evidence they left behind, but it might be tough."

"If one of them was my family, then their prints would already be here." I accepted the fact it could've been Peter or my dad. Or both of them. They had keys to the house, so getting in would've been easy.

"We did find evidence of messing with the side garage door lock. Is that the same lock as the rest of the house?"

"Yes." Well, that was new. Peter and my dad *had* the keys, so they wouldn't need to tamper with the lock or go in the side way, unless they wanted to keep suspicion off themselves. "It could be intentional."

"Yeah, it could." He sighed and led me into the living room, where three other uniformed officers were at work with flashlights, cameras, and scowls. A heavy weight filled the air, making the entire situation even more serious than what it warranted. "Are you okay?"

"No, but I feel better now that I'm not alone."

"Marissa," the detective said in a hard voice. "Someone else called the police a minute before you did, stating there was a break-in at this exact address. The call came from the house diagonal to yours, and when we went to ask questions, no one was home."

I gulped. *Ethan.*

"Now, we haven't verified it, but the frantic call, the language used . . . my gut says it's Ethan. The caller's words said *Marissa's in danger.* Would you know anything about that?"

I slid my gaze toward the TV and jutted my chin under it.

Luna smiled. "We got rid of the device. You were right. It was a microphone live streaming all audio."

Fuck. I recoiled, thinking of how much had been heard, for how long. Ethan and I had long talks in the living room, *fooled around* in the living room, had family moments. The fact someone had been recording all that made me a type of angry that terrified me.

This had to end, soon, or I wasn't sure what I'd do. The feeling gripping my mind and body was turning darker, more desperate, by the minute. It was time to tell Luna the truth—80 percent of it.

My teeth chattered as I said, "Ethan told me to call the police."

"He *told* you?"

"Through songs." Tears fell down my face as I betrayed Ethan. But I had no choice now. Not when Logan and I were in danger. *Real* danger. That changed things. Because throughout the entire night, one thing stood out to me. It was a line from the letter he'd given me at the library. *If I'm right, it'll set things in motion.*

I'd checked those emails thirty minutes before shit happened. Ethan had said checking would set things in motion, but was having two people break in to the house with me and Logan home *part* of that plan?

"We used to play songs on our Spotify accounts when he was at work. It's how we stayed connected through all the crazy hours. We can see the last song played, when it was played, or what we're currently listening to." I wiped my eyes with the back of my hand and bounced my feet up and down.

The detective sighed, but he didn't seem *annoyed*. "This has been going on since day one?"

"Yes. Well, day two. The first day was an added song to a shared playlist that said *Trust Me*." God, telling him felt like lifting a vise from my body while also sending a sharp pain through my chest. I'd disobeyed Ethan's first ask. "Ethan told me to trust no one, and I wasn't sure if that included you or not. I still don't—I don't know why this is happening."

"I understand why you kept it. I wish I would've known that earlier, but I understand. It proves my theory that this was planned, by him, for some reason." He wiped his hands on his thighs as he stared at the spot where the ceiling met the wall. He studied it for so long, it made me stare at it to see if there was something there.

There wasn't, as far as I could see.

He cleared his throat, making me look at him again, and his eyes darkened. "I looked into that case you mentioned. Christopher Malinowski."

My throat closed up. "What did you find?"

"The report said he drowned."

"You don't sound convinced."

"I'm not. Ethan left you that name for a reason in a book that's all about a family covering up a secret."

"Wait, the Harlan Coben book?" I frowned and looked down the hallway. "I never actually read it."

"Yeah, the husband thought he lost his wife for real, and her family knew she was alive the entire time. Great book, but the plot was too much of a coincidence with everything going on."

Ethan had bought that book *months* ago. It was hard to accept all those afternoons we'd spent with my family, hanging out like nothing was wrong, he'd been planning this. Him laughing with my dad and giving Peter shit. He'd acted like nothing was off. I swallowed and rubbed my palms together, all my thoughts blurring.

"Be right back." I grabbed my laptop and returned to the room. "Ethan is probably freaking out if he was watching the house."

"By all means." He watched me as I fired up the device.

"Are You Okay?" by Donny Electric waited for me.

I responded with **"For Now" by Sam Fischer**. "It's not enough for me to figure out what the hell is going on, but at least I know he's alive."

"Tonight's the first night a real crime took place. Up until the break-in, it was all speculation. It's not a missing persons case anymore." He pushed up from the couch just as one of the younger officers beckoned to him from the kitchen.

"Luna, you gotta see this."

The soft expression in his eyes shifted, and another wave of *badass* came off him. Luna marched toward the kitchen with me on his heels, and he stopped at the entrance to the garage. "I'll be damned."

"What is it?"

"Look for yourself."

CHAPTER NINETEEN

Sunday, 7:00 a.m.—One day "found"

YOU WON'T GET AWAY WITH THIS.

The big *red* words had been written on the windshield of my car. All caps, blocked, clean, neat. The threat clashed with the paint color that reminded me of homecoming parades as a teenager, but this wasn't a celebration or a spirit week. Not even close.

Hours later, after most of the crew had gone and I was left alone with a unit sitting outside the house, I kept thinking about why.

Every lie or deceit had been intentional up to this point. Ethan clearly planned this with precision, so would it be safe to assume the writing on *my* car had also been on purpose? That was a threat aimed at me.

Not Ethan.

My head pounded the same way it had when Lo was just born and I functioned on two hours of sleep. There wasn't enough caffeine in the world to get me through this, but sleep was impossible. The thuds of the footsteps in the hall haunted the silence, the hushed voices of the intruders repeating in my mind.

I wanted a break, a clean escape from it all, while not tipping off my parents that I knew something. *So what if they realize it, though?* Would they hurt me? My gut screamed they never would, but that was foolish. There was too much unknown to assume I was safe with them. I chewed on a hangnail and took a few steadying breaths. I needed a plan.

That meant getting a new laptop. That meant going to the office without my dad or brother seeing me. That meant getting out of this fucking house that had become a prison.

I packed a bag for me and Lo, fueled by adrenaline and thinking that this was the right move. I grabbed the envelope of money and the password sheet. Changing the song to **"Hotel California" by Eagles**, I hoped Ethan understood the message. I'd be going to a hotel, away from our once-safe home. Another wave of irritation washed over me as I thought about my husband. In a world of technology where he'd hid half his life from me, he couldn't find a better way to contact me without my parents finding out? I was certain he very well could. So he *chose* not to.

Despite the lingering connection via Spotify, I was alone in solving all these moving parts. No one was coming to rescue me, and clearly, no one was going to tell me a fucking thing.

I put on **"Ridin' Solo" by Jason Derulo** before Logan woke up and I fed him breakfast. It was still early, and as Logan shoved bananas in his mouth, I typed a message to the family group text four different times before settling on this:

> Hey all, there was a break-in at the house last night, and I need some time away. Everything is fine, but I'm taking Logan to a hotel to relax for a day or two. The police couldn't do anything, Luna dismissed it as a prank. I'll keep you posted, but I need some time to deal with this. Last night terrified me.

I cleaned up Logan's breakfast, got our stuff in Ethan's car, and hoped we were leaving early enough to avoid my family. They would ask questions; I had no doubt. But it wasn't unheard of for me to ask for alone time. When I'd visit over holidays from college, I'd hole up in my room for hours at a time to recharge my introvert batteries. After a breakup in high school, same thing. They knew I could get lost in an album or a book for a few days and come back refreshed. I *really* needed them to accept this.

Almost ten seconds after I hit Send, my dad called. I ignored it. While a part of me knew my parents loved me and Logan, the trust was gone. The urge to confide in them and let them comfort me also had left, and deep down, I knew things would never be the same. Peter sending the photo, the monitoring device, and them doubting me as a mother crossed all the lines. I'd finish this maze Ethan had laid out for me, but then I'd do what Peter said all along—cut them out.

My phone buzzed nonstop as I backed out of the driveway, staring at my home. Former home. It would take my family twelve minutes to drive here, so that meant we needed to get out now. Logan babbled as we headed down the road.

What if they installed a GPS in the car?

Did I care if they knew where I was? No, not entirely. If they did find me, there'd be no way to explain how they knew unless they admitted they were tracking Ethan's car. *Shit. I should leave my phone off too.*

I could drive to a phone store, get a new one, then head to the Hawkins office and call a rideshare. That had to work. My pulse raced in my throat as I sped down the road. The street was empty, but it didn't matter. They'd be here soon. I knew it in my core, which should've freaked me out. A week ago, I never would've called my parents aggressive or intrusive. Just involved.

I headed south, ignoring the pang of never wanting to return to my marital home. It was the place I'd fallen further in love and had Logan, but it was a prison of unease now. The same park I'd visited with Detective Luna had a little parking lot, and I crept in behind the playground. I'd waited too long to leave, and if my parents were on their way, I'd pass them on the narrow road to get into our neighborhood.

I was hiding in a car from my parents. The reality of the situation was enough to almost make me sick. I turned the stereo on, about to play kid music from my phone when I remembered I'd left it off. No tracking. I sighed and settled for the radio just as my parents' familiar SUV sped down the road.

My stomach hardened as they flew into the driveway. They'd really left seconds after I hadn't answered the call. Sweat beaded on my forehead, and my fingers shook as Peter jumped out of the front seat and opened the garage with the spare controller I'd loaned them. My dad followed with an urgency that sent a chill down my spine, and I didn't wait a second longer. I slammed the car into drive and sped out of the neighborhood.

I needed a cheap phone, a new computer, and to ditch Ethan's car. Then I could settle in a hotel for a couple of nights, free to do my own research and not have to pretend everything was okay with my family. Because nothing was okay.

The room smelled like cleaner and regret. The hotel wasn't the nicest, but it was safe and affordable. I was thankful for the wad of cash, and a part of me wondered if this was what Ethan had meant with *JUST IN CASE*. Had he planned for me to need to run away? Had he guessed that I'd turn on my family?

With a queen bed for me and Logan to share, it gave me space to just be. Logan chewed on the few plastic toys I'd brought with us, and I fired up the new laptop. It was the cheapest one, since I just needed internet. I logged in to my Spotify account and searched Ethan's last played, and it was still from the night before.

The pressure in my chest grew. This was the longest he'd gone without changing a song or talking to me, but that didn't mean anything was wrong. I put on **"Hotel Room Service" by Pitbull** and left that browser up. Something caught my attention, though, as I scrolled through my playlists. I had a new follower on my account.

I wasn't one of those people who paid attention to those things, but my previous number of followers was 365, and who could forget that number? I scanned the list of names on the off chance Ethan had switched to another account. Maybe my dad or brother had found his other one so he'd changed.

He'd have to pick a name I'd recognize, so I went through the list and frowned. No secret names or code words that we'd been using so far. Nothing like that. I chewed my lip, unsure if this additional follower was *a thing* or not. It could've been a coincidence. Or not.

But my gaze landed on one user that had me suck in a breath.

Badger1234

Fuck. I got up to make sure the window was locked and the hotel door secure. The chain was connected, and Ethan's car was at the office. There was no way someone would know I was here. Specifically, my dad. I'd used cash. I'd done my due diligence.

Badger1234.

That had been our family password for everything growing up. TV permissions, the shared iTunes account, streaming. He wrote it down in a special notebook only our family could touch. I could picture it with big bold letters. *Why in the ever-loving hell would he follow me?*

My scalp tingled with fear. Was my dad following me now, out of desperation, trying to figure out the clues? If so, why had he picked a name that I would recognize right away?

Unless . . . my knee bounced up and down so fast, I hit the mini desk in the hotel room. My dad might've assumed I wouldn't remember because tech stuff wasn't my forte, it was Peter's, and in a moment of quick thinking . . . he'd created the easiest name he could think of. Or maybe Peter had done it as some twisted way to warn me that our dad was watching? But why? He was in on this too. I changed the song immediately to my top songs from the previous year until I figured out my next step.

With Logan occupied with his toys, I powered on the cheap phone and called the detective.

"This is Luna."

"It's Marissa Creighton."

"I've tried calling you a few times, went to voicemail. You all right?"

"I'm at a hotel for the time being, and I got a new phone. I couldn't be at the house, especially with my family so involved." My voice shook with all the pent-up emotion. I wasn't allowed to break down with Logan nearby. I couldn't scare him, so that meant hiding my fear and powering through. "Did you find anything out?"

"Not about who broke in last night, no. There were no usable prints on the doors or the car. It was all wiped down."

I figured, but my shoulders sagged. "I'm at the Days Inn if you need to get a hold of me. I'm not telling my family where I'm at."

"I think this is a good idea for a day or two. Let us figure out who broke in to your house and get more details." Something crackled from his end. "I gotta go, but call if you need anything, okay?"

"Thanks." I hung up, and my eyes prickled with the threat of tears. It took one person showing me a little sympathy for me to crack. Unacceptable. I couldn't be weak. I had to protect Lo.

With my playlist still running, I checked Ethan's lack of response and logged in to online banking. I went through each account one by one and changed the password. I couldn't have my parents logging in and seeing where I used the credit card. I reconnected them all to the new email I'd set up at the library, and bam, I had an alter ego online.

Kind of like Ethan.

But why? My motivations were clear, but his weren't. I was protecting myself from my parents. The back of my neck tingled, and an awareness settled over me, making each limb on my body double in weight. What if . . . he was doing the same thing?

Tell no one.

Don't trust your folks.

I shook my head, pinching my nose for a second to settle myself. Logan made a *swoosh* sound as he tossed a toy onto the floor, and I exhaled. I couldn't jump to any conclusions. Things were too messy. I needed facts.

The key to finding out *what* was going on was with Ethan. That was clear. With a new device and free from monitoring, I logged in to his Gmail account and planned to do some digging. Two things I wanted to know:

His browsing history and the Christopher Malinowski emails.

I went to the emails first. My poor bottom lip throbbed from the constant biting, but I clicked to the folder labeled *CM* and tensed. This had to be revelatory. The answer to the puzzle. I needed it to be.

SUBJECT: Info

The recordings are verified. It runs to the top—the inner circle is involved. Hope that answers.

Here is the link to the files you wanted.

CM

A link! Holy shit! I clicked it with my pulse racing in my ears, but the browser said *The link is broken*. I tried again and again, with the same result. Maybe the link expired? I'd heard of that happening, but if he sent a link, that meant the files lived somewhere in the cloud.

Without a link to follow, I read the email again, trying to decipher what it meant. Recordings. Okay. That was easy to comprehend. Some recordings somewhere were real. Verified. *It runs to the top . . . the inner circle.* My lungs constricted inside my body, ice filling my veins. *The top* meant my dad—the owner—assuming they were talking about Hawkins Associates. Which, why wouldn't they? They'd both worked for them, both had gone missing, and one had ended up dead.

My fingers trembled as I clicked on the second one.

SUBJECT: (empty)

It's still happening. Account isn't closed.

The list is long. You're not alone.

I know where it's stored. We need to meet.

We're being monitored.

CM

Account. Long list. Not alone. Stored. Needing to meet. This was the email Christopher had sent Ethan before he died. The same weekend Ethan had been at a golf outing with my dad's business. My ears rang.

I took a picture of that email with my new phone.

Christopher Malinowski's emails didn't answer a single question. They just solidified that whatever he'd needed to meet with Ethan about could be the reason he was dead. *Ethan could be in trouble.*

Still no song on his end, and Logan made a loud sound with his toys, making me jump. "You okay, big guy? You having fun?"

"Pop Pop," he said, the name he used for my dad. "Pop Pop, Pop Pop."

God, I shivered. There was no way for them to find me here, I was sure. But hearing Logan say his name, like he had with Ethan at the library, made me bolt up to check all the locks again. As I made sure the chain was secured for the third time, the hotel phone rang.

Who the fuck would be calling my room?

CHAPTER TWENTY

Sunday, 11:00 a.m.—One day "found"

It rang and rang as I clutched my throat. What if it was room service? But I'd checked in an hour ago. The room was done. Completed.

What if it's Ethan?

I dove for the phone with my heart beating so hard, I could feel it in my fingertips. "H-hello?"

"Marissa, oh, sweetie, are you okay?"

My mom, not Ethan.

Fuck. HOW!

My entire body sagged with disappointment and anger, and my insides burned white hot. "How the fuck did you find me? Why are you calling? I asked for space."

"Honey," she gasped. I could picture her blinking a whole lot and gaping.

I rarely cussed or lashed out at them. After years of being told that wasn't ladylike, I'd become the version of myself they wanted when they were around. It was easier. But now? I didn't know who I was anymore, besides the fact I wasn't some weak, mild woman.

"What? I asked a simple question. I texted that I needed to be away from it all. Everything. You're not respecting what I asked." I paced the small section between the bed and desk as Logan watched me with wide eyes. I knew I needed to settle down to not startle him, but my self-control was slipping. Fast.

"What did you expect, Mar? You're our daughter, and you shut off your phone. Did you think about us at all and how worried we are?"

Of course it's about them. Old me would feel terrible. New me didn't.

"I asked for space," I reiterated.

She ignored my comment entirely, like she'd never heard it. "We've been calling every single hotel in the area asking to be transferred to your room, and thank goodness you're okay. I'm so happy to hear your voice. Here, your father wants to talk to you."

Of *course* he did. I pinched the bridge of my nose as something shifted inside me. Up until this point, I'd held a little hope that a part of my relationship with my family could be saved. That maybe there was some crazy explanation that made this all make sense. But the panic in my mom's voice, the absolute shock at me lashing out . . . they didn't even care about crossing my boundaries.

"Marissa, come back home," my dad said, his voice firm and hard.

"Why?" I fired back.

"You need your family. We are here to support you. You're not capable of handling this on your own."

"Okay, then I'll call you if I need support. I want silence. Alone time. Just to be away from that fucking house." I tossed all the shit I could reach into a bag. We were getting the hell out of here. I pulled up my other phone and ordered a rideshare. *Seven minutes out.*

"Stay with us. We have the guest wing. Come on, we'll head to the Days Inn right now and pick you and Logan up." His tone got more desperate.

Keys jingled in the background, and I snapped, "No. Leave me alone, please."

"Marissa, this isn't the time to be a hero. You could've been killed last night, and you being all by yourself with Logan at a hotel? That's not safe. I saw the threat on your car. Ethan is gone, leaving you and

Logan alone. Why are you being so childish right now, hiding from us? Who would protect you besides us?"

I squeezed my eyes shut because he'd hit on every point that made it hard to sleep. Ethan had left us, and we were alone, caught in the middle of something I had very few details about. "I'm not being childish. I asked for space. You're not giving it to me."

"Peter will be there in fifteen minutes. Be smart about this," he said. The lingering threat in his tone caused the hair on my neck to stand.

"Or what, Dad? That sounded like a real threat."

Silence.

Then, with a very different tone, he said, "We love you to death, you know this. You and Logan, okay? I'm sorry if my tone was harsh. I'm stressed about this. You. Ethan disappearing." He sighed. "Please let us help you."

A small part of me wanted to say okay. To shove all the half-truths to the back of my mind and bury them there. To go home to my parents' house and let my mom take care of me and Logan for a few days. To pretend none of this had happened.

But I couldn't. Even though I felt the familiar strings inside my soul being pulled to listen to my dad, to obey him, I shook my head. It reminded me that I was in charge right now. Not him. "I need to do this. Please understand that. Goodbye."

"Wait!"

I hung up the phone and unplugged it from the wall. We were on the fourth floor, facing the front of the hotel, and I frantically set to finishing my work. I had six minutes to put everything into a bag and get downstairs. Logan reached for an outlet, and I yelled, "No!" He wailed. Loudly.

My heart raced faster the more he screamed. My family would get to us in fifteen minutes, and the rideshare in six. That was too close for comfort. "It's okay, Lo. We'll be okay."

"No! Mama, no!" His cries set my nerves on edge as my need to comfort him struggled with the need to get the hell out of here.

Fuck. The car seat. I'd have to get it installed in the car, which usually took me a few minutes. I wanted to fucking scream. All our shit was in bags, and I held Logan in one arm, the car seat and duffel in the other, the purse slung over my shoulder. My muscles strained as I jogged toward the elevator with sweat dripping down my back.

Did my family not see how chasing me like this was so fucked up?

Once outside in the parking lot, I frantically looked around to see if I recognized any of the cars. Logan continued to wail as we stood waiting for another rideshare, and my eyes prickled with frustration.

Ethan's actions had put us through this; my anger wasn't just directed at my parents.

I paced, staring at the phone screen as if to make the rideshare arrive faster. Logan's cries made everything worse, and I was seconds away from snapping. *Peter is gonna be here any minute.*

If he got here before we left, I'd run. I had the wad of cash still in my pocket. I could hide and try to get a car out of town. Anything to keep myself and Logan safe.

Every nerve was obliterated by the time the older woman arrived in front of the hotel. "Please, we need to hurry. Someone is after us." I took a shaky breath, and she nodded. Her eyes widened, and her hands shook.

"Put your stuff in the back. I'll set up the car seat." She took it from my hands and connected it within a minute. It took me longer than normal to buckle Logan in because I kept scanning the parking lot for my family. Were they watching us, waiting to follow to the next hotel? It had only been twelve minutes since the call.

Soon enough, we were en route to another hotel. I unloaded, got a room, and settled into the second hotel for the day. I told the front desk to not reveal I was there and that I wanted zero calls. My adrenaline drained now that I felt safer. I unplugged the phone first thing.

Every so often, I wished I were more social and had more friends in real life. My online friends were great, but they couldn't exactly help me now. After this was over, I'd join mom groups. I'd go on a trip and meet some of my internet friends. I'd be done living in the shadows, because it had become glaringly clear I had no one.

This room had a large bed, and Logan had his teething toys in his lap as I fluffed the pillows to lean against the headboard. Research. Silence. Safety.

Ethan had once told me that clearing your cache and history was a safe way to make sure no one could hack your accounts and to prevent your device from slowing down. I'd put it on my calendar to do once a month after he'd lectured me about it. I didn't have high hopes of finding anything in his browser history, but it had to be done. An item to check off, since the Christopher Malinowski emails were more problematic than helpful. I logged in to his Google account and synced information.

Recently closed tabs.

Tabs from other devices.

History.

There was nothing exciting on the recently closed tabs. Email, news, MLB news. I scrolled through the list of sites, hoping to find something like *how to disappear from your wife*. Nothing stood out. Each site was very much an Ethan thing and not surprising.

The tabs from other devices, though . . .

Ethan's MacBook Air.

Ethan's Tech Air.

Wait. Did this mean he had two devices? One had to be the computer at home . . . but the other?

This was his personal Gmail account. EthanCreighton. So why . . . was he logged in to this on two different devices? Where was the other one?

The time stamp read *2 days ago*.

He'd logged in to his personal account, somewhere, two days ago.

Or someone had logged in to his account two days ago. There was also that explanation. I blew out a breath and scanned the websites. Google searches, email, social media—wait.

Mr. I'm Off the Grid was on social media?

I squeezed my eyes shut for a moment, enjoying a few more seconds before I found out if my husband was one of the ones who had secret accounts to talk to women. My poor heart was beat up, bruised, and purple from all the betrayal, but I needed all the facts. No matter how much it hurt. Even with Peter's warning that the affair video was fake, it still gutted me to realize I didn't know my husband at all.

My finger hovered over the track pad, refusing to click on it. My jaw tensed, and my body pulsated with anticipation. Lines and lines of social media links filled the *Ethan's Tech Air* device, and I clicked one right in the middle.

Beatrice Hernandez.

He'd spent a lot of time looking at Beatrice Hernandez's account. I'd stumbled across more secrets. My breath lodged in my throat at the photos of a woman with long brown hair and green eyes. She laughed in all her photos.

I clicked on the next link.

Hannah Theroux.

Veronica Gage.

God, was he having multiple affairs? That didn't seem likely. He didn't have enough time. So why research these women? How did that tie into my family drama?

I sniffed as moisture pooled in my eyes. My chest felt ripped apart. I wiped the tears away and took a few deep breaths as my stomach cramped. This was horrible. The worst. Of all the *worst-case* scenarios I could've chosen for my life, I was living them.

Missing husband.

Possible affairs, and if not cheating, still weird, unexplainable behavior.

No family to trust.

I grounded myself by watching Logan play and chew on the end of his shirt. He was the only good thing right now. I stepped away from the device and sat next to Logan, pulling him close and smelling his head. His sweet baby smell was shifting to full toddler, where sweat and crumbs and sunscreen mixed with the sweetness. "I love you, Lo. So, so much. You're in my heart, little guy."

He turned around and put his hand over my heart and said, "Boom boom."

I kissed his forehead and reached into the toy bag to pull out some stuffed animals. Cows and elephants were his favorite, and he reached for them with a huge smile. "Mama Dada Dada Mama."

"That's right, buddy." I ruffled his hair and eyed the computer like it was a ticking bomb of what little sanity I had left. It was going to blow.

As I slid into the uncomfortable desk chair, I clicked on the other links, scanning various profiles that were all women. These were all looked at when he was missing. That was weird. *Just, oh, I ran away from my wife and her parents, so I'm going to cyberstalk these beautiful women?*

Intentional or no?

I should go back, see what he was looking at weeks before he disappeared. Assuming he hadn't cleared his history. I clicked History and scrolled to the week before he'd left us. There were still social media links all over, typically viewed late at night.

Meaning, after I'd gone to bed, he'd gone onto his computer and looked at these accounts. Cool. Cool. It was fine.

Those nights we fooled around and he held me . . . I fell asleep, and he tucked me in and went to search Heather Smith's *account. Wow.*

The ball of emotion in the back of my throat actually hurt, and I clicked on her profile picture. A myriad of feelings went through me as I stared at her face. The most shocking one was recognition.

Did I know her? Had I seen her before?

It would be horrible if this was a neighbor or someone I saw at the grocery store.

One photo stood out, though. It wasn't a profile picture. It was one she was tagged in. It showed her and two boys.

Two kids who looked really familiar. So familiar, in fact, I knew where I had seen them.

In the old shoebox in the closet.

The school pictures. The woman. The *secret* prelife of Ethan I knew nothing about. A rush of adrenaline coursed through me. *His other family.*

Whether or not it was true, that's how I pictured it in my mind. *Did his last name used to be Smith, or is her last name fake too?* The name *Smith* seemed too generic and easy to blend in. This was the woman on the video footage, the one who'd gone to his office and looked panicked.

Wait. The security guard had given me a different name when I asked. Not Heather Smith. Two identities, same woman. Photos of her and her kids in my house.

What the fuck was going on?

I scanned my Spotify account and put on **"Why Is This Happening? (Song for John)" by Paul Andreas**. It was a desperate plea. As I watched and my anxiety grew because Ethan hadn't played a new song *still*, a semiplan formed in my head. There were two things I very much needed to do.

The first—go to the office. Figure out why Heather Smith used two different names. Each visitor had to fill out an information sheet when they signed in, and if I could access that, then I could find her address, number, something. I could also try to get the information Ethan needed to see if Dennis Paulson had met with Lexington LLC three months ago.

I stood up from the chair, my mind whirling. It wasn't like I could go to the office today, not with the car there. Plus, I wasn't even sure they were open on Sundays.

That left Monday morning to strategically go into the office and get the information I needed. That gave me tonight to get my shit together for it all to make sense. I grabbed sheets of paper from the hotel desk and wrote everything down.

Ethan disappearing.

His secret life.

The women—the footage. Heather Smith's two names. The kids' photos.

The break-in. The threat.

Ethan's letter.

My parents' misbehavior.

Peter sending me threats.

Christopher Malinowski.

One of Ethan's secret emails, May, mentioning my father's name and a year.

A listening device in our house.

Detective Luna.

What was connected? What wasn't?

God, what I would give to talk to the woman or Christopher Malinowski's family, just to ask questions. To see what they knew.

I studied Logan as he yawned. It was almost nap time.

I got his lunch ready, and he clapped and squealed at getting to eat on the bed without his bib. His laughter made me smile, no matter how short lived it was. He ate, and I turned off all the lights and let him snuggle me for a nap. Once he settled, I quietly got my laptop and focused on Heather Smith.

I went to Facebook's home page and tried logging in as him, resetting the password with his email until I could log in.

His name on the account was Ethan Creighton—so if he was trying to hide his identity, this wasn't smooth. His profile picture was literally him. His smiling face.

He's had this for our entire relationship. He got it the year we met. This isn't even his real name. Fuck, this was a lot to deal with. Okay. I could do this.

I logged in as Ethan and was bombarded with hundreds of notifications. I wanted to know recent activity. Did he post a lot? Did he even say he was married, had a kid?

Nothing.

No indication he was married or had a family. No posts. No political rants. Just . . . fifteen friends.

That was weird.

He'd had this for a decade and had fifteen friends?

I clicked on the list, and names I had never heard of popped up. Leslie, Frank, Theoren, Paige. I clicked his messages, and there was nothing.

No secret convos.

Was the only point of having this account to creep on other women?

My shoulders slumped at the lack of answers, and I clicked the notifications as a final attempt to get something from this cyberstalking. There were just updates from his fifteen friends, but he'd been tagged in a photo—a day ago.

No fucking way.

My heart leaped up my throat. I clicked ten times, my laptop not moving fast enough, and I waited as the page loaded.

And waited.

And waited.

Heather S mentioned you in a comment.

It's a go.

Flashers Grill. Six. Tomorrow.

I could barely breathe.

I googled Flashers Grill—it was a pub a mile away from the hotel. And six o'clock was in a few hours.

Every nerve ending was amplified to the point the movement of Logan's breathing made me jump. Was I brave enough to show up, see Ethan and this woman?

Fuck yeah, I was.

CHAPTER TWENTY-ONE

Sunday, 6:00 p.m.—One day "found"

Logan threw a fit. He was an even-tempered kid, but as we stood outside Flashers Grill, he screamed. "Baby, shh, please." I patted his back and cradled him against me. At this point, he could be crying from change, from my stress, or because he wanted to eat the plant leaf just out of reach. It was an equal chance for any option, so I just bounced him on my hip. "It's okay; you're okay."

People gave us dirty looks. I wanted to flip them all off. They had no idea what I was going through, and I narrowed my eyes at them. We weren't even inside the bar. I could've been inside, right in the middle, making everyone hear him scream. But no, I was outside, trying to stay hidden.

It wasn't going well.

I wasn't sure what I was hoping for—to see him actually cheat on me? To see them both to ask questions? To be proved wrong? I tried not to join Logan and cry, as he wouldn't settle down. This was going horribly. There was no sign of Ethan or Heather, and every person who gave me a double glance had me on edge.

Were they watching me?

"Excuse me," said someone with a deep voice, making me jump back a foot. A very large dark-haired man appeared out of nowhere. "Are you waiting for someone?"

"Um, yes. I am. I don't see them, and I'm trying to settle my son down." Tears flowed down my face now. Logan was screaming, Ethan and Heather weren't in sight, and this guy looked like a terrifying John Cena.

"Would you like to wait inside? I have a little one, and maybe it'll distract him." He smiled, the kindness so unexpected that I almost stumbled.

The guy blinked and took a step back, clearly put off, and I sniffed. This was no way to try to sneak around. Maybe I wasn't cut out for this. Maybe I should go back to my parents, back to the house.

After all, none of this shit was my fault.

"Come on, inside will be better." He frowned as he pointed through the gate. I followed because I wasn't sure what else to do, and he led me to a back booth. The entire grill had dark, red vibes to it, with black walls and red lighting. It seemed like a club, almost, and nothing like a grill.

The back of my neck prickled as I sat down with Logan next to me. Something felt off. More than everyone staring at my kid. At least he'd stopped screaming. The napkin dispenser distracted him, and the large man stood at the end of the table, staring at us with a frown. "Wait here, okay?"

He didn't let me respond before walking away, and the sounds of conversation around us died down. My spine tingled, and my gut told me to *get out*. Nowadays, I never ignored that feeling, and I grabbed Logan, tried to exit the booth when a woman slid into the side opposite me. "Sit down, Marissa," she snapped.

Heather Smith.

The woman who'd sent my husband photos of her sons. Of . . . their sons, possibly. I'd refused to acknowledge it when I'd first seen them, but they had similar features to Ethan. The jaws, the eyes, the smiles.

There was a high chance he had a second family. Instead of being ballsy and brave, my mouth hung open like a dead fish.

"You need to stop what you're doing." She swallowed hard and jutted her chin toward Logan. "You'd do anything to protect your son, right?"

"Obviously." I took note of the knife sitting on the table. The large man stood at the door, essentially blocking the exit, and I tightened my grip on Logan. "Seeing as you have two of your own, I imagine you can relate."

She blinked, and I swore she paled. It was hard to tell with the lighting, but she narrowed her eyes. "What did you hope to gain by coming here?"

"Answers. My life flip-flopped since Ethan went missing, and I want to know why." My face burned, and I didn't like the way the woman looked at me. Like *I* was the other woman who'd ruined her life. She clearly knew about me, which sent another layer of hurt through my body. Ethan was living a double life but had only told one of us about the other.

Her gaze moved to Logan, and her face softened for one second before the hard glint returned. "This doesn't involve you. Honestly, the less you know, the better. It'll be easier this way. Go back to your house. Stop sneaking around. There's too much going on for you to fuck it up."

"Fuck *what* up? That's what I want to know! Why does my husband have a secret life? Why is it better that I don't know what's going on? Why does he have social media and get messages from you?"

People stared at us now. Heather sucked in a breath and leaned forward.

She was so close, I could see the freckles on her nose and feel her breath hit my face. "What do you think you know?"

"What?"

"Tell me what you know." Her gaze was intense, dark, and for a moment, she reminded me of Ethan. He had the same expression when he was feeling competitive. Her demand wasn't fair. Didn't she understand I wanted to get answers?

"Do you know where my husband is?" I asked, my voice scratchy and filled with desperation.

Logan started crying again, and I patted his back. Heather's left eye twitched, and I saw the large man wasn't standing in front of the door. I slid out of the booth, torn between wanting answers and getting out of there.

"You have no idea, do you?"

"Clearly," I deadpanned. "Is Ethan coming or not? Do you have a way of contacting him?"

"He's never late, and he's not here," she said with a sigh. Her shoulders slumped, and her left hand was clenched in a fist. "Have you heard from him?"

"No."

"He might've seen you and bolted. There's a specific reason you're left out of this. Use your head and figure it out. Why would *you*, his wife, not be told what was going on?"

"That is what I'm trying to figure out! Jesus Christ." With my one free hand, I rubbed my temple.

"If you ruined everything by coming here, I swear to god . . ."

"If I ruined it? Ruined what, exactly? Were you two planning on running away?"

"No." Her jaw flexed. "We're trying to take back our life."

"Meaning . . . I took it in the first place?" My head felt light and dizzy. The theory that had formed in my head all week got a stronger voice as evidence stacked up. *I* could be the other woman.

Heather's gaze shuttered for a beat, and she pushed her hair out of her face. "In a way, you did."

"In a way?"

"Look, I can't say more. Not to you." Her gaze cooled. "You should go before you fuck this up even more."

Anger exploded down my spine, painting it with ice crystals. "Maybe if I knew a single thing going on, then I'd have the ability to ruin whatever this is, but I don't. You've offered me nothing." She sniffed, and I sneered at her. "You don't get to play the victim here."

"Oh, you think *you* are?" she yelled. We were officially causing a scene now.

My heart hammered in my chest, and I buzzed with adrenaline. I needed to go. Soon. Like, now.

"I think the rug has been pulled from under my feet, and I've been trying to figure out why. Why do you send photos of your children to my husband? Why are they stored in a secret box in our closet? Are they his? Does he see them?"

She sat up straighter and widened her eyes, looking all sorts of pathetic. Her lip trembled. "Ask your dad or brother."

Again, the connection. I stilled, her words covering me in a blanket of ice. "What?"

"You heard me. Ask Franklin or Peter about them. Hell, show them the pictures." She smiled, fear and relief coming from her. Her grin kept growing, almost like she enjoyed how miserable I was right now.

"How are they involved? Why would they know about your kids?"

She pursed her lips and tilted her head to the side, another reminder of how Ethan did a similar gesture. God, they spent so much time together, they had similar mannerisms. Heather ran a finger over the top of the table and looked up at me with wide blue eyes. "I can't tell you how your family is involved. It's too risky, and we've already lost too much."

I didn't have time for this. That was the reality of it all. Ethan could've confided in me, told me the truth, trusted me to believe him. But instead, he'd used this woman—hell, women—to talk to. Based on the children's ages, Ethan and Heather had been connected for a while. That was the thought circling my mind as I marched out of

Flashers Grill with Logan crying on my shoulder. My own tears weren't far behind.

That was the woman Ethan had left us for? She was horrible. As I walked back to the hotel, each step took all my effort. Ethan had another life. That was clear. That woman, Heather, was a part of it somehow, and I needed to go over the conversation again in my head, but I couldn't get past the hurt.

My soul felt pulled apart piece by piece. I couldn't say for certain that I wasn't the other woman anymore. What if Ethan had been with her before . . . he became Ethan Creighton? What if this entire time, I was the one pulling him from his real family, his real life?

What have you done, Ethan? And why are my dad and brother involved?

◆ ◆ ◆

"Hurt" by Johnny Cash.

"Say Something" by A Great Big World and Christina Aguilera.

"I Can't Do This Anymore" by dxrrvn.

No response from Ethan. It'd been too long. So not only was I furious and unsettled from meeting Heather, I was worried.

What if Ethan had seen me there and run away? No one knew I was at the grill, so why would he avoid me?

Oh.

Of course, he wouldn't want to see his two lives collide like that. The library was safe and clear of his . . . past.

I was at a loss. I swore going to Flashers had seemed like the right choice to finally learn something, but it had made me feel worse. More confused. Heartbroken and so alone.

Logan breathed heavily in his sleep, and footsteps thudded in the hallway, making all the muscles in my body tense. I strained my ears, waiting to hear the twist of the handle, but none came. The footsteps faded farther down the hall, and I could breathe again.

I got up from the bed and went to the desk, where I had my mess of notes. Heather had said I could ruin *everything*. Ethan chose not to tell me about it. When I'd asked about seeing his (potential) kids, she'd said to ask my dad and brother.

So, my family knew about Ethan's secret life? The one before me?

That seemed . . . not likely. They wouldn't have taken him in as their own if they'd known he'd abandoned a family. They wouldn't have offered him a job at Hawkins. I would've bet my money on that.

Hawkins.

Franklin Hawkins, 2008. That's what an email had said from *May*. But what if May was Heather? My blood hummed. In my gut I knew . . . but there wasn't proof yet.

I scanned all the notes on the desk, my gaze moving from one pile to the other, and I drew a line from topic to topic. Every single one was connected to something.

Hawkins Associates.

That was the common denominator. My dad's business. I pinched the bridge of my nose, something else seeming familiar about the year 2008. It was quite some time ago but . . . wait.

Didn't Detective Luna say Ethan's identity was untraceable from 2009 and before? Almost like something happened in 2008.

I typed *Franklin Hawkins 2008* into Google again and scanned headlines. Nothing big. They'd bought out a minor tech start-up the year before but kept all employees on staff. Most of that year was a blur, but nothing stood out. I went into more pages of results, desperate for something new.

How would I know, though? These secrets had been around for years, and I'd just found out about them. I eyed the notes with *clues* from Ethan and tried to find meaning in each one. He'd wanted me to get his computer password. He'd wanted me to see the document that said we were being watched. His songs told me to trust no one. He'd wanted me to find the Harlan Coben book with Christopher Malinowski's name.

CASIO was still unclear, so I put that off to the side.

Heather was wrong. Ethan might not have told me explicitly what was going on, but he'd left me pieces of it. Maybe I wasn't doing a good enough job at solving the puzzle.

I needed access to Hawkins Associates records, specifically from 2008, and from three months ago to see if Dennis Paulson had met with Lexington LLC or not. I needed to know why that was important and how it connected with this entire thing.

Ethan had talked about the server and network at work, how it was accessible via VPN, but only a few people had that ability. So it hadn't been weird for him to run in to the office to work on something for an hour if it was confidential.

I really needed to go into Ethan's office, without my dad or Peter there. I could pretend that I'd found Ethan, email them to meet up.

But then they'd know I lied when we didn't show up. *Wait.*

The emails I'd forwarded to myself had been deleted from *my* inbox by someone else . . . emails from Ethan's inbox, sent from Christopher Malinowski. My mind whirled at an idea.

Yes! This could work.

I wasn't an athlete, but the one time I'd played volleyball in gym and served the ball all the way over the net on the first try, my body exploded with pride. Every sense had gone into overdrive, and my smile had stretched across my face. This was like that.

It took two minutes to create another fake email. I wouldn't put it past my dad or brother to have the ability to track emails, texts, calls, which meant . . . I had to schedule this to send out tomorrow morning. To time it just right. Because they'd come to the hotel if it traced all the way here.

To: FHawkins@hawkins.com, PHawkins@hawkins.com
From: Malinowski_Eyes@gmail.com

Subject: I KNOW WHAT YOU DID

Unless you want me going straight to the authorities, we need to meet. I want cash.

Today. Noon. Felix Park.

Bring no one.

I know what you did, and we both know what Christopher found. You know he told others, right?

My soul left my body as I reread the email. I had no idea who I was anymore. Threatening my dad and brother? Typing fake emails? Planning secret visits to Ethan's work? God, it was terrifying, but I felt powerful. More powerful than I'd felt in years. Like the old Marissa was back, taking charge of life.

The email would be sent 10:00 a.m. the next day; I'd be in a new hotel by that point and waiting outside the office for them to leave in a panic. My knee bounced up and down so hard the table shook, and I scanned my Spotify, hoping, praying that Ethan responded with a song.

"Are You Home?" by Amber Run.

"Nope" by OMFG.

"Burning Down the House" by Talking Heads.

Wait . . . what? My new cell phone rang, making me jump a foot in the air. I yanked it from the desk and went into the bathroom to not wake Logan. Only Luna had my number.

"H-hello?" I said, my nerves fried. "What is it?"

"Your house is on fire. We need to talk. Now."

CHAPTER TWENTY-TWO

Sunday, 11:00 p.m.—One day "found"

Standing on my street while the smell of fire penetrated my nose didn't feel as traumatic as it would've before all this. Seeing our first home up in flames? Knowing that our quiet three-bedroom house wasn't *home* anymore? I would've been devastated if this had happened three weeks ago—hell, even seven days ago.

All my stuff was burning. All the memories. My ability to care left as I watched the flames. And like a phoenix, my soul was reborn.

"Neighbor called it in about twenty minutes ago." Detective Luna stood with his hands on his hips, his face as serious as I'd ever seen him. "We'll need to wait for the official report, but from the looks of it, the fire started in the front room."

"Ethan's office." My voice sounded distant, hollow, and without emotion. Logan slept in the car seat I'd placed on the street, his little body wrapped with a warm blanket. I moved my attention from Logan's sleeping face to the fire truck. The lights flashed in the dark night, the red and white reflecting off the empty windows of the neighbors around us.

Was Ethan in one of the houses, watching? Or was he with Heather? How had he known the house was on fire if he hadn't been here?

"Thank Christ you weren't at home."

I chewed on my lip. The list of people who'd known I wasn't at home was small. Luna, my dad, mom, brother, and Ethan. Planned or not? Was this retaliation for the search on Ethan's email or related to the people who'd broken in and written on my windshield? "I don't know what way is up or down, Detective. I don't trust my mind anymore. Is this my family? Ethan? His potential affairs? Related to Christopher's *accidental* death?"

He swallowed hard and narrowed his eyes just enough to show a flicker of worry. "There's nothing we've concluded that's moving the case forward. We'll continue to ask questions and—"

"Have you found anything out about who Ethan was before he became Ethan Creighton?"

He blinked slowly. "Most of those records are sealed."

"That wasn't a no." I crossed my arms and eyed him, unsure of why his answer annoyed me. I knew nothing about procedure or the right steps when it came to crimes, but maybe we could trade info. "I'll tell you what else I know if you share what you're obviously hiding."

"That's not how this works, Marissa. By not sharing, you're obstructing an investigation." He sighed as a large man with a radio walked over toward us.

"Got a minute?" he asked the detective.

Luna gave me a hard look before walking away with what appeared to be the fire chief.

A car raced down the street and came to an abrupt stop where they had blocks to prevent traffic. My stomach dropped at the familiar figure of my father.

He left the car door open as he jogged around the cement block. "Marissa! My god!"

His wide eyes and frantic hand movements seemed manic. He sprinted to me and threw his arms around me before I could get a word in. "Fuck, are you all right? Logan?"

"We're okay," I mumbled into his chest. His familiar scent sent me a painful reminder that I didn't trust him anymore. "We weren't home."

"I just . . . Who would . . . ?" He pulled back, stared down at me, and shook his head. "We need to talk. I think there are things you should know about what Ethan did for us at work."

I stumbled. "Wh-what?"

"I've kept you out of the loop for a reason, sweetheart. You're my princess. My baby girl." He swallowed hard and tightened his grip on my shoulder. "There are things that don't belong in your world, but I'm afraid I can't hide it anymore. I see how you look at me, like I'm a monster. I'm not. It all makes sense, I promise."

This was the most frantic I had ever seen my father. I'd guess he was hammered, from the red eyes and pale complexion, but I couldn't smell a drop of liquor. He'd offered the thing I craved most of my life—to be included, to be given answers. But was it too late? I pursed my lips, a deep blanket of calm settling over me as I weighed my options.

I could continue this investigation alone, trying not to break down. Or . . . I could pretend to join forces with him. My gut swirled with the same unease that had remained since Ethan disappeared, but there was a slight pull toward my dad, like *maybe* his secrets would help explain everything.

I wasn't being a naive daughter either. I didn't trust them anymore.

"Marissa, where'd you go? You blanked out for a second." He cupped my face and pulled me into a hug. "I'm sure you're rattled—god, I am too." He waved toward the detective and kept a hand on my shoulder as he approached us.

"Please tell me you know who did this. This is too much. A fire? Burning down my daughter's house? I want this fucker arrested." He almost spat with the anger in his voice.

"I'm working with the fire department to do everything we can." Detective Luna looked at me and sighed. "They managed to keep it contained to the front two rooms."

My stomach heaved. Logan's room was one of the front rooms, and without warning, I hunched over and dry heaved.

We were safe, I had him in my vision, but the what-if scenarios still played in my head on a loop.

"Damn it." My dad rubbed my back and practically snarled at the detective. "Call me if you need to speak with her. Look at her—she's falling apart. I'm taking her back home."

Every muscle in my body tensed, and as I wiped my mouth with the back of my hand, I swore Detective Luna nodded just a millimeter at me. Almost *telling* me to do it.

"I think that's a great idea, sir. We'll be in touch when you can come back to collect some things you need until the investigation is complete." He held out his hand to my father, who shook it. If I'd had enough fucks left to give, I'd make a comment. Like why the hell was Luna shaking his hand, or why did he speak with formality now, calling my dad *sir*?

But I was on empty.

The detective gave me one last long look, like there was a clue swirling in his dark eyes, but I couldn't decipher *what* he was trying to say.

"Let's go home, sweetheart. I'll have your mom get your room ready."

My dad guided me as I picked up Logan in his car seat, and we got it situated into the back of his car. A heavy silence greeted us when I got in the front seat. Shivers exploded through my body, my heart rate and breath speeding up. Dread filled me. I was going back to *their* home, with *their* rules, and *their* manipulation.

A cold sweat formed down my chest as I gripped the door handle.

Did I call him out immediately, or did I wait for him to start talking?

"Coming after you and Lo? Too much. I won't stand for it. Too fucking far," he muttered as his grip on the wheel tightened. I wasn't sure if he was talking to himself or to me, but the more he spoke, the more he gave away.

"A fire? Jesus. That shouldn't have happened. No. A scare, sure? But a fire. No. Absolutely . . ." His spine straightened as he slid me a worried look. "Marissa, look—"

My dad was losing it. I could use this to my advantage. "What if Logan had been in that room, Dad? He could've been hurt or—"

"Fuck!" He slammed his hand on the wheel. "Never supposed to be harmful. Not to you or him. Never harm. That was the rule. We have rules for this."

What is he talking about? "Rules for what?"

"Guidelines. You and Logan were off limits. Never physical harm." He swallowed hard and stared at me for a second. His eyes bulged out of his head as his phone buzzed with my mom's name on there. "I can't deal with her now." He silenced it. "What to do, what to do?"

He said the words in a singsong voice, one that sent a chill down my back. He reminded me of a villain from a movie, almost like he was debating his own plan. I could pretend to be the scared flower, the daughter he always considered soft. Or I could push back on him. See how much I could get him to reveal.

"I know Peter paid someone to drop off that threatening photo of me and Logan." I kept my voice calm and monotone, not wanting to poke the bear too much. "I also know your company is behind some of this shit. Whatever caused Ethan to run, to disappear, is about Hawkins Associates."

He swallowed hard. "Who have you told this to?"

"No one. I have no one left." I brought my knees to my chest, my pulse pounding against my rib cage to the point of pain. Should I be worried about him asking that question first? Yes. Without a doubt. But I had one thing going for me—Detective Luna. Sure, we were both keeping things from each other, but he knew I was going home with my father and mother.

And I was 90 percent sure my dad wouldn't hurt us, not after that genuine reaction. He'd been scared for me. The only conclusion I could fathom was that he'd never expected me to be involved. *Too damn late, daddy dearest.*

He opened his mouth a few times as he came to a red light. There wasn't much traffic out this late at night, and the moon was extra bright. If Lo were awake, he'd point and scream at the moon until we all cheered.

"I hoped Ethan would come back if he thought you and Logan were in danger."

"Did you arrange the break-in at the house too? Tell them to write on my windshield? Think it'd be fun for me to think my son and I were in *danger*?"

"No." He cracked his knuckles just as the light turned green. "Not directly."

"Not a clear answer." I shivered despite the warmth in the car. "*Not directly* means you didn't order it but you knew it was probable?"

"We can talk tomorrow morning after we get some sleep."

"I don't think so." I dropped my legs back to the floor. I was wide-ass awake. "You said you *kept* me out of things for a reason. But, Dad? I'm in them now. Whether you and Peter want me to be or not, I'm in. So you can either fill me in on what the fuck is going on, or drop me and Logan off at a hotel. Because I don't trust you anymore. Are the affairs even real, or did you make those up for me to feel weak? As if my mind can't possibly fathom hard, complex things, like you and Peter? Make me question my own husband when it's really your bullshit causing this?" My filter evaporated like the smoke billowing from my house. Gone were the delicate lines I'd danced along my entire life. No more tiptoeing around my father and his critiques of me. *Fuck* this shit.

"Marissa, Christ." He gripped the back of his neck and jerked the car to the right way too fast.

My stomach swooped through my entire body as I screamed, holding on to the side bar as we came to a stop. A small part of me thought he was going to kill us, just smash us into the side of the road. My scream got stuck in my throat as fear paralyzed me from the waist down. "What the hell are you doing?"

He put the car in park and faced me with the same disturbed look I'd seen on his face when he first approached me after the fire. Agitated. Falling apart. The look in his eyes had me gripping the door tighter. *How can I distract him and get Logan out of the back seat?*

I'd experienced almost every emotion the past week, but this . . . this terror gripped me like a fist crushing my trachea. I couldn't get myself and Logan out safely. There was no way. It was worse than a dream—you know the kind when you're stuck and can't run but you force yourself awake to get out of the horror? It was that, without an escape. "Dad!" I screamed, my hoarse voice betraying the worry taking over me.

I moved to open the door, but my dad's fingers closed around my wrist, to the point his nails dug into my skin.

"No."

The authority in his tone had me stop, for just a moment. "Give me one reason to stay in this car—hell, in this fucking family."

"You don't know Ethan."

"My husband? The guy I've been with for ten years?" I said the words to hide the overwhelming truth that my dad was right. I'd *thought* I knew Ethan, but the hidden accounts, the photos, emails, Heather . . . yet admitting that when my dad seemed ready to snap would've been stupid.

He released my wrist, and then rubbed the palms of his hands over his eyes for five, ten seconds, his shoulders tensing all the way up to his ears. "Peter and I did some digging."

"More than the *supposed* affairs at the office?"

"Shut up and listen for a goddamn second, Marissa. This isn't a fucking game. This is *real* life." He spat the words, the *real life* comment taking me back to when I'd been a kid who daydreamed.

You're always in your head, Marissa. Join us in real life sometime.

You live in music; we live in the real world.

You're hopeless on your own. You need an MRS degree.

My left eye twitched, and I snuck a glance at Logan in the car seat. Still no movements or sounds. Still sleeping. "Enlighten me then."

My dad's bushy eyebrows stood in every direction from his hands constantly rubbing his face, and maybe it was the streetlight, but he looked older. His wrinkles seemed deeper, the skin around his eyes darker and more sunken. Aged. "Ethan lied to us. All of us."

"Get to the—"

"His real name is Alexander Roux, and his family never died in a car crash. They're still alive."

CHAPTER TWENTY-THREE

Monday, 1:00 a.m.—Two days "found"

The ringing in my ears grew and grew to the point my head spun. *I'm gonna be sick.* I flung the door open and puked on the side of the road, the weight of what my dad said resonating with me as the truth.

I had no reason to believe my father, but the name aligned with all the secrets I'd learned about *Ethan*. My husband. The orphan who'd welcomed my family with open arms because he'd *had no one left*. I rubbed my temples and breathed in the sharp cold air. My dad wasn't lying.

"How did you find out?" I wiped the back of my mouth, shut the car door, and forced myself to sit upright again. Each breath took more effort than normal, and I tapped my fingers on my knees in a rhythm to calm me down.

"That's not the worst of it, honey." He cleared his throat, his bloated and pale face whitening further. "We believe he's following the same path his father did."

The father who never died? Rage rooted me to my seat. "And what is that? I have no idea what you're fucking saying right now."

His eyes flashed. "Language, Marissa. Ladies don't—"

"Give it a fucking rest." I pointed at his chest, pushing my finger into it and shoving. "What did his now-alive dad do?"

My dad shook his shoulders, clearly uncomfortable. "His father used to work for me, actually."

"What?" Another fucking connection to Hawkins Associates. For an artsy girl who couldn't do *math*, I sure understood the common denominator. Hawkins was in every scenario.

"I know how this looks—"

"Do you? Do you *really*?" I cracked my knuckles to prevent myself from punching him in the face.

"His father, Graham Roux, worked for us for only a year or two. Smart man. Kept his head down. Always did his work on time and had never complained."

"Not exactly painting a picture here worth listening to. Get to the point."

Another flash of irritation crossed his face. He masked it fast, a totally fake look of worry replacing it. "Dennis—well, the who doesn't matter—but one of our guys found some flags coming from his IP address. We have tight security measures in place since we deal with confidential situations and data."

"What did you find?"

"His father was extorting people for money. Using private information from their devices to blackmail them. Totally went against our company name and policy. Still upsets me to my core that someone could intentionally harm a customer for money. It wasn't even that much, just a few thousand dollars."

I swallowed the ball in the back of my throat, filing away all the information my dad had shared. So *Ethan's* dad blackmailed people. Not ideal, but it wasn't murder. Not like . . . *Christopher Malinowski.*

I paused on bringing up that name. The email was still scheduled to go out in just a handful of hours, and I wanted the freedom of having my dad and Peter gone still. I chewed on my lip, my sweatshirt visibly moving with my rapid breathing.

"What happened then?" My voice came out worse than an old scratchy record. "How does this relate to Ethan? Or—wait, Alexander, I mean?"

"We confronted him. He denied the entire thing. Caused a real scene. During the investigation, we found five more examples of him extorting money from customers. Took him to trial—guilty on all accounts."

My head spun. Ethan's dad. "So he's in jail?"

"Graham Roux is in jail, yes." My dad cleared his throat and glanced down at his phone on his left leg. The light stood out in the darkness of the car, but it was clear he attempted to hide whatever was on the screen from me. "We found similar things on your device at home."

"When did you do that, exactly?" I bit my hangnail, hating that the tiny shred of doubt my dad had planted grew wings. Even if everything he'd said was false, I had no way to prove it. There was no trace of Ethan Creighton before he'd turned nineteen. "How did you find stuff on our device, at home?"

My dad ran a hand over his face. "I'm sorry for breaking your trust. Peter put a tracking device on it, hoping to gain access to all the files Ethan had because he wouldn't be stupid enough to put it on his device at the office. And we found . . . the same behavior."

"I don't . . . I don't believe you."

"Ever come across a bunch of women connected to him? Secret payments?" He pursed his lips, his eyes gleaming in the moonlight.

My stomach dropped so fast, I thought I was going to be sick again. *The women on Facebook. The hidden bank account. The PayPal.* "Why does . . . What do you mean?"

"He had a list of women he extorted money from. All relatives of clients. We also found evidence of an offshore bank account." My dad's voice softened, like I was some delicate flower.

This flower was a weed now. I wasn't going away. Even if my insides were on fire with disgust that my dad's words made sense. I swallowed the ball of rage and blew out a slow breath. My son was in the car, and

I needed to remain calm. "You think Ethan . . . Alexander followed his dad's footsteps? And that he was about to get caught, so that's why he fled?"

"Yes. That's what we think." He nodded, more to himself than me. "I don't know the amount he's earned, but I imagine he learned a thing or two from his dad. Not to make the same mistakes. I just can't believe we didn't see this earlier. The event with his father happened over a decade ago. I'm sorry he lied to you so much, sweetie. I know you loved him, but he lied. His family wasn't dead."

Family. My dad had only mentioned his father, and getting all the facts seemed extra important. Like a piece of the puzzle was just out of reach, tangled with all the others, and I needed to re-sort all the information.

"What happened to his mom?" The ball in my throat grew to a large pillow as I tensed, waiting for my dad's answer.

"The event was all over the papers. After the trial, she took their children and moved away. Haven't heard from her since, actually. Alice was her name."

Alice Roux. Graham and Alice Roux, not dead from a car crash. Alive. Family. Children.

Ethan had a sibling. He had other people. He'd lied.

Just put it on the lying tab. He was over a million at this point.

Had he been able to visit his mom without me knowing? Why lie about it? Hell, did he visit with his dad and learn tricks of the trade? Had Ethan known who I was when . . . ? Oh no. I gagged. Ethan had to have known who I was if my dad's company had caused his dad to go to jail. But if he was also stealing . . . why marry me?

Fuck. *Fuck.*

I was just another pawn in a game. Or was I?

My mind was a cracked window, each thought making the crack spread, and I was seconds away from shattering. Ethan had told me to trust no one. Detective Luna had told me to be careful. My family spied on me. Had paid a teenager to threaten me with a photo of my son. To cause a break-in! Who did I believe?

Another thought bulldozed in—*how* had my dad found out about the name?

"How long have you known Ethan was Graham's son?" I asked, keeping my voice even. If I was going to lose it, I'd do it quietly.

"I'm not sure that matters—"

"How fucking long?" My teeth clenched together, and my bouncing leg shook the entirety of the vehicle. "Did you know this entire time who my husband was? His secret life? You never thought to share that with me?"

"Marissa, calm down." He glared at me and glanced at Logan in the back seat. "I know this is a lot, okay? But no. Peter and I found the connection yesterday."

"How? How did you connect these dots?"

"His *work* computer." My dad sighed, the sound filled with defeat and regret. "Peter bypassed all his passwords and protection. Found an entire folder with articles about Graham."

"Ethan could've just found the articles and been collecting evidence. What makes you assume Graham's his father?"

"Why else would he have those articles, Marissa? Why is there no trace of Alexander Roux after 2008? He's off the map. Like Ethan is now."

"I see the coincidences, but there's no proof in what you're saying unless you're hiding something from me."

I was right. I could tell by the way he ground his teeth together and the whites of his eyes bulged. I had him.

"So what is it, Dad? You're either lying or keeping something from me."

He opened his mouth twice, then wiped a hand over his upper lip before his phone rang. He answered it like it was his saving grace. "What is it? Uh-huh. Yeah. I got her. Okay. Shit." He slammed his phone into the center console and jerked the car back onto the road. "We're heading home. Now."

"Who was that?"

No answer.

"Dad, who was that? Why aren't you answering my questions now?"

He went faster, the car revving as he skidded left, then right. Once he settled the car, he exhaled. "No more talking."

"That's bullshit. This is my life we're dealing with. My husband."

"*You don't even know him!*" he screamed, destroying any sanity I thought he had left.

Survival instincts kicked in, and I closed my mouth. Provoking him while he was driving would be idiotic. With a knot in my throat and my stomach squirming like it was filled with hundreds of worms, I remained silent.

The tension in the car was filled with occasional grunts from my dad and his constant fidgeting.

He's nervous.

I wasn't sure why the thought thrilled me after he'd shed light on Ethan's past and his lies. *If* it were true. But seeing my always-in-control father on the edge meant things were happening. Pressure was cracking down. For what? I had no idea. Was Ethan like Graham? Was that even his father? Was my husband a monster who'd targeted me to follow his dad's path? Or was this just lies to confuse me, cast doubt on my husband?

Because the common denominator was Hawkins Associates, and thank god I had the new phone because I had research to do. Lots of it. And the new phone had no connection to my parents' Wi-Fi in any way, so they couldn't spy on me.

Point to the artsy one, dear father.

"Where Are You Now" by Lost Frequencies and Calum Scott.

A small, angry, and petty part of me wanted to leave him hanging. He'd been listening to the song live, meaning he was in front of his device this second. At 2:00 a.m. Probably worried out of his mind, if he'd seen me drive off with my dad.

Good. Let him worry.

What did he think I'd been doing this entire time? Enjoying life?

Or was he worried at all? Was he thinking about robbing more people? What if *he* was the one to plant the listening device? *This sucks.*

I left my laptop open, washed my face, and crawled into my childhood bed. Logan was comfortable in a pack-and-play off to the right of me, blissfully unaware of everything.

I played **"Real Name, No Gimmicks" by Luca Musto**, my stomach tightening.

Then I hit **"Alexander" by Ghostcamp** after waiting thirty seconds.

There was something missing in my dad's story about how he and Peter had figured out the connection between Graham and Ethan. That was for sure. But with one quick Google search, I found an old photo of the Roux family. I gasped, all the air leaving my lungs as recognition hit me like an electric shock.

There was no doubt my dad had been right.

Alexander Roux was Ethan. Or Ethan was him. He had the same face, hair, chiseled jaw, and easy smile. My husband's entire life was a secret from me.

Heather wasn't the other woman. The woman I'd met at the bar? It was his sister. Hailey. Two years younger than him.

Those pictures of the kids in our closet? Her children . . . Ethan's nephews.

He'd hidden this part of his life from me. He lied to me. My entire marriage was a fucking joke. If I'd eaten anything, it would've come up as I fisted the sheets, grounding myself to avoid screaming. *Focus on Logan.*

I had to figure this out. Logan deserved the truth, no matter what, and that was enough to shove the fury down.

While this revelation answered *some* of the questions, it didn't answer all of them. Like why had he lied? Why did he keep this *all* from me, assuming he knew his dad had worked for mine? Had he been ashamed of his father, or was he a con man too?

"It All Makes Sense Now" by Woody Jackson, Ethan responded.

"Not Good Enough" by Joy Williams.

"Not What You Think" by LilCJ Kasino. He followed up with a quick **"I Promise" by Radiohead**.

"Your Dad" by Keith Paluso. I then added **"He Is Alive" by the Blythe Family**.

"Check Yes, Juliet" by We the Kings.

Annoyed that he responded *now* and not . . . in the ten years before, I quickly made a playlist with random songs and titled it "MY DAD KNOWS YOU'RE GRAHAM'S SON" and added it to the top of my lists. He should see it.

Damn, why hadn't I been making playlist titles this whole time? Way easier than song names. His song didn't change, so I went to his profile to view his playlists.

Nothing added.

My impatience grew as exhaustion took over. Lo would be up in a few hours, and then the Christopher email was going out . . . I had to email Heather that I knew she was Hailey and call the detective. My brain was spiraling, and Ethan needed to respond to me right now.

"I Want It That Way" by Backstreet Boys.

Oh. He *wanted* it that way? My father knowing about his connection to Graham Roux? After telling us for a decade that he was an orphan? And trying to steal too? Or had my dad been planting a seed?

I went to my public playlists and changed the playlist names so each title had one word in all caps. He needed to answer this. I couldn't move past it.

"AREna rock"

"YOUr top songs 2021"

"brb STEALING your man xo"

"DATAchamps"

"TOOnztoonstoon$"

I put on **"Answer Me" by PLAZA.**

"Not Once" by Colorblind Dinosaurs. Then he switched: **"I'm on Your Team" by Written to Speak.**

"PLEASE" by Omido and Ex Habit.

Ethan played **"My Letter" by Flaw**, then hit Pause. **"Need to Know" by Doja Cat.**

God. That had felt like a lifetime ago, when I saw him in the library. The relief at seeing him alive was like a breath of oxygen after being stuck in a lake. That had happened to me once—thought I was coming up for air but hit the bottom of the boat instead. Terrifying fifteen seconds. Seeing my husband had been amazing, but the feeling had faded, and I was drowning again.

In lies. In deceit. In uncertainty.

The damn letter. He'd asked for two things. I'd searched for the emails he wanted, which may or may not have caused people to break in to our home, but the second thing was about Dennis Paulson.

Wait . . . Dennis. My dad had mentioned Dennis in his confession in the car. He was involved with everything somehow. But Ethan wanted to know if he'd met with Lexington LLC three months ago. My gut was torn in two. I wanted to help him, but was that foolish?

"More Time" by NEEDTOBREATHE, I responded.

Then I added **"I'm So Angry" by Amos Pitsch**. I needed him to understand that this was life altering, soul crushing. He said he was on my team?

I couldn't function without sleep, so I shut the laptop, falling back onto the bed as exhaustion weighed me down. My eyes got fuzzy, and my thoughts blurred in dreams of black and white. I tossed and turned.

I woke up every hour in a full-body sweat and checked on Logan. Being in my childhood home was messing with me. I couldn't relax. As I fought nightmares and a sleepless night, a lone thought remained in my head—one of the secret emails mentioned *my father* and the date.

I was confident about one thing in all the fucking mess. Everything was related.

I just had to find out how.

CHAPTER TWENTY-FOUR

Monday, 8:00 a.m.—Two days "found"

I'd made a mistake. I wasn't sure when or how my purse had gotten lost in the chaos of the fire, my dad's confession in the car, and the real fear that he was going to run us off the road, but it was gone. My bag with everything important. *All my notes. The extra cash. The car keys—my only way of driving a car.*

Plus, my wallet and lip balm. I *really* needed them both, and I was struck with the foolish feeling I was an incompetent, *dumb* artist again. My head throbbed like I'd tossed back ten shots of rum last night, so I chugged a glass of water in my parents' kitchen.

It smelled the same, but it felt different. Like the pale-red cabinets knew things had changed and I wasn't safe. Even the photos of Logan, Ethan, and me on the fridge seemed out of place. The rare wines my mom had always talked about were stacked on the counters in custom-made cabinets. The flowers and still life art had changed to rich images of modern blobs, surely by some talented, sought-after artist. Photos of my parents on boats and lavish trips lined the hallways. All of it felt like *home* yet was accompanied by a horrible, sinking feeling of dread. I hated those braggy photos and ugly art.

Next to a fresh pot of coffee, my parents had left me a note, essentially abandoning me in the house without a way out besides walking. I decided to pour myself a cup before reading it.

> Marissa—I had to head into the office, and your mother had an appointment she couldn't miss. Stay in the house. We'll be back soon. We're so glad you and Logan are safe. We're family, we always protect family. Never forget.
>
> —Dad

Tears prickled my eyes as I read it again, looking for codes. *Protect family*, huh? Belittling me for years, gaslighting me, threatening my child . . . that wasn't *protecting family*. I called bullshit on that. I pinched my nose, the weighted feeling of dread taking over already.

Did my mom have any idea about what was going on?

I texted her from my old phone. Can we talk, alone?

Her response was immediate. We'll chat as a family soon. Give Lo a kiss from me.

Not helpful. *As a family.* They sounded like a weird cult.

The house creaked with its age, and I jumped, spilling coffee on the only shirt I had. Everything else was at the hotel.

We were momentarily safe. That had to be enough.

I wanted to call the detective, but I wasn't an idiot. It was easy to assume I'd be watched or heard while in the house. My dad or brother would have access to the most advanced technology, and it could be anywhere. It was like the eggshell-painted walls with custom trim were closing in on me. The ugly art would suffocate me as everything blurred together and enclosed around me. I couldn't breathe.

I need out of this house.

But without money, what could I do?

Rideshares! Duh! It was all connected to my phone, so I ordered a car to get there in ten minutes and bolted to get Logan ready. He was a grump in the morning and cried as I changed him with a spare diaper my mom always kept in the closet. I grabbed some Goldfish and milk, needing that to be enough for breakfast, and went out to wait for the driver.

As the white car headed down the road, reality hit me. Car seat! I bolted into the garage to grab the one I'd left there after we unloaded Lo last night, and it was gone.

"What the fuck?" I searched in the cabinets, under the tarp—nothing. Like my parents had purposefully gotten rid of it so I wouldn't leave with Logan. *Assholes.*

They wanted me here, stranded, trapped, alone.

My throat closed up at the revelation.

The driver rolled her window down, a large smile on her face, and said, "Marissa? Hi there!"

"Look." My voice cracked. "I have to cancel. I can't find the car seat for my son."

"Shoot, no worries. I have mine in the back. How old is he? Two-ish?"

"You have one we can use?"

"If you don't mind some crumbs, get on in!"

Kayla was a miracle. If I ever had another kid, I was naming them after her. My lips cracked at my too-large smile, but I didn't care. We were en route to the hotel to get my stuff! To get clothes! To get some goddamn freedom!

The drive went by fast with Kayla's upbeat chatter. I responded as needed but counted down until we arrived at the hotel. I'd need a way to get from there to the office, and an idea struck. "Kayla, can I ask a huge favor?"

"Sure. You look like you need a friend today."

"Can you add another trip to the app or something? I just need to run into my room to get clothes, some stuff for my kiddo. But this isn't where we need to be today, and I'm afraid I'm stuck without a car seat for hours."

"Absolutely. I'll set it up now." She grinned and met my eyes in the mirror. A real angel.

With the speed of a sleep-deprived cheetah, I hauled Logan into the room. I searched frantically—tossing aside pillows and sheets and scouring every corner of the room—for my missing purse. Nada. I grabbed our bag and hurried out the door with Logan. Nothing left behind.

I ignored the stress and anxiety growing inside my chest like a hot-air balloon and loaded our small haul into the car.

It was almost nine, meaning I had over an hour to kill before my dad and Peter received that email about Christopher. I assumed they'd rush out of the office, but I had to be certain.

They couldn't see me go into Ethan's office. There was a countdown ticking somewhere, an unexplainable feeling that shit was going to hit the fan, and before it did, I wanted more information.

But what to do until then? Research without being detected. It'd be tough with Logan and all the unknown technology tools my dad had at his disposal, but I'd try regardless. There were nooks in the huge office that were out of sight. At least, there used to be a mother's room.

Yes—I'd use that room. It was on the second floor and private. My body hummed in response to my plan and settled my erratic heart as we neared Callahan Lane. I'd grown up hearing about the address, the pride of my dad. Callahan Lane was important and special, a street businesses dreamed about being on. The location was right in the center of our small town's downtown, with coffee shops and stores lining every direction. A tall bank and business center were next to it, and I gulped at the sheer intimidation Hawkins Associates evoked with its height and dark colors.

Kayla dropped me off at the main entrance with a smile, and the building overwhelmed me, overtaking all my senses. The smell of exhaust and sounds of people arriving at work on a Monday echoed in my brain: car horns, brakes, keys jiggling. People talking in sharp tones, their caffeine not hitting them yet.

I clutched Logan against my chest, shouldering my bag as I stared at the front doors.

The building had a large circular drive with glass windows and doors covering the whole bottom floor. I'd always thought it looked professional and sleek. Now it was a fucking microscope. A magnifying glass just showing everyone I was there. I could see the reception desk, the line for the elevator, the small coffee cart off to the left, and even a group of men in black suits entering a conference room. There were no secrets here. It was on display, exuding power and dominance.

Logan babbled and pulled on the collar of my shirt until he fit it into his mouth, and I steeled myself. This was for my family. For me and Logan to get the truth.

Let's do this.

I kept my head high, determined to show that I fit in here despite the fact my clothes were wrinkled and had spills on them. I wasn't doing a damn thing wrong, and it still made my skin crawl, like I'd broken out of my parents' house.

Just get through security. Hope they don't ask for an ID. Change in the bathroom. Mother's room.

Having a list of action items focused me.

"Good morning, miss?" The head security guard frowned at me, his brows coming together before recognition hit his face. I knew of him, but he wasn't the one I usually chatted with—which was in my favor today.

"Creighton. Mrs. Creighton, how are you?" He stumbled, clearly embarrassed he hadn't known me right off the bat.

"I've had better days." I forced a tight smile, glancing up at the glass walls, expecting my dad to be standing there watching me. Or Peter. Or Ethan, for that matter. Instead, it was just the sun reflecting off the glass walls and people shuffling about.

While it wasn't what I would call reassuring, there was probably a system set up to let them know when I arrived. Sweat pooled down my back and under my boobs as more people stood around us, flashing their badges at the other line. Would they turn me away? Take me into a back office?

The guard nodded, sympathy softening his features. "I'm so sorry to hear about Mr. Creighton going missing. We're all praying for his safe return." He took my bag and ran it through the conveyor belt with cameras. I signed the paper form. There was no harm in documenting I was here, especially if something happened to me.

Logan and I walked through the metal detector, and the guard handed me our bag back with the same flash of pity. "Thank you."

He pressed his lips together and gave off the favorite-uncle vibe as he leaned closer. "You need anything, you let me know. Ethan was a stand-up guy. Always polite. Kind to everyone. I wish more people here were like him."

The compliment made my eyes sting because *that* was the Ethan I knew. Not . . . Alexander with a father in jail and a secret sister with kids. Just thinking about his hidden past was enough to have my steps falter, but an idea struck.

"Hey, can I ask you a question?" I eyed his name tag, not placing Edward into any recent memories. He seemed older, weathered. Like he easily could've been here for over a decade. "How long have you worked here, Edward?"

He tipped his cap. "Fifteen years, ma'am."

Back when Graham worked here!

I glanced around us, not recognizing any faces. Almost everyone had a phone pressed up to their ear or in their face, so I took a chance. "Did you ever know anyone named Graham Roux?"

It was subtle, but his body weight shifted. He leaned more onto his left leg as his hand came up to rub his jaw. "I knew him, yeah. Haven't thought about that name in a while. A damn shame what he did to those families."

"Blackmailing them?"

"That, and stalking them. Tracking their movements." Edward shook his head and sighed, wrinkles forming all around his eyes. "I don't pay much attention to technology, and I know I'm old, but it's gone too far. It's even worse now with—oh hey, Dennis."

My spine steeled as Edward left me standing there. Dennis. The man I'd heard about and needed information on. I felt like a fucking mouse in a trap, like he knew exactly who I was and what I was doing. Without waiting a beat, I calmly walked away from security and toward the bathrooms. Each step felt like a thousand-pound brick was tied around my foot, like I was sinking into the beautiful marble floor of Hawkins Associates.

"Ma'am?" said someone with a deep voice, right behind me.

Please no, no, no. My throat tightened, and my mouth dried up. I walked faster.

"Ma'am, hold on, please."

Fuck. Logan bit my shirt, his teeth digging into my skin and making me yelp. My eyes prickled with tears from sheer adrenaline as a soft hand gripped my elbow. I had no choice but to turn around.

"Wh-what?" I asked, my voice shaky.

Him. It was him! The big burly man who I saw at the post office stood before me. Did the mafia secretly infiltrate my family firm? Were my parents being threatened into committing crimes? Oh god. Did this man and Ethan work together and have a falling out? My mind raced as fear danced along my spine.

His dark-green eyes moved from my head to Logan before he stood up straighter. "Marissa," he gasped. He took a step back.

I didn't like that he knew who I was immediately, but before I could figure out how to respond, he wiped a hand on his jacket over his three-piece suit. And why was he acting surprised at seeing me? He'd been following me. I was certain.

"I'm Dennis Paulson, one of the senior advisers for your father. We haven't officially met, but I feel like I already know you from hearing your dad, brother, and Ethan talk about you. And this little guy. Logan, aren't you adorable?" He scrunched his nose and smiled at my toddler, the easygoing vibes radiating off him clashing with my initial impression of who he was.

I'd pictured a creep, an old guy with evil eyes and a devil tail or something. Not this . . . handsome silver-haired man who got Logan to giggle. My mind split in two, unsure what path to take. *Be kind? Be mean?*

I had to take the path of least attention seeking, but I was at a loss. "It's, uh, nice to officially meet you."

He grinned for another second at Logan before moving a hand to my shoulder. His face softened with worry as he clicked his tongue. "I can't imagine these circumstances are nice at all. I'm so sorry for the stress, the situation Ethan put you in. I know your father has been losing his mind. He's generally hard to be around, but this? Boy, you should see him pace." He let out a small fake-sounding chuckle. "Are you holding up okay?"

"As best I can."

"Right. Of course." He closed his eyes and let his hand drop from my shoulder. "Is there anything I can help you with? Anything at all?"

I shook my head, real tears slipping down my face and onto my already distressed shirt. He tracked them, something dark flashing across his face before he stepped closer. Panic gripped me in a choke hold as he neared, the possibilities of what he would say exploding exponentially in my mind. All things I wouldn't have an answer to. He was close enough that his minty breath hit my face, sending chills down my body.

"Does your father know you're here?" He pulled out a white handkerchief and wiped my face, the look of sympathy gone and replaced with disgust. This felt too intimate to do to someone you'd just met. Way too intimate. I stood frozen, unable to form words as he cleaned up my tears with his beady green eyes boring into me. "He doesn't, does he? Interesting. Seems like maybe you're not the only *Creighton* keeping secrets, hmm?"

He pocketed the tissue, narrowed his eyes at Logan, then smiled. "Such a cute little toddler. I have a meeting I need to be at in one minute. Great meeting you, Marissa."

And with the energy of a tornado, Dennis Paulson strutted away from me and toward the elevators. He didn't spare me one glance, but it wasn't until he got into the elevator that I could breathe again.

I had no fucking idea what all that meant, but I knew that I didn't have long before my father knew I was here. That meant I had to get into Ethan's office *now*.

CHAPTER TWENTY-FIVE

Monday, 9:30 a.m.—Three days "found"

It wasn't the time for Logan to scream bloody murder, but he did anyway. People stared at us as we got into the elevator, condemning me for what could be numerous things. The way I looked, my screaming child, my tearstained eyes. The list went on, but I coached myself to not care. It was hard after a life of pleasing everyone around me. My shell was cracking.

Their lives weren't shaken to the core. They could fuck all the way off with their dramatic eyebrow raises. I cradled Logan's head, kissing the top of it as I rocked side to side. "Almost there, baby. I promise."

His response was another scream. It was possible he could feel the erratic beat of my heart and was feeding off my worry. I focused on breathing slowly and calmly.

My anger at Ethan multiplied the longer the ride went, because *he* was the reason we were in this situation. His lies, his disappearance, his secret life I was searching for, like trying to find Logan's favorite pacifier in the middle of the night in pitch black. I thought of a million things to say to his face if I saw him again, none of them good. I had the entire argument planned out in my head by the time the doors opened on the seventh floor, and I bolted out, not even bothering to apologize to everyone else in the elevator.

Logan settled the second we got off the elevator, thankfully, and I sighed in relief at the quiet around me. I handed him his pacifier, and for one second, things were okay. Changing clothes would have to wait, though—getting into Ethan's office was top priority.

From the elevator, I could see his office clearly. *Good, I'll be able to see if Dad or Peter come to this floor.* Ethan had a large corner office with a glass door and large window. There was crime scene tape over the door, blocking any discreet entrance to it.

"Hi, excuse me?" I went up to the small circular desk right in the center of the hall. Each floor had its own secretary, who fielded visitors and general calls. "Sammi?"

The beautiful black-haired woman eyed me head to toe before smacking her hand on her forehead. "Marissa, hi. I wasn't expecting you. Did you call beforehand? No, why would you?" She brushed her bangs out of her face, her cheeks flushed. "Oh gosh, you must be a mess. You poor thing. And Logan! Oh, sweet baby."

"A bit of a mess, yes." I forced a smile; I'd always enjoyed her genuine niceties. "I really need to get in there. Think that'll cause an issue?"

"I don't know." She chewed her lip. "Mr. Hawkins put the tape up last week and said a *no one is to cross this line* type of speech to all of us. He rarely comes down this way, so it startled everyone."

I *loved* that people forgot he was my dad sometimes. That's how little I came into the office. I used that information to my advantage. For all she knew, my only last name was Creighton. "I don't want you to get into trouble, but there's something Ethan left me that I really need. Is there . . . a task that could pull you from the desk for ten minutes so you wouldn't have a clue I was here?"

Her eyes sparkled. "I could go make copies for Mrs. Fields. I've been putting it off."

"Yes, I'm sure she'll be pleased." Finally, a fucking break. "Say that takes ten minutes?"

"Maybe fifteen if I stop and chat with Kathy at marketing." Sammi beamed and already had a stack of papers in her hands. "I hope you're doing okay. Ethan loved you and Logan more than anything. Not to creep on him because he's so happily married, but I want my future partner to talk about me the way he talked about you."

My face heated at the compliment. Full-on red cheeks and blush. Sammi didn't wait around, though. She headed in the other direction, essentially starting the countdown. Fifteen minutes.

Was that enough time to go through all of Ethan's things?

I went through the yellow caution tape, careful not to mess with it, and all the lights flashed on. The shades were down, blocking me from view.

I set Logan down on one of the large soft chairs with some teething toys and went to Ethan's desk. He had the same setup as home, with a few trinkets and photos here and there. He kept his workspace simple, though—no fluff. God, it smelled like him. Cedar.

I went through his drawers, his shelves, and didn't find a single thing out of place or calling out to me. No clue that matched anything he'd left me. I even ran my fingers inside the drawers to see if there was a hidden compartment. Nada.

But did he ever mean for me to come into the office? That was the part I wasn't sure of. He asked me to figure out Dennis's schedule, which couldn't happen unless I was here, so maybe he had planned for me to be here? The elevator dinged, almost like a countdown.

I felt it in my bones: *Search faster.*

Fuck. Time was running out, shrinking me, and I didn't know what to do. I couldn't log in to his computer without a password.

I pulled at my hair as I spun around in his computer chair. Our wedding photo sat on his shelf in the frame I'd gotten him after a concert. It had mini cassette tapes on the corners. It was super cheesy, and I couldn't believe he actually had it here for others to see.

Smiling, I picked it up and stared at our happy faces as the red font on the mini cassette tapes jumped out at me. *CASIO.*

I choked on my own saliva as I gasped. Could this *possibly* be the answer to the password? My fingers tingled with excitement to the point that they shook. There was nothing written on the photo or the frame. Nothing.

No indented words or symbols. Grinding my teeth together, I felt the hope slipping away like a small leak in a balloon. It was clear I was desperate for anything, a clue, a connection that I could've made without it being real. "Fuccccck," I groaned. Refocusing, I picked up the frame for the final time.

"Okay, Ethan, did you want me to see this?"

The elevator dinged again, the bell causing my breath to stick in my throat, and I waited, tense as a gargoyle, but no one exited the elevator. *Weird.*

With a new determination, I flipped the frame over.

The only thing off about it was a small red heart on the back. It was just a sticker. Maybe it was intuition or luck or the drive of this neon-red plastic sticker, but I undid the back of the frame and held the photo in my hands.

Ethan had written a password on the back and taped a small black SD card.

Holy shit.

EastportBlue.

The memory assaulted me. We'd been coming up with passwords we'd remember together for joint accounts, and EastportBlue was created after two glasses of wine. It was my stripper name—my childhood street and color of underwear that night. We'd laughed at our own little inside joke.

Now it was a branch I held to save myself, us, and Logan from the storm.

I clicked the mouse, bringing the screen to life again, and eyed the white bar. Ethan had a Post-it with the password to enter his computer—that was unsafe. He must've done that intentionally. He wanted to bait my family, while leaving this for me.

I logged in and inserted the SD card, my lungs constricting from the nerves. This had to have the answers.

Encryption code required: EastportBlue

Enter.

Those three seconds were the longest of my entire life. But I was in. Now . . . what was I searching for, exactly?

The SD card was clean, organized into just two folders.

CHRISTOPHER MALINOWSKI

MARISSA

The elevator pinged again, stopping at this floor, and I wasn't going to be lucky a second time. I double-clicked Chrome, signed in to my email with my throat pulsating in fear. I just had to email myself these folders.

Wait!

I didn't need to email them. I could upload them to my Google Drive. That was it.

The elevator doors opened, Dennis and Peter walking out on a clear mission. *Jesus Christ.* I swallowed the panic as I dropped the files into my drive, waiting for the circle to complete and tell me the transfer had worked.

I didn't make copies of the folders—I moved them entirely so it would remove any trace from Ethan's computer or the SD card and the hands of my dad and brother.

Fifty percent done.

"Marissa? What in the—" Peter stopped at the edge of the office, his gaze moving from Logan to me, then to the computer I was clearly using. His eyes widened, and he raised his hand just an inch. "Did you sign in? Are you . . . okay?"

I didn't get a chance to answer before he paled. "Does Dad know you're here? You shouldn't be here, Marissa."

"I missed him, okay?" I stood up, desperate to give the device more time to load the folders. Anything. The chair squeaked, and I moved in front of the desk, between Peter and Dennis and the files I needed more than air. "He loved this place, and it smells like him, and the house burned down, and Dad had to bring me to my childhood home, and I don't have any of Logan's stuff and—" Genuine tears fell, and my voice was all raspy and smoky. All real, not performative.

The adrenaline worked in my favor to distract my brother and Dennis for at least a second.

"Hush, Marissa. You don't want to cause a scene." Dennis clicked his tongue and waved an arm through the caution tape, undoing it entirely before shutting the office door. When he turned around again, his sharp eyes were solely on the computer. "You thought coming into his office and sitting at his desk would help you?"

"Dennis, don't use that tone. She's been through a shitstorm the past week." Peter frowned and clenched his fist a couple of times. He stepped toward me with his lips flat when the computer made a *ping* sound. It was subtle, but it was like hearing the back of an earring drop onto tile. Like you weren't sure you heard where it fell, but you knew something had happened.

I had half a second to save everything.

"I need your help!" I blurted out, the hysteria making both men cringe. "You said if I needed anything, you'd help, right? Both of you? Well, I need it. Badly."

"Anything, Mar. What is it?" Peter moved closer, and *god*, I wish I knew the keystrokes of how to log out. Five seconds. All I needed.

"It's . . . benefits, beneficiary stuff. Like, if he never comes back, what does that mean for me and Logan?" I sniffed loudly, making Dennis cringe. It was clear any kindness he'd showed downstairs had been performative. Knowing he could turn it on and off like that sent a different kind of chill through me. "Payments, finances. How do I . . . ? I don't make enough."

"You know Dad and I will make sure you're okay." Peter sighed as worry lines formed on his forehead. "I'd do *anything* for you. Tell me you know that." His voice lowered and deepened with some underlying meaning.

My brain was past the point of deciphering any more clues, yet the hair on the back of my neck stood on end. My body sensed danger, even if my mind couldn't pinpoint what.

Keep talking. Convince them. I dug my nails into my palm, keeping an eye on Logan as he crawled toward Peter. I couldn't yank him out of reach; that would cause too much suspicion.

"I was really hoping to find files or paperwork explaining all the finance and benefits stuff, since there's nothing at the house after the fire. This is . . . awkward." I pushed my hair behind my ear and looked at the floor. I'd played the shy woman my whole life; I knew the role well. I grabbed my water bottle out of my bag to do something with my hands. "Dennis, any chance you could help me out?"

Dennis sneered as Logan yelled, "Pee Pee!" My son ran to his uncle Peter, and my brother scooped him up in a hug. Well, shit. There went my moment to prevent either man from holding my son. Peter and I shared a look, and he tilted his chin down at me, almost like he was saying *Don't worry.*

How the fuck could I trust him anymore? My faith in humanity had crashed and burned.

My brother kissed my son on the head before saying, "Let's head to your office and talk about options."

Dennis gave a curt nod before freezing me in place with those emerald eyes. "But first let's have Marissa show us what's on Ethan's device. She's too sweaty to be innocent. Just like her old man."

I was *nothing* like my father. Anger flared in my chest.

Dennis strode toward the computer, but I had a couple of steps on him. I prayed that the folders had gone through, that enough time had passed. I had moved the files from the SD card to my drive—no evidence left behind if I damaged the computer.

I did the only thing I could've.

Please work.

I uncapped my water bottle and poured the entire thing on the tower—over the blinking lights and the plugged-in cords. Everything froze, even the oxygen trying to get into my lungs. The sixteen ounces dripped over the black cords and over the grille, spilling into the device. *Destroy it. Please.*

There wasn't the sound of an explosion or hissing like I wanted. Just silence.

Then Dennis growled, "You *fucking* idiot."

CHAPTER TWENTY-SIX

Monday, 9:45 a.m.—Two days "found"

Dennis shoved me to the ground in one swift motion. I barely caught myself in time before my face met the light-red carpet. Pain exploded up my forearm and into my shoulder, sending a jolt of energy through me as my nerves prickled. I winced and cradled my arm to my chest while I rolled to my back. My stomach muscles strained as I pushed myself up off the floor. Sunlight streamed through the windows, showcasing dust spiraling into the air from the kerfuffle, and the beams hit Dennis's face, making him look more than a little devilish: his eyes greener, more menacing, the twist of his lips meaner . . . he enjoyed my pain.

I had to get the hell out of there—now.

"Dennis, what the fuck?" Peter set Logan down on the chair and rushed over to me. Logan's face crumpled; we had seconds before he wailed, since Peter was one of his favorite people. My heart leaped in my throat, waiting for the explosion of sound. Peter held out a hand for me, and I took it, noting how sweaty his was. Up close, there were beads of moisture around his forehead and large dark bags under his brown eyes.

I wiped my hand on my shirt and picked up my son.

Everything had happened at once, in a blur and without reason. Even the clouds covered the sun momentarily, casting a dark shadow over the office. Dennis growled as he plopped into Ethan's desk chair, the leather squishing in that gross, deep sound with his weight.

Please be glitchy. Please don't work. Please.

"You saw what she did." Dennis furiously clicked on the mouse and hit the side of the computer with his hand three times. "She found *something*. Fix your sister's priorities, Peter."

Fix your sister.

Of all the threats lobbed my way, either explicit or implied, *fixing* me seemed the most terrifying. It could've been the way his lip curled or the narrowing of his eyes as he glared at me. The man was *sinister*, and my gut tightened thinking about all the things he could do.

Logan belted out a wail like he'd broken a leg, and I shifted him onto my other hip. "What do you mean by *fix*? I'm heartbroken right now."

"You foolish girl." Dennis stood up, straightening his shirt before motioning toward Logan. "Do you know how easy it would be to ruin your life?"

"Dennis." Peter's tone had a thick warning, the low timbre not one I'd heard on him before. "Enough."

"I refuse to let Franklin's fucking daughter and her rat husband ruin—"

"Shut up." Peter shoved him in the chest. "She's not a part of this. Never was, never will be. Leave her and her son out of it, or I will fuck everything up."

"Wow, feeling brave without your old man around? Would he like to hear how you speak to me?"

Peter's eye twitched, and he stepped in front of me. "Marissa and Logan are off limits. That was always the rule. You agreed to it."

"And you think she's gonna forget this lovely conversation? Just listen to music and ride off into the sunset? No. She's involved and fucking it all up."

"She doesn't understand—"

"Then *make her understand*, or I will."

Roots grew from the balls of my feet into the plush carpet, freezing me in the spot despite the warning bells blaring in my mind to *run*. My fight-or-flight trigger broke, and I could only hug Logan tightly and stare at the exchange in front of me: Dennis looking down at Peter like he was nothing and staring at me like I was the lynchpin in their plans. I had no idea what their plans were! I wanted to find the truth about Ethan. Couldn't they see that? I didn't care about whatever they were doing.

My skin warmed as an idea formed. "It's . . ." I paused, gulping down the anxious ball of dread in my throat. "Ethan, all right? I don't know what's going on or why you're threatening me—"

"I'm not threatening you, Marissa." Dennis licked his bottom lip. "Don't put words in my mouth. No one would believe you. I'm simply stating fact: you're involved in things beyond what your pretty little mind can handle."

If I'd thought the room was tense, it worsened twofold when Dennis narrowed his eyes into slits, reminding me of a venomous snake on the verge of an attack. *This* was the guy who'd caught Ethan's dad, cruel and vile.

"I, uh—" I stumbled, swallowing the fear. "I wanted to delete the photos of the affair."

Dennis clicked his tongue. "Little liar. If that were true, then why, dear Marissa, did you ask our security guard Edward about Graham Roux, a name that hasn't been mentioned in over ten years?"

Peter sucked in a breath, barely audible over the roaring in my ears. It was like a freight train passing through a cornfield in the middle of a tornado. Dennis had a glint in his eyes. An evil one. Almost joyful with a side of sinister. The roots in my feet doubled in size, growing up my body and wrapping around my limbs to paralyze me. I had no answer. No excuse. No reason. Nothing.

Dennis's smirk increased the longer my silence grew, and the shrill of Peter's phone cut the thick air. They shared a look before Peter answered with a curt "What?"

The sound shook away the metaphorical vines holding me hostage. I slid my bag onto my other shoulder and stepped toward the door. I had no real plans but to get out of the office and away from this building. I could walk to a hotel. There had to be one nearby. Or a café. *But without my purse and the only money I had?*

Fuck.

"Is it *him*?" My brother's voice rose an octave at that last word.

It took every ounce of effort to not react as my pulse spiked. *The email. They got it.* They weren't paying attention to me now, not with that bomb. Peter blinked fast as Dennis's lips parted. The victorious smirk he wore shattered like glass crashing into a brick wall.

"He forwarded it to you," Peter said. He nodded like *my dad* could see him. I knew it was him on the other end. It was ten on the dot.

"Give me the phone, now." Dennis yanked it from Peter's hand. "It's me." He nodded twice, the muscles in his shoulders tensing. Then he barked, "Let's move."

Dennis marched past Peter, not glancing at me once as Peter followed.

My brother stopped at the door, faced me, and mouthed, *Run. Take Logan and run.*

I shivered.

Their expensive cologne left with them, and I took a real deep breath for the first time since they entered.

Escape. This was my chance.

I bolted through the door with Logan on my side, every sound making me jump. The laughter of someone down the hall. The light music coming from someone's office.

Was this a trick and they were waiting behind a corner to scare me? Would they try to kidnap us? My parents might not have *officially* locked me in the house, but they'd taken away every means of a rational escape. What would be next? Locks on doors?

Shaking away my immense regret, I headed toward the stairwell instead of the elevator but paused. Was that the smarter choice? Fewer cameras . . . fewer people . . . easier for them to hurt us. Stuck with indecision, I froze.

"Everything all right, Mrs. Creighton?" Sammi returned, her smile gone from her lips when her gaze landed on my face. "Oh, you're pale."

"I, uh, have to leave." My throat was too dry, too hoarse. "Thank you for everything."

She chewed her lip as her frown deepened. "You don't look well. You should sit down."

"No, no, I need to leave. Get out of the building." My mind started spinning, and I took a slow, forced breath to get oxygen into my brain. Passing out would be the worst thing to happen right now. "Somewhere safe. Somewhere not here."

She grabbed my elbow, gently, and guided me toward an empty office just next to Ethan's. "Sit, I insist."

"Sammi, no. I need out." I shook against her hold, but her fingers tightened around me to the point her nails dug into my skin.

"I have a message for you. From Ethan."

"What?" I snapped my head in her direction so hard, a nerve exploded in my neck, and I winced in pain. "When? What is it?"

She shoved me into the empty room and shut the door. "He told me one day that you might come in here looking flustered. If you asked to see his office, I needed to let you, but then tell you this: *Use the guest network. You'll find the one.*"

"*Use the guest network*? What the fuck does that mean?"

Sammi shut her eyes and took a deep, shaky breath. "When he told me, he made me memorize it and practice saying it but didn't give me any context. I can tell you he looked serious. He always was when he talked about you and Logan."

"Guest network?" I repeated like an idiot.

"We have internet set up, and sometimes, we'll have a guest network if we have a third-party vendor come in for a presentation. The big bosses don't want to risk our network being hacked, so we never let nonemployees use it. Maybe that's what he means." She glanced over her shoulder, hunching as she looked down the hall. "I don't know what's going on, but Ethan was weird the past two months. Something big is brewing. I can feel it in the bones of this place."

I nodded because I, too, knew something weird was going on; I just had no fucking idea what. "Thank you again."

"Of course. Ethan's the best boss I've ever had." She smiled at me, lines forming around her eyes, and I knew in my gut I could trust her.

"Is there somewhere I could hide where there aren't any cameras?"

"Hmm." She tapped her finger against her chin. "There's a mother's room on one of the floors and the bathroom, obviously." She clicked her tongue before she stood straighter. "Shit. I gotta get back. Good luck, Marissa."

She quickly ran out of the room, smoothing down her gray skirt before sitting at her desk.

I was alone but not without a plan. *Guest network, Ethan? Let's go.*

While Sammi was otherwise occupied, I snuck behind her desk. *God bless her.* The woman was organized to a T. Labeled, clear as day, was a set of hooks: *Company Cars.* I snatched the first key I could find. I couldn't fulfill Ethan's request about Paulson and the LLC. Not now. My time here was running out.

Ethan had told me he'd sit in his car in the parking garage and answer emails there because he'd be interrupted less. My father demanded such excellence—he made sure there was enough internet to be used anywhere on the property.

Well, hiding out in a car sounded pretty damn good right now. Plus, if I had to make a quick getaway, I could. I'd just buckle Logan into the seat with me and pray.

My shirt stuck to my back, and if anyone really stared, they'd see the pit stains forming all the way down to my ribs.

Get to the parking garage.

The dull sounds of chatter filled the air, the occasional click of a heel or rolling of a suitcase echoed on the fancy tile. I felt like an easy target, exposed to everyone in the open foyer. I walked faster, my burner phone buzzing in my pocket. That would have to wait.

My pulse echoed in my ears as I approached the sleek black door to the garage. There was no sound as I pushed it, my breath lodging in my goddamn lungs as I spotted the company cars to the right.

The key chain read *VEHICLE 10*, and god bless this place—it sat less than ten yards from me. A car screeched somewhere else in the garage, the sound stilling me as I imagined the worst case. *They're coming for us.*

I unlocked the door and jumped in, setting Logan on the passenger-side seat. Then I waited. Just to be sure no cars were appearing behind us. We were situated between two other company cars and shielded from the main view, so unless they were looking specifically at this vehicle, we were safe.

Now show me what you got, Ethan.

After giving Logan a box of Goldfish, I got out my new laptop and tried connecting to the guest network. There were so many options.

Too many.

Hawkins 5G

Hawkins Employee

Guest

Tom's iPhone

Kimmys5gspot

Fuck.

But then I saw it.

Evan Dubb Network.

Evan W. Evan Williams. Our joke names for each other. I typed in the address where we lived and *holy fucking shit.*

I was in.

Not two seconds later, a chat box popped up in the corner of my screen. Almost like an instant message from back in the day.

Margarita, is that you? It's me.

CHAPTER TWENTY-SEVEN

Monday, 10:15 a.m.—Two days "found"

What's going on? I typed into the pop-up notification, feather-like prickles dancing around my neck and spine. If Ethan had set this guest network up, then had he been waiting for me to sign on? Relief flooded me, my limbs collapsing with joy that I could finally talk to him. Not in person, but in chat. After all this time. Maybe I'd get some real answers. All thousand questions I had swirled like a damn pinwheel.

> Can we talk about your dad? Were you able to get the information on my desktop?

Okay then. I bit my hangnail to the point of blood. Right to business. No *are you okay* or *are you alive* or *how's Logan* or *I'm sorry I put you through this.* He wanted information.

He had to mean the folders with Malinowski and my name on them. Irritation made my jaw tense as I typed back, Yes.

> Send it to me. It's urgent.

Yeah, no shit, Ethan. This whole thing was urgent. God, why did he need these so badly? Was there a countdown? A clock? A hostage situation?

Fuck, what if there *was* a hostage situation . . . ? I shook away the thought. That woman might be his sister and those boys his nephews, but that secret part of his life had never crossed mine in the last ten years, until now. If my dad or brother or *Dennis* found out, though . . .

Are your sister and her kids okay?

Fine. The files, Marissa. Now.

The tone. He must be stressed as hell to be this bossy.

He'd set this whole thing up—the network, the clues—and sending the files was the least I could do to help him, because I did want to help my husband. Even if he had lied about his family, it was clear my dad and brother were up to shady shit. Dennis too. And for some foolish reason, I believed there was a possible scenario at the end of . . . this . . . where Logan kept his dad and I wasn't fully betrayed. It was unclear what that looked like, but I held on to that 2 percent of hope. Because without that hope, I wasn't sure if I would survive.

He wanted the files. I could do that.

I cracked my knuckles before checking both side mirrors and signing in to my Google Drive, desperately praying that the folders had uploaded in time before I spilled water on his computer. What a fucking miracle that the water damaged the computer. It was a long shot, but seeing Dennis's rage had been worth it. I tapped my finger against the side of my laptop when the drive loaded, but something tugged at me.

My scalp tingled, and I paused my urgent clicking. Something wasn't right. I craned my neck to make sure no one was creeping up on the car and even started the engine just in case I had to make a quick getaway.

The files hadn't been on his desktop; they had been on the hidden SD card. Ethan would remember that. That meant . . . *fuck*.

It wasn't him.

Think. I wanted to toss my fucking laptop out the window and run it over, but I couldn't alert the fake Ethan that I'd caught on. If it was my dad, Peter, or Dennis . . . wait.

The tone. I read it again, and it was the same condescending tone as my dear father. Marissa. Now.

Totally him.

It didn't work. The copy didn't go through.

What do you mean? You didn't save them?

Again, the Ethan I knew would've asked what happened. He would've wanted to know the process to see how the end resulted.

With my dad, the blame went straight to me.

I was almost caught. I had to destroy your device. I'm sorry, but they didn't catch me.

I needed those files, Marissa. To save us.

Where are you? Can I come to you?

Even though my gut told me this wasn't Ethan, the clues to *get* me here had all been from him. So that meant either my dad had gotten really smart about my inside jokes with Ethan, or he'd hacked into this network Ethan had set up.

Or, the third option, which hadn't hit me until right this second, was that Ethan was in trouble. I'd assumed when they all took off earlier, it had been due to the Malinowski email, but did I have any proof of that?

The timing was suspicious, sure, but the red flags were waving in the wind. I got out the new phone that only Detective Luna had the number for, and saw I had a missed call from him. My stomach ached as I called him back immediately.

"This is Luna." He answered on the third ring.

"Hi, this is Marissa Creighton. I'm worried something happened to Ethan."

"Weren't we from the start?"

"Yes. Well, no. I'm afraid my dad, brother, or Dennis Paulson have him or are going to hurt him or something." I spoke too fast, my sentence running on like I'd had way too much to drink. It seemed urgent and important the detective understand the severity of the situation. "I'm at the office, and they—"

"You're at the office? Why?" His tone sharpened, making my gut twist uncomfortably. "I called to tell you not to head there."

"To search Ethan's things. To try and get information from what clues Ethan left me. But I think something's wrong. This chat feature he installed, it's not him."

"Catch me up. What you're saying doesn't make sense."

I brought him up to speed on the morning's activities, minus the part about sending the fake email about Malinowski, just as "Ethan" responded.

Not yet. I need those files, Mar.

"Whoever is chatting as him knows enough but not everything. Are you able to get eyes on my family?" I wasn't sure if that was a real thing he could do, but I had to try. "Maybe call them into the station immediately or something?"

He sighed. "I could arrange for an update at the station within an hour."

I nodded, even though he couldn't see me. The question nagged at my mind, and with the overwhelming sense of time running out, I asked, "Did you know about his father? Ethan's father? He used to work for my parents and was arrested for exploiting customers?"

The detective was silent. "We made that connection, yes."

"He's in jail. Ethan's family is alive, not dead, like he told me all these years. My dad insinuated Ethan is doing the same thing as his dad, stealing information, and that's why he fled."

"There has been no evidence of that, Marissa."

Hearing him state those words settled the minor debate in my gut. My dad had planted the doubt to rattle me, and I'd fallen for it yet again. He'd gaslit and lied to me for years, so why would it change now? I handed Logan his sippy cup as I asked the other question on my mind: "In your opinion, *why* would someone keep their past identity a secret?"

"I can't speculate on Ethan's reasons, but I promise you, we're digging into it. There are things I can't share with you yet, but I want you and your son safe. Can you leave the office and go somewhere out of town for a few days?"

"I don't have any money or a car seat for Logan." I wanted to pout—he'd kept crucial information from me! But I also hadn't shared everything. My missing bag had the keys to Ethan's car—leaving me stranded again.

"We can arrange for an officer to pick you up from there within thirty minutes and bring you to the station. Would that work?"

"Yes." My shoulders slumped in relief of soon getting out of this parking garage. It was creepy, dimly lit, and had me on edge. "Detective, what's your theory on all this? The secret past? The hidden family? Him disappearing intentionally? My dad trying to frame him like his father?"

"My guess is that Ethan was trying to expose something at Hawkins and didn't feel safe enough to do it with his current situation. I can't confirm that, but that's my gut talking. Now, I appreciate you connecting the dots, but after the fire at your house, I need you to back off and let me do my job."

I nodded again, clearing my throat before replying, "Yes, sir."

Something chaotic went off in the background, like people yelling, and he sighed. "I gotta go. I'll call you when there's an officer out front."

He hung up, leaving me alone again with the chat box. He wanted me to be safe and to stop searching. Well, I would, once I got out of here. Until then, it was back to talking to fake Ethan in code.

How do I know you're Ethan? I've already been lied to by everyone I love.

There, play the emotional card. My dad hated that shit.

Casio.

My heart leaped in my throat at the mention of the song name, but it fell just as fast as I remembered the note had been left in the company car. That was information my dad and brother knew.

More.

While I waited for the other side to respond, I went to my drive and sucked in a breath at the two files sitting there. I double-clicked on *MARISSA*.

There were ten varying files listed. Some audio, some video. I did the same for the other one, and holy shit—videos and files galore. At least fifty of them.

I clicked on the first one; an image of a large black-haired man with a gnarly beard came up. His face was sweaty, his eyes frantically looking around the room he was in. He seemed familiar, but I couldn't quite place him. My neck tensed as I hit Play, my grip tightening on the device as I prepared myself for whatever I was about to see.

"They fucking know. They're gonna get me, I swear." He gulped and took a shaky breath, looking into the camera directly. "I made copies of everything, all the proof needed to put Franklin and Dennis away, but it might not be enough to save me. How fucked that my choices are death or rotting in jail like Roux."

He took a drink of water and some spilled down his beard. "If you're watching this, have a plan. They are ten fucking steps ahead, even more. God, they're gonna kill me and get away with it. How many others have been in this spot, vulnerable and waiting for fate? I wanted a tech job to make money and start a life. Not . . ." He cringed. "The shit they made me do. Maybe I deserve what's coming my way."

I noted the date—three years ago, a week or two before the camping trip. Wait . . . was this Christopher Malinowski? He looked nothing like the photos from the press around his death. God, my entire body shivered with a bone-deep fear. The terror in his voice shook me to my core, rattling my soul. He'd spoken about my dad like he was a murderer, but that was . . . fuck. It wasn't as unbelievable as it would've been a week ago.

I breathed deeply, forgetting I was waiting on a response from Ethan, and by the time I clicked back, the chat box was gone.

Then, before I could watch another video, the screen went black.

CHAPTER TWENTY-EIGHT

Monday, 11:00 a.m.—Two days "found"

The knock on the window was enough to make me scream. My mom's face was *right* there, with her painted lips and pretty smile. "Honey, open the door."

A million thoughts raced through my head, like how the *fuck* was she here? How had she found me? *Why* was she here? I stared at her, frozen in place like a mouse caught in a trap. She rattled the door handle so hard, the metal made a screeching sound.

Before I could engage the lock, she yanked the door open and moved her gaze from my head, to my outfit, to the black computer screen in my lap. Then it darted to Logan.

She looked so out of sorts with her burnt-orange flared dress, perfectly done hair, and her sweet perfume tingling my nose. She had no place being wedged between company cars in a dark parking garage. Alarm bells went off in my gut, but I didn't know what they meant. *Why is she here?*

"Look at you." She clicked her tongue in disappointment and reached for the laptop with her manicured hands. She gripped the sides of the screen before my limbs lost their temporary numbness.

I tightened my hold and held it firmly. "No."

She narrowed her eyes, just slightly, like she would when Peter or I annoyed her as kids. "You're a mess. You can't come into the office looking like this, not when our family name is plastered everywhere. We have a reputation to uphold, and you're ruining it." The muscle in her jaw twitched, and she tried taking the laptop again.

I shook my head, reverting back to my stubborn teenage self. "Mom, no."

"I'm not taking your precious laptop, Mar. I'm trying to get you up so we can fix your appearance." She closed the device, and I finally let her slide it off my lap. She set it on the roof of the car, and I released a pent-up breath.

She didn't take it and sprint off into the dark garage. Not that she would in her kitten heels, but the thought was there. A lot of irrational thoughts were there. Did my dad have her watch me? Had she been following me the entire day or just at the office?

I wasn't foolish enough to think *not one* camera had seen me grab the keys and come into the garage. They had eyes everywhere. But my mom? This was a lot. Made me twice as nervous about what happened to Ethan. The screen going black after that video . . . god, that video.

The way Christopher had spoken about my dad.

"Why are you here?"

"Me? I should ask you the same question. I even took Logan's car seat, and you still came? That is foolish, Marissa. Now get up. I'll hold my grandson so you can put yourself together."

"No!" I blurted before wishing I could take it back. "I'm just . . . so much has happened, I'm paranoid, okay? Detective Luna said an officer is coming to pick me and Logan up to go to the station soon."

"Then you're getting cleaned up before you represent this family like a slob. Being distressed doesn't grant you freedom to let yourself go. Your father and I assumed you'd be at the house, resting, showering, so we could make a press release together. Yet you took it upon yourself to make the wrong decision. We know what you should do, honey. Now get up. That's an order. After that, we'll have a little chat."

I held on to Logan tight, shouldering my bag and making sure the laptop was secure under my arm. She sounded like my damn father, patronizing me. And what was with *a little chat*?

"Like about why you're in the garage?"

"That, among other things." Her lips pursed into a fake smile as she reached over and ran a hand over my face. I held back a flinch. Her touch felt so foreign, so different and disgusting. "You are my beautiful, artsy, and sweet-souled daughter. I love you, Marissa. I love our family, always. You are my reason for existing."

Her words were one thing, but the underlying threat in her tone sent another wave of unease through me. I eyed my watch. It had been ten minutes since I called Luna—that meant I had to buy twenty minutes before an officer would show up and I could escape this extremely uncomfortable run-in with my mom.

We walked in silence toward the black double doors that returned us to the main building. Her shoes clicked on the pavement, and my shoes made an awful squeak, our differences becoming more apparent with each step. She pushed the doors open, her face transforming into a beauty queen smile, and she reached over to grip my wrist. "We're going to the bathroom, dear."

No one spared us a glance at first, but as we went farther into the foyer, everyone turned our way. Myriad echoes of *ma'am* and *Mrs. Hawkins* chorused from each of the workers, and she replied to them all by their first names.

It was equally impressive and shocking she knew them all—my mom tended to give the impression that she didn't give a shit about what my dad or brother did at work. The blasé comments about tech boring her when she could be off with her friends and doing charity events, or the wave of her hand every time they talked shop. *Oh, stop the boring talk. I'm sick of it.*

Yet she knew at least ten employees by name.

But my dad had owned this place for two decades. Maybe that's why. Christmas parties and holidays. Yeah. That made sense.

I was never invited, though.

I shook the confusing thoughts away. I had my own survival and my son to worry about, not the way my mom knew everyone.

I swallowed down the unease and turned toward the security guard I'd spoken with earlier. His eyes widened at me as my mom directed me with a tightening of her nails. I wasn't in a position to fight her, so I let her lead us into a bathroom.

She let go of me, stalked to the other wall, and pushed every stall door open with her hand, her bracelets clinking with the motion. "Good, it's empty."

She then waltzed by me and locked the door.

That little click was enough to make me stand straighter. "Mom, what are you doing? Why are you bolting me in here?"

"To protect us, honey. I don't want anyone walking in. Now, do you have clothes in your bag?" She took Logan from me and kissed the top of his head. She jutted her chin at the bag. "Get dressed."

I set the laptop down on the sink, making sure the counter wasn't wet, and set my bag next to it. With her and Logan visible in the mirror, I could see every movement. Not that I thought my mom would hurt my son, but I just wasn't sure who to trust anymore.

"Why did you take the car seat?"

"What are you going on about?" She brushed Logan's hair out of his eyes and adjusted the neckline of his shirt. It was wrinkled, and she definitely noticed.

I stood straighter, raised my voice. "You said you took Dad's car with Logan's car seat this morning. Why?"

Is she . . . trying to manipulate me? I blinked and kept going. "You didn't think to take out the car seat?"

"Someone set your house *on fire* last night, Marissa. You and Logan are in danger, and all I want to do is protect you both at our home, away from it all. You've been through so much, honey, it's incredible that you're still standing here, more confident than I've ever seen you.

Ethan leaving might be the best thing to happen to you. You've grown so much."

"But you didn't answer—"

"Now, you didn't want to come to your dad's office looking like a mess, did you? It would make him look bad, and we have worked so hard to build this business to what it is. Hours and years, and yes, you've had a stressful week, but image is everything."

Her voice was intense, but her cheeks were a little pink. She was getting flustered.

Interesting.

"I still don't know why you thought coming here was a smart choice. The stress must be making you irrational, and that's forgivable. Understandable, even. That's an easy excuse to explain this." She wasn't looking at me now. She stared over my shoulder.

Okay . . . Is she talking to herself . . . or a mic somewhere?

The hairs on my arms stood on end.

"I wanted to see Ethan's office. Not Dad's office. My *husband* is missing, Mom."

"Oh, the guy who had a *secret* identity? The guy who will end up in jail, just like his father?" She pursed her lips, clearly having opinions on the matter. "Your father told me everything, obviously. Graham Roux. Such a shame. It's telling, though, that your husband didn't mention his past life to you. I'd say that sort of betrayal isn't worth fixing. What kind of woman would go back to her husband after a decade of lies? What kind of woman would forgive him for stealing from *her family's* company? It can't happen."

I gulped, the nugget of fear multiplying by the second. My mom never spoke to me like this. She mostly twisted my words and made me feel small. Stupid. *Just like Dad does.* No more. I wasn't that Marissa anymore. "I'd like to hear Ethan's side of the story."

"What side? He lied to you, to us, for *years*. He could've tried to take down the company! Don't you see that? He could've done significant damage to your dad's business with a revenge scheme or selling secrets. I certainly can't forgive him for lying about who he was all this time, not when his criminal father is behind bars for what he did to people. To think he was with us all the time! No, I refuse to have that around my family. We don't need that kind of garbage."

"The father of *my son* is garbage?"

Logan whimpered, clearly upset at the growing tension.

"Listen to yourself!" Her voice rose for the first time since all this happened. Her rattled mannerisms scared me more than everything else because she *never* lost her cool. "You're worried about your heart. I get it. It hurts. I know the feeling, Mar. I've been heartbroken too. Lied to, sure. But this is bigger than your little marriage. Lo will have enough people in his life loving and supporting him. Ethan *won't* be missed."

"You're speaking like you know what happened to him, Mom." My own voice chilled as I slid out of my dirty shirt and slipped into a fresh black one. "You holding back on me? Do you know where my husband is?"

Her eyes clouded. "What are you insinuating?"

"Thought that was pretty clear. You've locked me in here and written Ethan out of our lives without allowing for a possibility of an explanation. Makes me curious why you're speaking in past tense."

She blinked, twice, and then she was back to herself. "Regardless of what happened or will happen to Ethan, he won't be walking back into our family because of the lies. I refuse to allow that, and your father . . . psh, he'll lose his position at the company for what he wants to do to Ethan. This could cost us everything here."

Nothing about me or Logan. Just the business.

The shell around my heart hardened. "What if he has a good reason for the lies?"

She arched a brow, clearly taken aback by that question. She shifted Logan from one hip to the next and stared at me with a new light. "Your father always underestimated you. I told him not to, that just because you weren't like your brother didn't mean you weren't intelligent."

"Thanks for the vote of confidence." I put on deodorant, fixed my hair into a braid, and put on new jeans. Immediately, I felt better. Black pants, black shirt. Black parts of my soul where each member of my family had created a hole. "I've learned a lot about myself the past week."

"Well, please share, since you're taking that tone." She scoffed and glanced at the locked door.

Was she waiting for someone to join us? Or barge in? I didn't like the way she moved with rigid limbs.

"I can piece things together despite all the *lies*. Ethan wasn't the only one keeping things from me. Isn't that true, Mom? There are all sorts of things Dad, Peter, and you know that I don't."

Her blush increased. "Business doesn't pertain to you, of course."

"You all made *sure* of that. You don't think Ethan shared things with me?" I applied some lip gloss, taking my time and watching her in the mirror. It was subtle, but I got exactly what I wanted: a reaction from her. Her cheek twitched. Just enough to let me know she was worried.

She *desperately* wanted to know what Ethan had told me.

"I'm sure he shared things, but without context, you wouldn't understand. An offhand comment means nothing without the full picture."

"Mm-hmm." I pursed my lips, popped them, and smiled at her. "Does the name *Malinowski* mean anything to you? Do you have enough context for that?"

Caught ya. Her *deer in the headlights* look told me all I needed to know.

"I'd like my son back." I eyed her, steeling my shoulders back with courage I hadn't had before. The tide had turned. It might've been foolish, but I'd laid a significant card on the table, and it was her turn. She didn't know what I knew, and I wasn't even sure myself, but that name was enough to send alarm through *everyone* in my family.

She stilled, swallowed hard enough for me to hear, and gripped him tighter. "Do you think I'm a *danger* to your son? My grandson?"

"I think I'd like to hold on to *my* child now." I stepped toward her, my mind already sizing her up. She was a petite woman. Never really worked out and had always been slim. I could elbow her in the neck if I had to, and she'd be bruised. I could pull her earrings, her necklace, or her hair to stall her.

I'm planning to physically hurt my mom?

What was happening to me?

"No need to be so dramatic. Here I was, complimenting you, when you treat me like this, like I'm the villain here. It's not like I've kept an identity from you, Mar, or left you and Logan in the dark without help." She gave me Logan, and once he was secure against my side, I kissed his head.

If someone were to come through the door, I'd be able to protect Logan. That brought me comfort. "Can we be real now?"

"Were we faking it before?" She crossed her arms for a second before shifting and adjusting her diamond earrings. So erratic. She stared at the door again, and I searched the bathroom for anything that could be a weapon. Paper towels? The air freshener? That could work if I sprayed it in someone's face.

It wasn't likely I could fight in here, if it came to that, but I still wasn't sure *why* my mom felt like a threat.

"You don't want Ethan found." I bounced Lo on my side. His nap time was damn near approaching, and he'd have a full fit soon. "I'm still figuring out *why*, but he knew something. Something big. I think that's why he left and you all want him to stay gone."

"After all the lies, of course I don't want him back in my family, and Marissa, if he was like his father, stealing company secrets . . . we can't have him sell people's data. It would be horrible, and we can't have that on our conscience. Last time, it was horrible, and it still eats at me."

"He knew something, and he wanted me to figure it out."

She gulped again just as a loud pounding hit the door.

"Mrs. Creighton, are you okay? I'm Officer Rogers. Detective Luna sent me."

"Yes," I replied. "Could I have another minute?" Then I narrowed my eyes at my mom, disgust weaving down my spine and twirling with apprehension. The *hate* on her face startled me. She'd never looked at me like that in my entire life, and it felt like little knives poking my skin. I lowered my voice so the cop wouldn't hear me. "I'm going to find out what it is."

"You shouldn't be in this game. I can't protect you anymore. None of us can. That's what this has been about, Mar. Protecting you and Logan. You're too innocent, too sweet for this."

"Well, it's a little late for that, isn't it?" I arched a brow, tossing gasoline on the fire. "I've seen the videos he left for me. Feel free to pass that on to Dad. And cut the *protecting* bullshit. None of you treat me with respect, so you can fuck right off with that."

With that, I unlocked the door and met the officer. I wasn't brave or bold. I let life pass me by most of the time, but not anymore. I was taking charge.

I knew something about my parents—they messed up when they were angry. And I'd pissed them the hell off.

"We're heading to the station for a bit, okay? Everything all right in there? The security guard told me to hurry and get you out."

"Oh, just my dear mother locking me in the bathroom." I plastered on a fake smile just as my original phone buzzed in my bag. I pulled it out and eyed the screen as we stepped into the foyer, and my momentary joy evaporated at the text I got.

ANONYMOUS: They got him. They got my brother. What did you do, Marissa?

CHAPTER TWENTY-NINE

Monday, 12:00 p.m.—Two days "found"

What did I do? Please. The rush to defend myself outweighed the sinking rocklike feeling in my stomach as the meaning of the text hit me. *They got him.*

Ethan.

Who had him?

"We've arranged for you and your son to be safely transported. Are either of you hurt or injured that I should know about?" the officer asked, his tone concerned. His eyebrows furrowed into a deep line as he stared at us for a beat.

"We're fine."

Ethan probably wasn't fine. Inside, I certainly wasn't fine, but I couldn't get my mouth to form more than that simple answer. I quickened my pace, and he mirrored me, so we were soon near the exit. The security guard I'd spoken to earlier straightened at our approach, and I swore his shoulders sagged with relief.

"Mrs. Creighton, glad to see you're okay." His eyes widened, and he looked over his shoulder, worry written on his face.

"Thank you for *everything*." I held his gaze for a second too long, hoping he got the weight of my gratitude. He clearly knew more about

Ethan's dad *and* had enough suspicion to send the officer to the bathroom where my mom had locked us in. If the time came, I had a gut feeling he'd be a character witness to some of the madness that happened around here.

Now I needed to text Hailey back and find out what the hell was going on.

It had been hours since I changed Logan, and I used the back of the police car to quickly put him in a clean diaper. The poor kid had been an angel today, clearly reading the atmosphere around him and behaving better than normal. The love I had for him had no bounds. We got him into the car seat that the officer had brought, buckled in and safe, and then we were on the road.

Finally, I was getting away from the damn office and my family. The arrogant, shiny building disappeared from view, and I stared at the text on my phone, my heart in my throat as worry for Ethan tripled.

Yes—he'd lied to me and had enough secrets to ruin us.

Yes—I still wanted him alive.

Yes—he could be doing something illegal or wrong, but after learning how horrible my family was . . . was it forgivable?

Hope didn't make me weak or mean I was thinking with my heart, as my mom had said. A full-body shiver took over, and I trembled. The way my mom had spoken about him, in the past tense, like his lies were a personal betrayal to her. It had surpassed weird and gone straight to worrying.

Marissa: What do you mean, "they"? How do you know?

Hailey: He was supposed to text back forty minutes ago and never did.

Marissa: Well, he hasn't responded to me in days, Hailey.

Hailey: He left to meet you at the office. Said you'd follow the steps. Did you see him?

Marissa: I never saw him. Are you sure?

Hailey: Yes, I'm fucking sure. Had a way to get into the parking garage.

I gulped down a breath to calm myself. Everything felt weak—my legs, knees, lungs. He had a way to get into the parking garage. *Was he there the whole time and didn't approach me?*

Did he not want to approach me, or did something happen?

When I thought something felt off . . .

Sweat beaded on my lip, and I wiped it off, mistyping three times before I could settle down and get it right.

Marissa: He set up a secure network for us to chat but it felt off, like it wasn't him on the other end. The words weren't right.

Hailey: Your family has him. I know it. Fucking Hawkins ruining the men in my life.

Marissa: I want to find him alive, but I need you to tell me what his plan was.

Hailey: To ruin your family. Destroy the last name Hawkins for all the shit they did to us, and to others. They'll continue to get wealthy by screwing with others' privacy.

Marissa: So he waited ten years to do this?

Hailey: It took that long to find what he needed.

Marissa: Which is?

Hailey: Evidence.

Marissa: To what? Work with me here. We're on the same team.

Hailey: No, we're not. Your family needs to pay, and you're one of them. Why do you think he lied to you? He wasn't supposed to stick around this long. You were just a target, all right? An easy way to get an in with the family.

I was a target. A way in. No, there was no way . . . I shook my head hard, my temples throbbing. It had been in the back of my mind ever since my dad mentioned Ethan's father used to work for the company, but seeing it written down? Horrendous. The most disgusting, vile feeling of betrayal coursed through me. It made it real.

Marissa: There's no way. We met in college.

Hailey: Yeah, because he staged running into you. The day in the record store holding The Decemberists album? Yeah. Planned. He followed you and learned what you liked to make you fall in love with him. Your entire life together was just a waiting game for him to get revenge for our dad, prove his innocence. It just took longer than he wanted.

I swayed, left to right, like I'd twirled in fifteen circles and suddenly stopped. The world shifted underneath me, ice cracking on a frozen lake and submerging me into the deathly cold waters. I'd never expected the truth to be twice as horrible as the scenarios in my head. He didn't just want a divorce. He wasn't just having an affair. He hadn't just lied about his family's past. He'd been *using* me. To get revenge?

My stomach rolled, and I frantically searched for the button to roll down the window. There wasn't one. I was in the back of a police car because Logan and I weren't safe, all the fault of the people I trusted and loved the most. "Could you—you open the window, please?" I barely got the words out.

"Sure thing."

He cracked it a few inches, and I took a deep breath of fresh air, needing to ground myself in the moment. The urge to go deep into my mind, forgetting all this and escaping into the world of a song, was strong. To say *to hell with it.* Pretend I didn't suspect my family, that I didn't care about what shit they did, and let them baby me and Logan. Ethan had *used* me.

God, of all the questions to ask . . . I was weak. Pathetic. But I had to know.

Marissa: Was his plan to leave me and his son when it was done?

Hailey: Logan complicated it. I'm not sure what he was going to do anymore.

Logan complicated it. The words bolded in my brain, underlining themselves as I thought back to all the *weirdness* that had occurred since I found out I was pregnant.

Obviously, I'd be easier to leave if it were just me. A child made things more difficult. I glanced over at our son, who had Ethan's eyelashes and personality.

Was it all fake? Did I even know my husband anymore, if it had all been an act to *use* me to get near my family? The jokes? The laughs?

Nothing had ever split my soul into two before. Not like this. It was almost too much to recover from. I'd been fighting for my family, but now? Who was my family anymore? Once I got access to my wallet or reissued a credit card, Logan and I could leave this mess—just the two of us. Start over somewhere.

Tears prickled my eyes even after all that had happened; these felt different. I'd read once that tears had their own makeup depending on what incited them. Utter heartbreak had caused these, and for a second, I wondered what they looked like. Would they be achingly beautiful, or would they show the destruction happening in my soul?

Hailey: This is bigger than you. If you even hope to keep Ethan in your life, you need to find him. Your family had to have something to do with it.

I needed to respond to her, put on a front that I wasn't falling apart. It seemed important. Maybe it was the smugness about her when we'd met at the restaurant or her lack of helping at all. She felt she had a leg up, and she did—and I didn't want her to think me weak.

Marissa: I have nothing to do with what my family does. Ethan knows this. You should too. We both want Ethan alive. Now do you have the evidence or know what it was about?

God, my heart raced to the point where my ears throbbed and my neck hurt. His sister was being so difficult. Did she have the evidence needed? I'd seen the video from Christopher Malinowski, the fear on his face naming my family, the dread of the reality facing him.

Marissa: What evidence did he find? Did those files he saved for me contain it?

Hailey: You have the files?????

Marissa: Not sure yet. My computer was hacked when I clicked on the first one.

Hailey: Fuck! Your family has him, I can feel it. You need to figure out where they have him. He's never ghosted me in ten years. TEN YEARS. And nothing now? He'll die, and that's on you. Your family has been silencing people to protect their secrets for years. Just ask Hannah Theroux, Veronica Gage, Beatrice Hernandez.

Those names . . . they were familiar. Where had I seen them? I squinted, my knuckles aching from how hard I held the phone. They felt like old acquaintances you went to school with, that you'd connect with on Facebook years later—wait.

Facebook.

Ethan's small friend list with random women. Fuck. *My family silenced people?*

Did that mean *kill*?

And *people*? *PEOPLE*, as in plural?

My brain couldn't comprehend the words despite understanding their meaning. I was past the point of being a fool—Logan and I couldn't afford it. So I had to accept the possibility that what she was saying was true.

Even if it disgusted me and clashed with everything I knew.

Marissa: Are you sure?

Hailey: Jesus. YES!!! Stop being annoying. Talk to your dad. Find out where he is.

Marissa: I'll try and find out something.

"Do you or your boy need to stop for anything before we get to the station?"

"Wh-what?" I jerked my head up and met the officer's gaze in the rearview mirror. He repeated the question as heat flooded my face. "Oh, we're fine. Thank you."

He tapped the wheel, and I stared back at my phone like it was the map that led to the treasure. She needed to *work* with me, damn it.

Marissa: What evidence does he have? Does he have proof they killed someone? If he does, you might be right about what lengths they'd go to.

She typed but never sent anything. That went on for five minutes, and I slammed my head against the back seat. It was clear she wasn't going to be my ally.

My mind stewed for the rest of the drive, trying to imagine the reality she lived in. If someone had framed *my* dad . . . would I have gone to this extent for revenge? Did it make me horrible to know I wouldn't?

Sacrifice and pretend to be with someone for a decade to find evidence? That took some drastic dedication. I chewed my lip as the officer parked the unit. The air cooled my skin when I was let out, and I took a deep breath. I'd asked for this to happen, for all of us to meet at the station.

That meant seeing my family . . . the ones Ethan's sister insisted had killed or silenced people.

"We'll let you sit in one of the unoccupied rooms until Detective Luna gets here. He wanted you to have a moment to yourself before you debrief."

I nodded and hoisted the car seat with a sleeping Logan. It was time I shared everything with the detective—the names of the women, the accusations, the money, the file I'd seen. He was the only potential ally I had left. My throat ached like I'd swallowed metal darts, but I kept my head high as we walked down the sterile hallway, and the officer led me into a beige room with windows. He gave a polite smile before shutting the door, and Logan and I were finally alone.

In a safe place.

Not a hotel or a parking garage or my childhood bedroom.

The first thing I needed to do was check if those files were still there. I held the power button down for a few seconds, hoping it would restart the device, and when the familiar hum of electricity filled the silent room, I almost cheered.

My device isn't trashed.

I immediately scanned for Ethan's song, and he played **"I Escaped" by Jason Ray McKenzie**. Relief flooded me. He was safe, somehow.

Out of habit, I clicked on Ethan's profile and noted he'd created a new playlist that morning: "MARISSA—First Letter."

Goose bumps prickled over my forearms as I clicked it.

First letter . . . I chewed my lip and scanned the entire list of songs. Okay, this was something people did online sometimes, left clues with titles and bolding the first letter.

Why not spell it out, though? Why not *name* the playlist what I needed to know? Why make me jump through hoops every day since this shitstorm had started?

"Sígueme y Te Sigo" by Daddy Yankee.

"Enemy (with JID)" by Imagine Dragons and JID.

"All Star" by Smash Mouth.

"Redbone" by Childish Gambino.

"Cold Heart - PNAU Remix" by Elton John, Dua Lipa, and PNAU.

"HeadBand (feat. 2 Chainz)" by B.o.B. and 2 Chainz.

"THATS WHAT I WANT" by Lil Nas X.

"E" by Matt Mason.

"Ride Wit Me" by Nelly and City Spud.

"MAMIII" by Becky G and KAROL G.

"Rap God" by Eminem.

"One Right Now (with The Weeknd)" by Post Malone and The Weeknd.

"Vegas" by Doja Cat.

"Electric Feel" by MGMT.

"Roar" by Katy Perry.

SEARCH TERM ROVER.

What the fuck?

I gritted my teeth and opened up my drive, annoyed Ethan's playlist didn't help at all. God, he'd spent time doing that while I was searching his office? He couldn't have just called the damn phone and told me what to do? He had to have known I was struggling.

God, the room smelled like stale soda and fries. It made my stomach roll.

While it was safe, I felt stifled.

My shoe made a consistent tapping sound against the tile as I waited for my files to load. *File uploaded at 9:40 a.m.*

A bitter taste entered my mouth before it hit me.

The truth *smashed into me.*

It felt like a shot of espresso.

I knew what I had to do! God, Ethan was a genius.

The timing was *perfect*—something had happened to him . . . which he might've predicted.

Ethan had known that the chat box wasn't safe and had given me *this clue* to search.

So I did. I went into the folders I'd downloaded from his SD card and searched *ROVER*.

A file came up.

I double-clicked it.

CHAPTER THIRTY

Monday, 1:00 p.m.—Two days "found"

The video was grainy, dark, and gray. My dad sat in the corner of an office, not his current one, but the same building. Dennis was there. So was Christopher Malinowski.

The atmosphere was tense, that was clear even through the video, but Christopher had a spark about him. It was in how he sat up straighter and seemed confident.

"I know your plans," Christopher said, intertwining his fingers like a villain and tapping his two pointers together three times. "You won't get away with it. Not after what I found."

"Stop speaking in code, Chris." My dad ran a hand over his jaw, his eyes narrowing at Dennis every other second like they were having their own internal conversation.

Dennis stood up and slowly walked behind Christopher, placing his hand on the shoulder of the chair. It was a sheer intimidation move. "Here's the thing—regardless of what you think you found, it won't hold up."

"You framed Graham Roux, Brandon Theroux, Jesus Hernandez, and Preston Gage. I have documents proving it. I sent them to others so if something were to happen to me, you'd still go down." Christopher puffed out his chest, smirking despite the sweat clearly forming on his hairline. He was a large man and not someone who could easily be physically restrained.

"Ah, but see, the thing is, son, we've noticed suspicious behavior on your device for weeks now. I started documenting some worrying things I saw. One of the many roles I play for Franklin is to monitor his staff's activity. You sent viruses to clients' personal devices. You hacked their cameras and watched them. You even caught some of them in nefarious positions, right? It was brilliant, honestly. Your student loans are piling up, and it'd be easy to blackmail them into getting a payout," Dennis said.

"Such a disappointment. That's not the Hawkins way, Chris. Our clients are our family. The trust we have with them is crucial for success. How else have I survived for two decades?" My dad paced the office and released a long dramatic sigh. One I'd heard him do many times. "We even reached out to local law enforcement for web crimes."

"No, you didn't. If that were true, I'd be brought in for questioning."

Shit. Christopher lost his attitude. His smirk. He glanced back and forth between the two of them, craning his neck to see Dennis behind him. "None of this is true. I've never done any of that."

"What's stronger—your word or the evidence I have from your IP address? Your workstation? Your emails encrypted to look like someone else?" Dennis clicked his tongue, and this time moved his hand to Christopher's shoulder. "Here's how it's gonna go: You're not going to say a word to anyone. You're going to quietly, discreetly leave the company in two weeks, and if we're feeling generous, we'll write you a nice letter of recommendation."

"You're forcing me to quit?"

"Not forcing you. Giving you a choice. Do as I said, or all your activities go public. Simple as that. You go to jail for decades and miss out on life. I think it's an easy choice, don't you?" Dennis looked at my dad.

"Is this what you did to all of them? Blackmailed them to keep their mouths shut? Framed them so they couldn't tell the truth?" Christopher jerked his shoulder out of Dennis's grip and bolted up from the chair. His eyes were wide now, panicked. His jaw tensed, and for one second, he looked directly at the camera.

The sheer intensity of his gaze made me jump in my chair, the loud metal legs screeching on the tile floor. Shit. This wasn't real time; this was the past.

Something moved in my peripheral vision, and I lifted my gaze to see my dad glaring at me through the window.

Fuck.

The man I'd known my entire life, now accused of blackmailing and *killing* others, stared back at me with emptiness in his eyes. Any trace of warmth that had been there the night before was gone. His gaze moved over my face, his jaw tightening with anger, and it landed on my laptop.

Rationally, I knew he couldn't *see* what I was watching, but in my gut, I knew he suspected the truth. Somehow, despite all the challenges, Ethan had succeeded in one thing for certain—the truth about my family getting out to me.

My dad tried opening the door with a loud bang. It wouldn't move, and he hit it harder with his shoulder, causing me to gasp.

No. All the blood left my face, a tingling feeling gripping me head to toe, but the door didn't open. Yet I didn't remember locking it.

His left eye twitched as my mom joined him, their mouths moving but no sound traveling through the window. Peter joined them a few seconds later, his entire face solemn and void of emotion. My *family* stood on one side, me and Logan on the other.

If looks could kill, my mom's would wound me the worst. The beauty queen lipstick was still there, but the sneer, the utter disgust on her face, clashed with her flared dress and perfect hair. She'd even donned a bright-yellow sheer scarf, the cheery color out of place.

It was the staredown of a lifetime—them and me. Peter looked the worst, his eyes downcast and his shoulders slumped. His demeanor screamed defeat, while my parents looked ready for war. If anything in the video was true, that meant my dad and Dennis had done this numerous times. They were pros. But my mom? I still wasn't sure where she fit in, but the hatred in her voice in the bathroom still rattled me.

Hailey's texts kept coming to mind, her insistence about them hurting Ethan getting louder and louder in my head. I had to know what they'd done to Christopher.

With their eyes on me, I clicked Play on the video again.

"Son, we have a solid business that's had a few rogue employees. It happens. You've heard stories about fucked-up teachers. There are always people you miss in background checks." Dennis kept talking, but I kept my eyes on the past version of my dad.

He followed Christopher's gaze and spun around, his forehead wrinkling as he searched for something. I knew the second he found the camera. "Fucking shit." He yanked the device off the wall, the video itself becoming like a roller coaster and hard to watch. My head spun with the camera.

"You son of a bitch."

The sick sound of flesh on flesh had me gripping my throat in fear. I couldn't see the image anymore, but the audio continued to play. God, this was messed up.

Clothing shuffling, more thuds. A chair rolling.

A moan.

Heavy footsteps.

"Take care of the device?" Dennis said, his voice strained like he'd overexerted himself.

"Done." My dad breathed heavier as he got closer to the camera. He put it in his pocket, and even though I knew, rationally, that Christopher had died outdoors, I still feared for what he'd gone through in the video. Squishes and muffled voices carried over the audio, like my dad was walking.

Maybe he was—at work. I closed my eyes and tried picturing what the sounds were. Footsteps, for sure. An elevator ping. Voices without clear words. It went on like this for minutes, and I skipped ahead, seeing if it got any clearer. I jumped to twenty minutes. Thirty minutes. Forty. Nothing.

It felt anticlimactic. Forcing myself to look braver than I was, I checked to see if they were still staring at me, but Detective Luna was there, talking to them.

My dad *laughed*, and my mom had her typical supportive-wife smile as she leaned onto my dad's shoulder. God, how performative were they? Minutes ago, they'd been plotting against me, I was sure. And now?

Anger curled itself along my spine, sending the most aggressive urge to hurt them. How *dare* they act like that when I knew the truth? My fist clenched just as the detective glanced my way. He held up three fingers—*three minutes.*

Then he led Peter, my mom, and my dad down the hallway and out of sight. I swore the stifling air felt warmer without their chilling presence.

I regretted calling this meeting. I didn't want to sit in a room with them or hear any of the shit they had to say. Plus, I had a feeling I knew *exactly* what route they were going to go.

Before doing anything else, I copied the file to the device's hard drive, shared it to my work email, the fake account I created, and even Hailey. After getting the email of the police department off their website, I sent it to the station so they'd have a copy too. Christopher had died—circumstances unclear—and I owed it to him.

I had a minute left until I'd have to talk to my damn family, so I went to the audio files. I clicked one recorded the same day as the video file, but after the first minute, the audio stopped completely. I clicked on the next one, recorded with a different device, one my dad clearly didn't know about. There, I heard someone, loud and clear.

"You look like shit." My mom's voice had lost her usual saccharine twang. "Jesus, Franklin, don't go out in public like this. We have a reputation to uphold, per our vision."

"Shit got bad today. Dennis is taking care of it, but it was too close. We need to stop—this is the fourth attempt."

"No, you need a drink and to tell me what happened. We have a good thing going. We've mastered it, and funds are lucrative." Glasses clicked, and ice rattled. "Now, Franklin."

"Malinowski found proof about us framing some of the others. Threatening to expose them."

"And Dennis did his part?"

"Faking all the evidence against him? Yeah. That's easy. Have the files and everything packaged. This just feels different."

"Explain it to me."

God, my mom's urgent tone bothered me. She sounded desperate, angry, and honestly . . . in charge. It was so unlike her, the housewife who never spoke up or out of turn or raised her voice. *Let the men be men, Marissa.*

"He was smugger than the rest, like he had a trick up his sleeve, and then I found this goddamn camera!"

"Who knows where the fuck he recorded it or streamed it."

"You fools. Why were you in his office? You know better, Franklin."

"We were in mine. I don't know how it got there."

"You're getting sloppy." The sound of plastic hitting a hard surface had me envisioning her setting the camera on the counter. "Malinowski, the overweight programmer. Married. One kid. Eats brussels sprouts all the time and stinks up the lunchroom?"

"Him, yeah. He's good. Smart."

"Everyone who works at Hawkins is smart. It's about being smarter than them. It's about being superior and better. We are the best, Franklin. Never forget that. Now, how much damage can he do?"

Holy shit. *Superior. Better.* I rocked back and forth on the chair, the vile feeling seeping in my veins. Who was my *mother*? I had never heard her speak to my dad like this, ever. She sounded . . . evil.

"If the video gets out, some. He made it seem like he had proof of numerous people."

"*Seem* is one thing. He's bluffing."

"I'm not sure, hon."

"Did anyone see him leave your office?"

"Dennis took care of that, wiped the tapes, ghosted in as him so it looks like he was working. We know the drill—it's this goddamn camera."

"Let me see his file. Does he have allergies to any drugs or food?"

"I'll pull it up."

There was silence before my mom let out something like a cheer. "He's going camping this weekend. Posted all about it online. Problem solved, Franklin. Just like the last time. I know what to do."

"Aren't you planning to go to a music festival with Marissa?"

I gasped. My name. I didn't want *my name* mentioned anywhere on this tape.

"Another fucking music festival? I'll cancel." Sounds of typing carried over. "There's a golf course two miles away from this campground. Have Dennis make it look like this outing has been planned for months. Do it immediately."

"God, I married well."

"Don't fuck this up. You handle your end, and I'll handle mine. In three days, Christopher Malinowski won't be a problem."

CHAPTER THIRTY-ONE

Monday, 1:20 p.m.—Two days "found"

"I Figured It Out" by Alan Silvestri played on my device before leaving the room, and sure enough, Ethan's current song updated.

"When Can I See You" by Babyface.

He played it for a minute, then switched again.

"Where Are Ü Now (with Justin Bieber)?" by Jack Ü, Diplo, Skrillex, and Justin Bieber.

Any worry that something had happened to him evaporated. I wasn't sure what his sister had hoped to gain by texting me in a panic, but Ethan was alive. My parents were here. Dennis . . . that was another situation to worry about later. For now, it was about my husband and my family.

"Police Station" by Red Hot Chili Peppers, I played back, my finger hovering over searching for another song, but I hesitated. Was I ready to face him? To have the hard conversation I wasn't sure my heart would survive? No. I sure wasn't emotionally, but that shell around my heart thickened. We had to talk. With a quick search, I found what I wanted:

"Please Come Here" by Y O U T H F O O L.

Not more than thirty seconds later, he replied:

"On My Way" by Alan Walker, Sabrina Carpenter, and Farruko.

My son slept on as our lives changed forever. I carefully put the laptop in my bag and shouldered it. Then I scooped my arm through the car seat and carried Logan out of the secure room and toward the hallway. This was the moment where I knew my life would never be the same. There was a new path for me. I was turning in my family.

Even Peter. My chest ached at the notion my brother was a part of this. Even though he always protected me . . . he was in this too. All these times of him telling me to cut off our parents, to get away from them, lingered in my heart. Had he been trying to save me this whole time? I just didn't know, and I couldn't trust my gut anymore.

"Marissa." Detective Luna spoke with an urgent tone, his voice pulling me from the temporary haze clogging my mind. "We're all in the conference room. Please, join us. So we can all get on the same page."

Join them? See their faces when I accuse them?

My pulse spiked, but then it settled. "Okay."

He placed a comforting hand on my shoulder. "Don't worry, you and Logan are safe here."

I appreciated his words, even though I knew we were. No more gaslighting, no more insults, no more making me feel foolish. *I had* the information needed to have this all make sense. Could I share everything with the detective right now in the hallway? Sure. Of course I could.

Or . . . I could say it in their presence. Make them sweat and see what lies they could come up with. How much could I disturb them now? Make them feel even a drop of the fear I had over the last seven days.

Old Marissa was gone.

"Everyone is waiting in here." The detective held the door to a small conference room, where I felt my parents' gaze before I saw them. I didn't cower or bow my head.

I met them head on.

My dad had sweat through his shirt, ruining his crafted image. My mom's hair was askew, like she kept running her hands through it. Peter looked sullen, as if he were at a funeral. When he saw me, he sucked in a breath and rushed toward me. "Mar, you're okay, thank Christ."

He smelled like body odor and gum as he hugged me. "Take my credit card and run," he whispered, digging his nails into my arm. He pulled back, his eyes twisted in misery as he nodded.

I nodded back as he slid the plastic card into my pocket, out of sight from everyone else.

"Why wouldn't your sister be okay, Peter? She's fine. Both she and Logan are just fine. Now, Detective, I know you called us here for an update, but we have a concern to bring up. It might be hard to hear, Mar, so if you want to sit down?" my mom asked. "We learned more about Ethan, er, Alexander."

"No. I'm good standing." The pulse at the base of my neck was erratic, almost painful.

"Okay. It'll be shocking news, so you might need support. That's what we're here for. We're always here to support our family." My mom stood, too, running her manicured finger over the table. "Franklin, would you share the latest with Detective Luna?"

"Sure." My dad cleared his throat, his gaze shifting from me to the detective. "Well, you already know we found evidence that Ethan has been stealing data from our clients and using it as blackmail. In our search for clues of where he went, we discovered he had hundreds of files and payments from clients, and we tracked down videos he stole. This is disgusting and unacceptable behavior. His father, Graham Roux, used to work for us, too, and did the same thing. We also learned he was sleeping with one of the managers there. Kelly. You've met her. She came forward this morning, worried that her unexpected pregnancy might be a motive for him to disappear. Mar, I'm so sorry—"

"Bravo." I clapped. A manic laugh escaped me. "Great performance."

My dad frowned. My mom sucked in a breath. The detective cracked one knuckle as he watched me. For the girl always in the background—the person who did the soundtracks for big moments, was never the lead actress—I was thriving in the spotlight. Four pairs of eyes bored into me, all with various forms of interest.

"Care to explain your dramatics?" my dad snapped.

"I'd love to." I shrugged, just as Logan stirred. Helping my son out of the car seat gave me something to do with my hands as I stood up for myself in the biggest way possible. "First off, Ethan—or Alexander—wasn't selling data. *You* do that, and then when an employee figures it out, you blackmail them to keep them quiet."

"Ridiculous." My mom snorted, so unladylike and out of character.

I arched a brow at her. "I'm not wrong, Mom. This might be hard for you all to believe because you've always made me feel like some dumb, incapable woman who can't understand technology, but I figured it all out. You framed Graham Roux. You framed numerous others. Dennis doctors the footage and paints the picture to fit your narrative. If the person tries to speak up, you remove them."

"You have no evidence of these claims! We shouldn't be talking about this when Dennis is probably after Ethan as we speak." My mom blinked a lot and hit my dad in the shoulder. "You told me Dennis had been acting weirder at work. Maybe this is all him? He's going rogue? He could be doing this all behind your back. I told you Dennis came on to me and I turned him down. He was furious. Spat at me!" My mom's voice was like that of a cartoon character at this point. "This might be his revenge, tarnishing your business and turning your own daughter against you!"

My dad nodded, his posture straightening as he leaned in to the lie. "Dennis has been erratic lately. And he's worked with us for years, but after he hit on my wife, things were different. If he wanted to hurt me, he'd go after my family. That means Marissa. So yes, Ethan is in grave danger. I don't have proof, but I have a feeling Dennis has hurt others in the past."

"Could we search for Dennis now? Send out a squad? It might already be too late." My mom's eyes gleamed, like she'd formulated a plan on the spot. She squeezed my dad's forearm in a perfect act of worry. "I hope Ethan is okay so we can ask questions."

"Ethan is just fine. Let's not pretend that's why you're worried." I kissed Logan's head as he reached for my mom. "No, baby, it's just you and me now. Gam Gam made some bad decisions."

"Marissa, knock this shit off. You don't understand anything!" she yelled.

"Sure, I do. You guys tried to frame Ethan for having affairs, and when that didn't take hold, you planted the seed that he was stealing data and selling it. Please. He sure as shit wasn't doing that, and you all know it. He found out the truth about you and knew what happened to those who spoke up."

"And what truth is that?" my mom asked, her voice filled with venom.

"Didn't you cancel another ridiculous fucking music festival so you could take care of Christopher Malinowski?"

The silence in the small conference room was painful. I heard every breath my mom took as she stared me down.

"We have evidence of this, Mr. and Mrs. Hawkins." Detective Luna sat forward, resting his elbows on the table. "Now is the time you should call in your family lawyer."

"This is bullshit. She's a mess. Have you seen her stained shirts and horrible hair? She's a disgusting mess. You choose to believe her, over us?

We're upstanding members of this town, have numerous foundations and scholarships to help underserved youth. Why would *we* ever take care of that horrible man? It's a good thing he's gone, with how much his blackmail hurt people!"

I couldn't stand this act. I shook my head and rocked Logan back and forth.

"You can stop anytime now, Mom, and call the lawyer. I have the files where you admit to killing Christopher Malinowski after framing him wasn't enough. I also have the video that will clear Graham Roux of the false charges. So enough of the *you don't understand* and *this is business* with me, because I got your asses."

"You're delusional." My mom seethed as someone tapped on the window.

The little hairs on my arm stood on end as I heard shuffling outside. I swore the particles in the air shifted when I turned around.

Sure enough, Ethan stood there, outside the window.

Then everything slowed like a scene in a movie. Sound distorted. My vision became a tunnel. The stale coffee smell blended into the background. And all I saw was Ethan. Or Alexander Roux.

"No. No way," someone whispered.

Ethan's gaze landed on me, and his entire body sagged as he squeezed his eyes closed. Then he opened them again. Shook his head, like he couldn't believe this was happening. My heart pounded against my rib cage like a woodpecker on a tree, but I didn't care. Ethan's lips parted, and then he smiled. A full grin that stretched across his handsome face, showcasing his white teeth and week-old beard.

He looked the same—trim, in shape, handsome. He wore dark jeans and a black fitted sweatshirt. His brown hair had the same messy curls, since he hadn't cut it in a few weeks, and my throat closed up. My instinct was to sprint toward him, throwing myself at him with the relief of him being here, safe, alive.

He disappeared on me.

He lied to me for ten years.

He used me.

"Marissa." My name. That's all he said, and my eyes welled up.

He stared at Logan, his eyes softening before his entire face crumpled. Seven days of hell. Seven days of mystery and questions, and he was here, in front of me, yet still out of reach.

I wanted to shout at him, cry, slap him, and hug him so tightly, he couldn't breathe.

"How the fuck is he here?" my dad asked. "I thought Dennis had him."

"Clearly he can't follow simple directions," my mom seethed. "Fucking idiot."

"This was always about protecting Marissa and Logan," Peter said. "That's what you're missing. This wasn't about you or Mom or your business. It was about Marissa and Logan, regardless of the past, and that's why he's here." Peter laughed, drawing my attention to him. "Mar, Ethan and I both did things that you might not forgive, but they were always about protecting you. Try and see that, even if it's hard."

"Peter, what are you saying? Have you been working with Ethan?" my dad asked, his voice breaking. "How dare you? You are my protégé! My firstborn!"

"Stop talking, Franklin. You'll make it worse," my mom whispered.

"Enough." Detective Luna stood and opened the door. "Alexander Roux?" His firm voice was nothing like the tone he used with me. "We need to talk. Come with me."

He spun around and pointed at my family. "Stay here, all three of you."

When I didn't move, he jutted his chin toward the hallway. I followed.

The door clicked shut, and I stood a foot away from Ethan. *Alexander.* The man I'd loved for a decade, who'd built our life on lies. My heart ached for him, while the anger simmered. He'd put us through this without a warning.

"Dadadada!" Logan cheered, reaching for him. I turned, blocking it.

Ethan frowned but nodded, like he understood. He took one of my hands, swiping a thumb over my palm slowly.

"Wait for me. *Please*, Marissa. I have no right to ask you to after all this, but we'll talk soon, okay?" His intense gaze pleaded with me, but he didn't give me a chance to do more than nod before he moved toward the detective.

Much like I'd been doing the last seven fucking days, I'd wait.

Because Ethan was right about one thing—we *would* be talking soon.

CHAPTER THIRTY-TWO

Monday, 9:00 p.m.—One day home

I was cleared to leave the station after Ethan's lawyer showed up and briefed me. If I was needed for questioning or for a statement, the police would reach out to him, and he'd let me know. That meant I could go . . . home. Somewhere. A hotel.

The station provided food for Logan and me, so he was set for the night, but where did I go? To our burned house? It was still taped off until they finished investigating. Not that it was home anymore, anyway.

I had my bag shouldered, a borrowed car seat with Logan sleepy and secured in it, and a rental car that Ethan's lawyer had managed to get me in an insanely fast time frame. My purse was still gone, probably destroyed by my parents. I didn't care about anything in there now. Detective Luna assured me no one would be leaving the station, and I was safe. I didn't have to watch my back or check to see who was following me. They were looking for Dennis to bring him in, but my business with my family was done. Over. It was just Logan and me.

My old phone rang just as I started the rental car, and my breath caught in my throat at the sudden loud sound. "Hello?"

"It's James, Alexander's lawyer. He wanted me to pass on an address to you. He insisted you and Logan needed a place to stay, and he has everything you need there."

He rattled off the address, the location way closer to where we'd lived before than I would've imagined, and I thanked his lawyer. With a quick type into my map, I confirmed the house was four down from our current one.

How in the *hell* had that happened? *Wasn't that house for sale a year ago?*

Just put it on my *questions for Ethan/Alexander* tab.

My mind was quiet on the drive despite all the unanswered questions. I *should've* taken Peter's credit card, pulled out cash, and bolted from this town. This would be all over the news soon.

I could escape Ethan and my family, find a safe small town with Logan, and change my name, but the pull to get more answers was stronger.

And, if I was being genuinely honest with myself, I wanted Ethan to explain it all away.

The drive was short, and I arrived at the three-bedroom house just down the road from ours. I could still see the tape from the fire, the lingering smell of burning wood hanging in the air.

God, was that just yesterday?

I carefully got Logan out of the car, his peaceful face undisturbed from his sleep, and I used the garage code the lawyer had given me. A shiny black truck greeted me, and for one second, I wondered if someone else lived here.

Ethan wouldn't do that. My gut knew he wouldn't send us to harm. Lie to us? Sure. But not let us be hurt.

I couldn't help but wonder how Ethan had pulled the truck, this house, the entire thing off. He clearly had money in all those accounts. But . . . how?

My pulse raced as my fingers wrapped around the gold handle to enter the house. There were no sounds but my racing heart, and I pushed the door open. A faint smell of lavender and cleaner welcomed me, and I took a hesitant step.

A lone light was on in the kitchen; a black table with four chairs and a basket of fruit was right there. Bottles of water lined the marbled counters. Curious, I opened the fridge and found it was fully stocked.

I set Logan's car seat down in the dim living room, and that's when I found the folded sheet of paper with my name on it on the coffee table.

After almost falling over with how fast I dove toward it, I plopped onto the leather couch and ripped it open.

> Marissa,
> I wrote this without knowing how this would all end—so I hope, with the deepest part of my soul, that I'm either with you right now or will be soon. I'm sure you've figured out a lot about my past now, and I know it doesn't look good. But I promise I've had a good reason.
>
> My parents were happy, and we had a normal, active family before my dad started working for Hawkins Associates. After, I used to hear my parents talking about his concerns of shady things going on with data and how it made him uncomfortable. He started bringing things home and hired a lawyer. But as you know, your father and Dennis framed him to make it seem like he was selling data from clients. He swore his innocence the entire time, and as a teenage boy trying to do right by my dad, I formed a dumb plan to get revenge. His incarceration broke my mom. She's been a shell of herself and divorced him after the first year. She cut herself off from my sister and I because we refused to believe our dad was guilty, and we resented her for abandoning him. My sister went on a downward spiral of revenge, her entire personality

changing because of what Franklin Hawkins did. Again, my plan would show my mom his innocence and put our family together again.

I was smart, could learn technology, and my sister helped me find you. How perfect would it be to date Franklin Hawkins's daughter and get insider information? It sounds wild, but it was what I set out to do. Ten years ago.

A lot can happen in ten years, Marissa. Mainly, you and Logan. I didn't want to fall in love with you, madly in love with you at that. It wasn't the plan, but I did, Marissa. My life became more about you instead of this plan. Being with you and Lo changed my life. I'm sure you sensed my anxiety about having a child! He was another kid who could've been exploited or ended up in harm's way because of your family. Having him changed my plan, Mar. It wasn't just about proving my dad's innocence anymore. I had a son. I have a son. One I love more than life itself and a wife who I never wanted to hurt. I had to protect you both and that meant getting you out. I knew there was a high chance you and Logan would move on without me, and that was the better alternative in this shit show. God, you own my soul, Marissa, and I know it might not seem like it, but I really thought I could have it both ways. Prove the truth about your dad, Dennis, and your family, and continue to be your husband.

You might never forgive me for exposing them or for lying to you. I'll accept that. I deserve it after what I put you through, but can you see it had to be that way? If I gave any indication that I had information or they knew my past, they'd find a way to frame me or kill me. Like they did with Christopher Malinowski.

Like they did others. They might've suspected I found something out when I disappeared, but they couldn't just fake evidence that fast.

The proof had to come from you. It was the only way. You're so smart and incredible, I knew you'd be the only person who could save all these people your family has destroyed.

It took years of trying for me to get involved in your family business. They are a tight ship and good at what they do—lying, manipulating, framing. It took seven years of loyalty before I could work there, and even there, I had to jump through hoops. Do things I never wanted to do.

But then I found a video left by Christopher, hidden and encrypted. It changed everything. It was proof I was right, and even though I lost focus of my goal a few times, it was real and still happening. That set everything in motion—the plan to leave, dropping clues to you to be careful, and praying that you found what I needed you to find.

I'm sure I broke some laws while doing this, and I'll take what comes my way. But this house? It's yours if you want it. For you and Logan. The other one has too many memories—and bugs from your dad. It's yours to do what you want. Sell it. Live here. Rent it. Burn it down.

I hope you forgive me. If I survive this, and don't end up in jail, I'll do everything I can to support you. I love you and Logan. I will for the rest of my life, and I'll spend the rest of my days here providing for you and him, trying to earn your trust back. Our start wasn't ideal, but the journey was incredible. Give him a big hug for me, please.

Ethan

I still wanted to punch him in the face. My bruised heart felt 2 percent better, but that was it. Ten years of lies, of deceit. I had a decade of memories to overanalyze, to sift through to see what was real or not. I had no idea if I could ever forgive him for this. Genuinely.

But I understood why this had happened, and that was a blessing in itself. The last week had been almost enough to kill me, but I had answers now, at least.

It'd be hours, or days, before I heard from Ethan. I was sure. I quickly searched the three bedrooms, sighing at the pack-and-play already set up for me. With a calming numbness, I took it out of the main bedroom and set it up in the living room. It felt weird to just sleep in a bedroom right now. Made me uneasy. I wanted the couch instead. It was closer to the exits, both the front and back door.

I brushed my teeth with the toiletries in the bathroom, showered really quickly after washing Logan. Then I finally fell onto the plush couch. Only then did I look closely at my original phone. Countless text messages and voicemails from the past two days. Tons from my family. One from my boss. I ignored them all. I just wanted to hear from Ethan, his lawyer, or the detective.

A weird alert popped up. Item detected near you.

What the fuck?

I sat up, an uneasy feeling gripping my throat. Item detected? *Another* fucking bug?

I tapped the message. Then I hit Continue and Play Sound. I waited, my breath on edge and my goddamn pulse beating so hard, it hurt. I didn't hear a ping. Nothing. But that didn't mean much.

I carefully lifted a sleepy Logan into my arms, preparing to bolt if needed. I walked through the kitchen and each bedroom, straining my ears for *some* sort of noise. There wasn't any, again. Weird.

I spent another five minutes trying not to feel like the dumbass in a horror movie and grabbed a knife from the kitchen to be safe. It could stay under the couch, for a bit. I was rattled, that was all. The item could've been a speaker or a Bluetooth device or a laptop. Ethan probably had some around the house.

But then a million other images played in my head. The listening devices I'd found in our home, the warnings, the gray line of my family wanting to threaten me. The detective! I could call him, just let him know where I was. Yes, I'd do that.

I dialed, and he didn't answer, his voicemail prompting me to leave a message. "Hi, Detective Luna. This is Marissa Creighton. I'm at a house Ethan secured for Logan and me, and well, I just wanted to let you know where we are in case something happens. Is Dennis in custody? Is my family? I got a weird alert on my phone about an item being detected nearby, and I think it rattled me. Please, call me when you have news, even if it's late. Thanks."

There. That was smart. The right thing to do.

I couldn't settle down, even after the call and with the knife nearby. I held Logan in my arms, too worried to set him down. It would take too much time to pick him up and run if I needed to, and at this point, I thought about driving to a hotel. I double-checked all the locks before sitting on the recliner.

A random creak in the house had me bolting up. There was no way I'd get sleep; the least I could do was research why that alert had popped up on my phone. I typed it into Google on my burner phone and came across articles about Apple AirTags.

Fucking hell.

More technology that could track things, people, pets. What the hell.

To stop sharing your location, tap button to disable and follow on-screen steps.

Okay . . . the *item* was sharing my location? To whom? For what reason?

Who needed to find *me*?

Maybe I was being paranoid. Probably. But *what* was that sound?

It was a click, like a door handle turning just a bit. I jumped up and grabbed the knife, certain Ethan would say my name if it were him entering the house at ten at night. He'd know how jumpy I'd be after all this.

Even if it were his lawyer, he'd call or knock and not just come in.

Who else would know about this house?

Soft footsteps. Like socks on tile. A light came on, illuminating the kitchen that overlooked the living room. I shifted Logan to my left side so my right hand could hold the knife. Then I waited for whoever would make their appearance.

The footsteps stopped deeper in the kitchen, like they were near the stove. Did I announce myself? Go see who it was?

"You're awful quiet in there." The female voice was deep. Familiar but not in a way where I knew who it was.

At least it's not my family.

"Is there a reason you're sneaking into this house at night?" My tone sounded confident. It seemed after this entire shit show, I felt powerful. How dare this person come into *this* home and scare me?

"If I've been given a key, it's not sneaking." The woman came into view; Ethan's sister held a glass of wine near her hip. Her gaze moved toward the knife in my hand, and she snorted. "Put the knife down, Marissa."

"I'd rather not." There was something about her smirk that had me on edge. Like she knew something I didn't—more than the obvious things. "Is there a reason you're here?"

"A few of them, actually." She took a sip of the wine and studied Logan, who was sound asleep. "My nephew's cute."

"You're not here to compliment how cute he is. Hailey, what do you want?"

"More answers."

"More answers?" I repeated her words, hoping delaying her from whatever she was set to do was a good idea. It was 10:20 p.m. Would the detective call me back and stop by if I didn't answer?

"I thought they'd hurt or killed my brother for hours. You didn't think to let me know he was safe? I was freaking the hell out!" she yelled, her white teeth standing out in the dim light. Wine stained them, almost like blood. The bags under her eyes were dark, and her hair wasn't done.

"Because you were so forthcoming and helpful?" I swallowed. "Hailey, I've just fucking learned that my family is horrible. That they've done the absolute worst things imaginable. I understand why you can't trust me even though I'm the reason your dad will be cleared of charges. Not your brother. *Me.* I turned the evidence in to the station. I turned on *my family* to save innocent people in this, like your dad. All while I learned that my *husband* had targeted me to get revenge. I'm not one of them. So take your attitude and blame elsewhere. I am done putting up with people's shit."

She took a large sip of wine before assessing me as she walked closer. "Alex said not to underestimate you. That you're tougher than you look."

Pride had me sitting straighter. I sure as hell was tougher than I looked.

"He's not wrong. You'd be foolish to be like my parents and assume I'm some weak-ass bitch who rolls over. Now, my son needs to sleep. I need to sleep. I need to figure out what the hell I'm going to do tomorrow morning. Do I stay and ride it out? Do I change my name and start a new life without ever looking back? Those are hard choices and require a clear mind. So, again, what do you want?"

She frowned, some of the fight leaving her gaze. "You plan to keep Logan away from Alex? You'd keep his son from him?"

"I don't know, Hailey. He lied to me for a decade, used me, played me, and . . ."

Helped me find myself. Taught me how to use my voice. Trusted me to free innocent people.

My eyes welled up. "I don't—"

The front door handle twisted. The eerie clink of metal grating on metal made us both jump. Hailey's eyes widened as she moved closer to me. My heart pounded as I tensed. *Please be Ethan. Please be Ethan.*

"I didn't lock the door," Hailey said. "I'm so sor—"

"Mar?" My brother's familiar voice rang out as he pushed the door open. His face was lined in fear, and before I could ask what was going on, someone else walked in.

Holding a gun.

CHAPTER THIRTY-THREE

Monday, 10:30 p.m.

"Ah, there you are. *And* Hailey Roux. What an honor." Dennis waltzed in, kicked the door shut, and grinned at us. "What a fun, unplanned reunion. Peter, I'd like to officially introduce you to Ethan's sister."

Hailey paled.

Peter's face tightened.

"Now, how about we all have a chat? That sounds like a great idea." Dennis laughed, absolutely unhinged. His shirt was untucked, his hair in disarray. The familiar scent of whiskey floated in the air.

He's drunk.

And has a gun.

The urge to run caused a little cry to escape my throat, but I remained rooted in my spot. Logan slept pressed against my chest while a crazed man had a gun. The air suffocated me, the bone-chilling fear gripping me so tight, each breath took all my effort.

Dennis had found me.

Dennis helped *take care* of those who spoke the truth. I was one of those people.

"Can you put the gun away? It's not needed right now." Peter's jaw clenched every few seconds as he held up a hand. "Dude, come on. They are terrified."

"They should be." Dennis pursed his lips, his vivid green eyes way too excited. "Your dear sister fucked up everything, and this one is collateral damage. I mean, fuck, the Roux are nothing now. What's the world gonna be like without one?"

Hailey squealed and moved closer to me. Any uncertainty between her and I disappeared, and there was an unspoken understanding as our gazes met: *Survive this.* Her large eyes—just like her brother's—were wide and terrified. Sweat pooled on her forehead, and she glanced at my sleeping son, her meaning clear.

I held her forearm, squeezing it in some sort of mock assurance. I had no idea how the fuck we were going to get past Dennis, but I knew Peter wouldn't hurt Logan. He could restrain me, possibly hurt me, but never Logan. I dug my nails into Hailey's arm and looked at my son, trying to communicate to grab Logan if needed.

She nodded.

Dennis eyed me up and down, a sneer on his lips. "Couldn't just leave it all alone? Had to sneak around and ask questions? Your husband cheated on you and stole from the company. The one your dad built from the ground up! He paid for your life! How dare you repay him this way?" He waved the gun in the air, his finger near the trigger the entire time.

My hand twitched with the knife. My heart leaped in my throat. "Ethan didn't do that."

"You don't know shit, bitch."

"Dennis," Peter scolded. "My dad said to be smart. We're not *killing* them." Peter moved a few inches to the right, putting himself between Dennis and me. It was the first time I realized how big Peter was. He towered over Dennis.

"How would we explain them dying, Dennis? Think about it. If Marissa is the witness, she can't be dead. It'd mean the case had merit."

My brother spoke calmly, with confidence. To anyone else, he likely seemed in control. Only I heard the waver in his voice.

"Your mother had other plans, and I do what she says. I'd never go against her." Dennis moved around Peter but stilled. His eyes turned to the size of plates. "Did you hear that?"

"Hear what?" Peter asked. The muscles on his back flexed as he stood taller.

"A car door. Is someone else here? Did you fucking call the police, Marissa?" Dennis growled.

"N-no." I shook my head hard, slowly moving Hailey and myself a step to the left.

Dennis ran to the window, moving the blinds to look down. While he did that, Hailey grabbed my arm and held out a hand. *Give me the knife. You hold Logan,* she mouthed.

A million thoughts raced through my head on how we could get out of this situation.

We could run toward the front door, but he could shoot us. Easily. There was too much light and not enough distance between us and him. He had a fucking *gun*. A full-body shiver made my pulse race harder. My teeth hurt from my clenched jaw, the absolute fear rooting me to the ground. Logan was here. Near a murderer. Who had a goddamn gun. This wasn't good. At all.

Think.

"Check the back, Peter. Do it now." Dennis stalked toward the other window, shoving the shades aside as my brother slowly moved toward the back of the house. His gaze caught mine, and he seemed terrified. He mouthed something so quickly, I almost missed it: *Trust me.*

His words from the station replayed in my head. *The things Ethan and I do are to protect you and Logan.* Peter might've fallen into my parents' schemes, but I knew without a doubt he loved me and Logan.

He was the only chance we had at getting out of this alive.

Peter checked the back window but discreetly unlocked the patio door. It was so subtle, Dennis would have no idea.

Is this for us to run out? Is someone coming in?

His allies? My parents? They were at the station. But wait . . . How was Peter out? Why had he been allowed to leave, and how the hell had they found us?

The AirTag.

I had no idea what it was attached to, but that had to be it.

"I don't see anyone in the front, but I heard it. I know I did. Is there any other door into this place? A back window, maybe? I need to check." Dennis shoved the gun in his waistband and moved toward the hallway, stilling, and pointing his fingers at us. "Don't fucking move, you hear me?"

Hailey nodded as a tiny desperate cry left her throat.

I refused to nod. I stared Dennis down as he marched out of view. I kissed Logan's forehead as two truths hit me.

The first was that I couldn't just hope someone was coming to save me, Logan, and Hailey. If I wanted us to survive, I had to be proactive. I'd learned that the last week.

The second? I would *kill* for my son.

"What do we do?" Hailey asked, tears welling in her eyes. "This wasn't . . . I can't believe . . . How do we—"

"Breathe." I stood by her, keeping my attention on the hallway. "Stay calm, and we can escape."

"Mar," Peter whispered, still near the back of the house. He placed a hand on the window, but he faced me. "I am so fucking sorry about all this. I need you to know that. I wanted you out of it, away from it all. I can't . . ." He hiccuped, the despair evident in his sagging shoulders and crumpled face. "Please, I—"

"Everyone in the front room! Right fucking now!" Dennis screamed, interrupting whatever my brother had wanted to say. "Give me your phones, or I shoot Peter in the knee."

I hesitated, and he fired a shot into the ceiling, making me jump. Hailey tossed her phone near his feet, and I did the same. My damn burner phone was on the side table, too far away for me to reach it.

"Fucking fools."

My heart jumped in my throat at the urgency and desperation in Dennis's voice. He was losing it, slowly, and the longer we were here, the more likely he'd snap and shoot us. Peter's hand trembled as he walked by us, going toward Dennis.

He fisted his hand twice before turning around and pulling out duct tape. He couldn't . . . possibly . . . no. Each heartbeat was a stab in the soul. "Peter," I warned.

His eyes watered. "It's the plan, Marissa."

"No. I'm holding my son. Don't do this to us." A sob broke through, the brief resolve I had shattering as my brother stared at me like I was a target. "I—I'm not putting him down."

"You have to. I need to duct-tape you and Hailey."

"Think of your nephew," I said again, louder. Something caught my eye over Peter's shoulder, a flash of movement in the window's reflection. Peter's attention wasn't on me, it was over my head, and he widened his eyes at me, trying to communicate something.

It was lost on me. He had duct tape in his hands, approaching me. My fight-or-flight response kicked in, and I kneed my brother between the legs. He howled, falling to the floor, but Dennis was right there.

"Ah, you're feisty, Marissa. I usually like fight in my women, but if you touch us again, I will shoot *you* in the leg, so settle down." Dennis paced the living room. There was a TV and a couch, plus two armchairs near the front windows, and he tapped his gun on top of them every time he passed one. "Okay, I'm here to get information in any way possible. If that means hurting you, then I will."

"No. You're here to find out where the files are, who has them. That's it." Peter groaned. He moved to sit on the couch, leaving Hailey and me standing on the edge of the living room and kitchen. The duct tape roll sat on the floor, forgotten.

Good for now.

"Are you hoping to delete the files before they get out? What do you want the files for?" I asked.

"You don't ask the questions. God, you're mouthy. Franklin told me you were a pain in the ass. That's why I never wanted children." His lip curled in disgust.

The jab hit where he meant it to, right in my heart. But it dulled, just as fast as it had come. My parents were dead to me at this point. They'd sent their henchman after me, for Christ's sake.

"Yeah, no one wants you to have them either," I said.

He snarled. "Where are the files? Talk or I start shooting people."

The hair on the back of my neck stood on end, like the particles in the room shifted.

"If you *hurt* my wife or child in any way, I will destroy you and everyone you love."

I gasped. Ethan was here. Ethan was HERE.

He wore the same outfit I saw at the station, but he seemed darker, more intense, more confident as he strode in from the kitchen to stand in front of us. "Hailey, walk out the back door right now."

"Wh-what?"

Ethan kept his back to us. "You shouldn't be here. You're not a part of this. Leave. Dennis won't do a thing. This is about us, not you."

"But I can't leave you—"

"Go," I said, pleading with her. "Take Logan and go. Please. *Please*."

It was the worst moment of my life, handing my son off to a woman I didn't know, trusting her to take care of him. His chances were higher out of this house, but my soul cracked when I hoisted him into her arms. "Go." I nodded. I handed her the knife and my child, watching my entire life leave with her.

Tears fell down her cheeks as she backed up a step, then another. She squeezed him, ran a hand over my son's back, and gave me one fierce glance. It was a look only a mother would understand. It was an innate *I'll die to protect this child* expression that reassured me this was the right choice.

"You're lucky I have a soft spot for small children." Dennis moved closer to Ethan, his eyes glowing with anticipation. "I hate them, but

I've never hurt a child. He's probably too young to remember any of this, so he's safe. Your sister, though . . ."

"You framed her father, destroyed her family, and held her hostage. She's had enough from you." Ethan shoved Dennis's chest, provoking him. "Now, are you going to shoot me? Shoot Marissa?"

"It's early in the night, and we have a lot to talk about." Dennis laughed. "God, I need a drink for this. Peter, check to see if there's whiskey in the kitchen."

"No." Ethan was nothing like the soft-spoken man I was used to. He was firm, hard, and terrifying. "Here's what's going to happen: you're going to give me that gun and then let us walk out of here, alive."

"I never realized you were funny, Alex. Your old man was a dud of a human."

The muscles in Ethan's neck tensed.

"This room is live streaming as we speak, on the company website. You think you can recover from this in any way? You're done. Hawkins is done. Your only chance at a life is for you to drop the gun and run."

"Liar. You sent your wife, child, and sister to this house. You wouldn't stream it." Dennis glanced around the room, his attention lingering on the corners.

"I've been studying you for years, Dennis. You and the Hawkinses. Until you are all locked up behind bars for what you've done, I'm taking every precaution to protect what's mine. You don't have to believe me. That's on you."

Dennis showed his teeth, looking like a wild animal rather than a polished man. "Who has the files?"

"Everyone," I said. "I sent them to numerous accounts. Everyone deserves to know the truth."

"Everyone? Please. You probably sent them to yourself and the police. We can hack the police one easily. That's been done. And I already have someone in your account, deleting all traces of it. Who else?"

Wait. Was that true? Had I not sent the files to enough people? Would the truth not be released? My breath stilled. No. Detective Luna knew. He had been in the room when my parents snapped.

"Doesn't matter, Dennis. It's out. The truth is out, and innocent people will be free," I said, raising my voice. I wasn't cowering to this asshole. Logan was safe. I refused to be weak ever again.

Ethan moved to the right, putting more of himself between Dennis and me. He had his hand on his back, his fingers making the same three motions over and over.

Sign language. He was spelling something.

R.

U.

N.

Fuck. My throat tightened with fear. Peter seemed to notice the change in the air too. He leaned forward, his elbows on his knees as Dennis pointed the gun at Ethan. "I will shoot you."

"Doesn't stop the truth from coming out, and my murder will be on the company website. Your choice."

"Full of shit. Peter, get on your phone and show me the site."

My brother glanced at me for a second before he stood and pulled out his phone. He took his time as he nodded. "Yes. It's on there."

"Show me. Show me right fucking now before I kill you all."

Everything happened so fast.

Peter tossed the phone at Dennis's face, the movement causing Dennis to fire the gun in the ceiling. My brother then tackled him to the ground as Ethan yelled at me to run.

I didn't hesitate. I dove for the patio door just five feet from me, flung it open, and ran into the cool night air. Another shot went off, and my heart lurched. *Don't look back. Don't look back. Find Hailey. Find Logan.*

There were voices. Loud ones. Definitely including Ethan's. That was good. That meant he was still alive. I rounded the house and glanced at the front window. Peter's shirt was covered in blood as he lay on the ground, unmoving. Dennis and Ethan were out of sight when another shot went off.

They need help. I had to find a phone.

My lungs burned like they were on fire, and I sprinted down the road. The air was freezing cold. It smelled like fall, like bonfires, and crickets chirped all around. My feet hit the pavement in hard slaps, and I kept going. Beyond the street, beyond the intersection. My calves hurt, my bare feet ached from all the rocks, and my eyes watered. It could've been from the cold, the wind, or my emotions. The fact I was still alive.

"Oh my god, Marissa?" a panicked woman yelled at me.

Hailey. My son. Oh my god.

She sat on a bench, Logan crying on her shoulder as I approached her. "Thank you. Thank you so much."

"What's going on? What happened?" she asked, her voice raw.

I needed to hold my son more than I needed to breathe. She gently handed him to me, and I cradled him. I had my baby. We'd made it. We were alive.

Peter? Ethan?

God, I hoped so.

"I think my brother was shot. I don't know about Dennis or Ethan. We need to call for help. Are you okay to keep walking?"

She nodded. "This is crazy. I can't . . . ," she cried. "I can't lose my brother. I just got him back."

"Let's run. The gas station will have a phone."

We jogged there, my muscles aching and pounding from exertion.

Even if Dennis had shot Ethan, if he and Peter didn't make it, I knew I'd survive. I'd been surviving the last week, and if I learned anything about myself, it was that I'd do anything for my son.

More confident than I'd ever been, I sprinted into the gas station with Hailey right behind me, then finally took a calming breath. The attendant stared at me like I was a ghost, and I didn't blame him. I panted for air as I asked, "Could I use your phone to call the police, please?"

"Uh, sure?" The kid frowned and glanced at the door, like someone was chasing me. He motioned for me to come behind the counter. With Logan whimpering on my shoulder, I soothed him as I picked up the phone and called 911.

CHAPTER THIRTY-FOUR

Two months later . . .

Logan ran—not walked, not strolled—straight-up raced up the ramp with his little legs so he could go down the slide. Even though it was freezing cold and just beyond the holidays, he insisted on playing outside at the park near our apartment. It was a small one-bedroom where we had no personal space. He slept in his crib that was only three feet away from my twin bed, but it was how I needed it. Him close to me. The therapist I'd started seeing said it was normal and okay that I needed him close.

Maybe in time I'd feel better about everything, but I wasn't anywhere ready for my baby to sleep far away from me. Not after *all* that we'd lived through. Logan screamed for joy as he went down the slide three times in a row, and then he let out the *yippee* cry. "Daddy, daddy, daddy!"

Ah, Ethan was here. Well, Alex. Alex, Logan's father and my husband, walked up toward us with his hands in his pockets. He gave me a small smile before bending down and letting Logan tackle him. "I missed you, kiddo."

Ethan hugged Logan hard, our son's arms wrapping around his neck. We'd seen Ethan every other day, but things had been weird for a while.

Were we still married? Yes.

Did I need space? Yes.

Had he initially dated me to get into my family? Yes.

Had I forgiven him? No.

I wrapped my arms around my stomach as a gust of wind came through. It was a cold, miserable January day, and the sky matched my gloomy mood.

"You being good for your mama?" Ethan asked, pulling me back to the moment.

Logan nodded.

Ethan's gaze moved to me, his soft brown eyes warming. "How are you?"

"I'm okay." I tried to smile, but it still felt stiff.

Ethan walked up to me, set Logan on the ground, and brought one hand to my face. He cupped my cheek, his eyes searching mine as he sighed. I liked the feel of his hand on my face. It reminded me of the good times.

"Today?" His voice was just above a whisper.

My eyes prickled. He asked the same thing every time he saw me. If *today* was the day he could come back home. Try to be a real family without lies. I wanted us to be together, but it was still too much. He was adjusting to having his dad out of jail and being a part of his nephews' lives. Things were prickly with Hailey at first, but we were slowly becoming friends. She and I tried to get coffee once a week. She wanted to get to know her nephew, and since Logan had lost so much of his family, adding more seemed like the right thing to do.

When I didn't answer, Ethan dropped his hand and smiled, one of his dimples popping out. "Made a new playlist for you. I emailed it to you while I parked."

“Thanks,” I whispered. A part of me still wondered if I should change my name and move away with Logan. Leave every trace of this life behind and start over. But that part grew smaller and smaller each day. What if Ethan and I could get past this? What if Logan loved his cousins? He sure liked Hailey, and to deprive them of each other seemed cruel. Logan would someday get to spend time with one of his grandparents who was totally innocent, and I couldn’t take that away.

Oh, that had been an interesting morning, when Ethan . . . well, Alex’s dad and I met. He never once made me feel bad about who I was related to, and somehow, that made it even harder to consider disappearing. He was *genuinely* a good human. He’d thanked me for helping clear his name. Things were starting to come together.

Ethan had a new job in technology for some start-up, all remote work. I’d increased my writing to support me and Logan until I made a choice about my marriage. I had my own independence, for the first time ever, and it filled me with pride knowing I could do it. That was one thing I’d learned about myself after surviving all this bullshit—I was strong, capable, and tough.

I wasn’t weak or overemotional like my parents had always made me feel. I’d figured everything out and survived it. I’d always get through life’s obstacles.

“I don’t know how to forgive you,” I said. I shrugged as my heart raced. I missed Ethan so much, but if we were going to do this, we had to start over. Clean slate. We couldn’t go back to *before*. “So much happened.”

“Mar, I know. God, the fact you haven’t given me divorce papers is a gift itself.” He picked Logan up and rested him on his hip. “You take all the time you need, but I’m going to keep asking and keep showing up and keep sending you songs because I love you. I don’t deserve you or Logan after what I did, but I swear, I’ll spend every minute of every day making it up to you. To both of you.”

My throat got all tight, and I coughed, clearing the ball of emotion. Ethan had more gray hair at the temples than before, somehow making him look more handsome. His eyes still held the same lightness that had always been there, despite the life he'd had. He refused to tell me some of the things he'd seen on his work servers, but other than that, he'd answered every single question.

Like why his sister had ever come to the office.

Turned out that hadn't been the plan, and he was pissed as hell about her impatience. My family made up all the other affairs to frame him, based on seeing him with Hailey one time. And the reason he asked me to find out about Dennis meeting with the LLC? He simply wanted me to visit the office and talk to his secretary, hoping I would find the files. And all the people on social media? A support group.

Finally, I asked why he couldn't have just sent the files to the authorities.

He had been terrified it wouldn't work after seeing what happened to his dad. He wanted my parents trapped, where they couldn't just fly to a nonextradition country. The call had to come from *inside* the house, from a member of the Hawkins family. Plus, he'd counted on Peter folding if I was involved. Peter had been crucial to all this. He was the reason Ethan managed to escape before the showdown at the station. My brother was still in the hospital, where he'd be until he was cleared to go to a custodial facility. Because he'd made a deal and exposed everything, his sentence would be lesser.

I had gone to visit him a few weeks ago, and it still made my chest ache. After some determined inquiries from me, Peter had explained that I'd been kept in the dark all these years for two reasons. The first? I was a terrible liar and too *kind* for their world. I'd cry when someone else got hurt and was painfully honest. They hadn't wanted me knowing anything bad because I'd expose it. Which I sure had. The second was my parents' antiquated views on gender. It was ironic, how my mom was in charge and bossed my dad around when it came to the shady stuff, but for a woman to publicly join the workforce? Out of the question.

Peter shared that our parents had taken the fall to protect him that night at the station, in hopes of him following their legacy and enacting their backup plan. Because they had one. They had a whole slew of smear campaigns and attacks to silence anyone who threatened them. They just hadn't planned on me being the one to out them, so they'd had nothing personalized prepared.

I'd never forgive my parents, but I planned to remain in touch with Peter. He'd shielded us that night in the house. Dennis had shot him in the stomach, and Peter had almost died for us.

I couldn't leave my brother. He meant too much to me, which was another reason why I couldn't up and leave. Lo and I had family here. One thing was for sure, though: I'd never visit my parents in jail.

I sighed as Ethan kissed the top of Logan's head, then pointed to some clouds in the sky. "What does that look like, buddy? A dog?"

"Yes! Woof woof!"

Ethan was such a good dad, and watching him with Logan had my chest ache with longing. My husband was kind, playful, brilliant, and . . . went through some bullshit because of my family. I missed him so much. The memories of the three of us hit me every morning, but with everything that happened, the moments I thought I would die all led me to the same thought. Him. I wanted Ethan with me. I still loved him so much.

Could I do this? Trust him again?

I believed all his answers and reasoning. He vowed to spend the rest of his life making it up to Logan and me. I already proved to myself that I didn't *need* him or my family to live, so besides pride, what held me back?

I chewed my lip, and I knew, deep down, that I wanted to try again. I'd go in with more awareness of my strength and know our power wasn't so imbalanced, but as the decision solidified in my mind, my body tingled with excitement. "I might be ready soon."

Ethan whipped his head around, hope reflecting in his eyes. "Really?"

"Maybe. There'll be some stipulations."

"Whatever you want." He swallowed loudly. "Anything."

"I have my own bank account so I'm not entirely dependent on you."

"Of course, yes." He blinked fast, and his cheeks pinkened.

"The second you lie about anything again . . . I file for divorce." My voice trembled, but the knot in my stomach eased. My gut had been right from the second Ethan left, and I refused to ignore it now. I wanted to be *happy* and provide Logan with the best life possible.

"I will never lie to you again." He shook his head back and forth, hard. "I will choose you and Logan for the rest of my life. And if we have more kids, them too. I'm sorry I put us through this, but I don't regret them being caught."

"I know. I understand that." I swallowed, thinking about the families that would get freedom and closure. Christopher's wife and son were suing Hawkins Associates and would likely get a huge settlement.

Ethan smiled. It was one of my favorite grins because it made his eyes crinkle on the sides. "What's that for?" I asked.

"You know how an artist can experiment and try new things, becoming better with each attempt?"

"Um, yes?" I had no idea where he was going with this. None.

"We're like that. Us. Our relationship. When we do this a second time, really get it right, we'll have the foundation from before. Our earlier albums. And this one can be new. A soundtrack of hope, forgiveness."

"Trying to talk music to me?" I fought a smile. "You know I'm a sucker for that."

"I know. God, I'll talk music to you for the rest of our lives."

My stomach was in knots as I stepped closer to him, inhaling his comforting cologne. His eyes lit up, and I intertwined our fingers. This was the first time I'd instigated touching him since everything had happened, and we both sucked in a breath. "What would this new album of ours be called?"

"*The Soundtrack of Our Lives*? *Soundtrack of Second Chances*?" He kissed the back of my hand and pulled me into his arms. He rested his chin on my head while Logan snuggled between us, and for the first time since that day he'd disappeared, I felt good.

"All right. Let's start the record over."

And that night, Ethan came home.

Acknowledgments

While so much of this story is made up, there are some very real aspects that I want to acknowledge. First—my love of music. To be able to incorporate some of my favorite moments in life (the concert mentioned in the story was one of the best date nights of my life) and some of my favorite artists (Jungle and Glass Animals), while making it dark and sinister was a creative dream come true. I was raised with music. It is my therapy, my stress release, my way of communicating, and I hope that part of my life showed through these pages.

My dad was a DJ for a bit, played instruments his whole life, and is still in bands while in retirement; he taught me the power of music. I remember my first cassette tape and my first "burnt" CD with jock jams, blasting Van Halen and rapping Coolio. I am still in love with Hall and Oates and Earth, Wind, and Fire. The love of music that was passed to me is now with my children in all our family playlists and dance nights. Thank you, Dad, for having that be such a core part of my growing up.

I do need to explicitly say that my parents and how I was raised were the complete opposite of Marissa. My mom and dad led me to believe I could do anything I wanted, and I've always lived that way, not realizing there were limits. When writing this story during the end of the pandemic, I considered my family (mom, dad, brother, husband, son) and thought, *What would be the worst that could happen?* I took that and ran with it.

Andy—my husband of over a decade now—thank you for supporting me, pushing me, letting me cry and pretending I'm a big toughie when I'm really a marshmallow. I hope you enjoy the little nuggets of our life sprinkled throughout this. I took so many of our inside jokes and incorporated them into this story (Crescent Ballroom, amiright?), and DukeOfFranklin, and all the memories we've had together the last seventeen years. You've seen every setback, achievement, win, loss, and celebration, and I couldn't ask for a better partner in life, parenting, and working in the subjective field of art. I love that you make us family playlists, and I love how much you love our family.

I want to thank my agent, Jessica Faust, who read the query letter for this and requested the manuscript in a day. When I say it was a dream come true, I mean every word. Thank you for being a champion of this story and pushing me to find my voice. This adventure has been so fun and is only just the beginning.

A huge thanks to the Amazon team. Jessica—your endless enthusiasm and cheering can be heard across the country. I knew the second we were on that Zoom call this was a good fit, and I can't wait to see what else we can do! Manu—your edits and suggestions made this story even better, and I cannot thank you enough for your insights. Jena, your copyedits were some of the best I've worked with. Thank you so much for helping polish and find any holes. If it weren't for you, the timeline and days of the week would have no meaning. Tristen, your comments were so helpful and helped make the final version even better. The cover designer . . . the way I gasped when I saw the cover. Stunning. Perfect. I want to frame it and cover my entire house with this.

Writing is hard. I'm not gonna lie. You need a circle of people around you to get through the tough days, and my circle has grown and changed throughout the years. But a special thank-you to Kat Turner and Kat McIntyre, who read the first draft and were so encouraging. A huge thanks to Sarah, Megan, Rachel Reiss, Rachel Rumble, Mikeala, and Haley. Thank you for always having my back, cheering me up or whooping and hollering about good news. I adore you all so much.

I want to end with a special shout-out to two authors whom I admire, and I am a HUGE fan of their work. Both were such inspirations to me. Elle Marr has been one of my auto-buy authors for years (who has also pubbed with Amazon—and OMG, have you read her yet? If not, what are you waiting for?), and she's also so wonderful and kind. She let me ask her a ton of questions, and I cannot speak highly enough of her.

The second is Darby Kane. She is a romance author who dove into the thriller world and wrote such riveting, terrifying stories that I fell in love with her writing. She made me believe that I could also write romance and thrillers. Inspiration is such a fun thing, and I can truly say that Darby Kane helped me get over the hurdle of *Can I really do this?* So thank you so much.

I'll conclude with a thank-you to you, dear reader. I hope you loved Marissa's story, overcoming her own biases and beliefs and realizing her true power. Thank you for taking a chance on a debut author. I'm so grateful for you.

"Until the Next Time" by Dropkick Murphys.

—Elle

About the Author

Tell Me You Trust Me is Elle Owens's thriller debut. She also writes award-winning romance titles under a different name. Elle grew up in central Illinois and has been creating stories forever—roughly since birth. After discovering Nancy Drew as a teenager and David Baldacci as an adult, she started down the path to writing her own suspense novels. Owens draws upon her career in technology to blend the world of tech and everyday fears into her work. She especially loves sports and spending time with her husband and kids.

For the latest on Elle and her books, check out her website (www.elleowens.com) or follow her on Instagram (@elleowenswrites).

About the Author